Double Your Standards
SARAH BLUE

PLAYLIST

Spotify Playlist

Same Damn Time - Future
Double Fantasy - The Weeknd, Future
All-American Bitch - Olivia Rodrigo
Work Out - J. Cole
Feel Anything - Nxdia
Good For You - Selena Gomez, A$AP Rocky
I Like Him - Princess Nokia
FU In My Head - Cloudy June
Favorite - Isabel LaRosa
Get UR Freak On - Missy Elliott
Sweet Talk - Kito & Reija Lee
Hurts Me - Tory Lanez, Trippie Redd, Yoko Gold
One More Night - Maroon 5

Casual - Chappell Roan
3 - Britney Spears
Nasty - Tinashe

Fuck you, Will.

Kate

Celebrating

OVULATING in your thirties is violent, feral, and unfortunate when you don't have a partner to alleviate the unbelievable ache of wanting to get fucked within an inch of your life.

Not that I really know what that feels like anymore.

I sigh, glancing down at my manicured nails wrapped around a martini glass. I don't even have a tan line where my wedding ring used to be anymore.

My plan wasn't to be thirty-three, divorced, and trying to figure out what I wanted in life. But here I am, at my own divorce party with my two best friends, who happen to also be my co-workers, and truly the only two people I can count on in the world.

This bar is the hottest new place in Tampa. It's set right outside of a marina. A row of party boats lightly rock in the late night breeze off the bay. If it wasn't for the music and other bar-goers talking over one another, it would be peaceful, serene even.

The place is packed, my best friends are here, but I still feel alone.

I don't want a relationship, far from it. I know I'll never marry someone again, and truthfully, I'm rather disgusted that I both hate men currently and still want to mount one so desperately right now.

Savannah bumps my shoulder, nudging me out of my thoughts, and making me spill a bit of my drink over my knuckles in the process.

"Come on, Kate, we're celebrating. You're finally free from that tool," she says, holding up her own martini.

I give her a smile and take a sip of my drink.

"Is celebrating the right word?" Chelsea asks, her dark brows furrowed.

These two women are my everything. All three of us met at our teaching jobs at the University of Tampa. The one major thing we had in common was too much education and still, apparently, too little sense.

"'Celebrate' is definitely the right word. I mean, hell, when was the last time you came out with us, Kate?" Savannah asks.

I have to think long and hard about the last time we did something together and I'm filled with guilt. I've been a shitty friend, too caught up in my own failing marriage to do much of anything besides mope and mourn.

"I'm sorry—"

"Hey. I didn't say that to guilt trip you. We just missed you is all," Savannah says, wrapping an arm around my shoulder and squeezing.

"You deserve better," Chelsea says.

I take another sip of my drink, letting the vodka coat my throat. I know I deserved better than what Will did to me, but it still hurt. We'd been together since sophomore year of high school. He was all I knew, the only man I'd ever slept with. While he was with his mistress turned fiancée and their newborn, here I was, at thirty-three, figuring out what I was going to do next.

I had a job, a decent one, though I don't need the money. I'd gotten mostly everything in the divorce since it was my money that paid for everything.

There was this tangible sadness over this idea that I missed out on so much, that I hadn't truly lived. I gave all my best years to a man who stopped seeing me at some point, and I embarrassingly held on to him for dear life, even though he didn't want to be kept—at least not by me. In retrospect, I didn't want to be kept either, I just don't think I knew that at the time. I'm still trying to figure out what it is that I want.

"Kate," Chelsea says, reeling me out of my thoughts as she grabs both sides of my face. She's never been one to mince words and she doesn't now. "You gave too many years to that man for him to do what he did to you. You two haven't lived together for a year now; the divorce is final. You deserve to live it up, do all the things you wanted to for years but never did because you thought you had to be this perfect little wife. It's time to live for you. I mean, that's what you want right? You don't still have feelings for him do you?"

I look into her deep brown eyes. My beautiful friend, who only has my best interests at heart and knows me better than everyone else.

"I'm not still in love with him. In fact, I think I hate him. I'm just not sure what I want," I say, though I have some ideas.

Ideas I never even shared the true depths of with the man I was with for nearly eighteen years. Those ideas were hidden away in the dark for moments when I was alone with my phone and the web browser in incognito mode. I didn't want to date, but I wanted to have fun.

Fun that I've denied myself for far too long.

"At least we're all in agreement on that," Savannah says,

holding up her glass, and Chelsea and I follow. "To Will, we wish you well...in hell," she says cackling and we clink our glasses together.

"Alright, so are you wanting to date again?" Chelsea asks and I crinkle my nose. "Okay, no dating. What about some fun?"

"Isn't it weird for me to be in my thirties trolling for one-night stands?"

"Take that back right now," Savannah says, her big blonde hair bobbing as she speaks animatedly. "You never had a hoe phase, Kate. It's overdue. It's like every woman's rite of passage to have a certain amount of time dedicated to getting railed by as many men as your sweet, little heart desires."

"How long has your rite of passage been then?" Chelsea jokes at Savannah who grins.

"For some, it's a rite of passage. For others, it's a lifestyle. Plus, I do keep some of them for a few months until they bore me," Savannah says.

"I wouldn't even know where to start when it comes to hooking up with someone," I say. My cheeks feel like they're flaming hot.

"Kate, you're a Miami ten. Please, you could go touch the arm of any man in this bar from the age of twenty-one to nearly in the grave and they would say yes," Chelsea says.

A Miami ten was beyond generous. I knew I was attractive, maybe minus the scars that hadn't faded on my neck and collarbone, but I'd be lying if getting cheated on didn't take a hit to my ego.

I didn't know if I was good at flirting; hell, I wasn't sure I knew how to flirt. The last five or so years felt like a blur of resentment, loneliness, and frustration. I swallowed the rest of my drink, hating how unsure I feel about taking a step out of my comfort zone.

Tired of being on autopilot and accepting less than what I deserve. I'm ready to lift this fog and try, really put myself out there and figure out who I am. Life is too short to not actually live it, I just don't have a single clue where to start.

"Another?" a deep voice from behind the bar asks.

I glance up, and it isn't the barely legal young man that waited on us before.

No, he's all man, and he certainly doesn't look like a bartender. Not with the way his white dress shirt is rolled up against his forearms that are delicious. Could forearms be delicious? I'm not sure anyone else's have ever been, but his are thick, strong forearms lined with a phlebotomist's wet dream of veins.

The previous bartender wore a button down of drinking parrots on them, while this man looks like he just got off work at his finance job. But there's something about his smile, the dimple on his chin, and the way his hair looks like he's run his hands through it five hundred times today that tells me he doesn't work in an office. He looks too put together to be working behind a bar, but maybe that's his whole appeal.

He looks like a GQ model with his sun-kissed skin, strong jawline, and eyes that bordered between blue and green. I bet it depends on what color he's wearing and they'd shift in tone.

"We'd all like another. We're celebrating," Savannah says, ogling the man, and I wonder if my reaction mirrors hers.

"Oh? What are we celebrating tonight?" he asks, a dark eyebrow arching in my direction as he takes three martini glasses and starts mixing the drinks.

I watch in awe as his large skilled hands mix our drinks and wonder what it would be like to be that Boston shaker right now. He's assured in a way I never really noticed in a man before, almost effortless. I bet he doesn't have to flirt, he just asks a woman to get on her knees and she falls to the floor, her tongue lolling out, waiting for him to take what he wants.

The idea is...erotic.

"Our friend Kate here is finally divorced," Chelsea says and I can't decide if the heat on my cheeks is from embarrassment or from the alcohol they keep plying me with.

Mostly, when you tell people you're going through a divorce or have just gotten divorced, you get looks of pity, or they don't even know how to react.

Not this mysterious bartender. He smiles instead, placing the drink in front of me.

"Well, you'll have to let me know his name, so if he ever comes in, I can give him a free drink for the misfortune of losing you."

I blink at him, and he winks, helping the customers next to us. Goddamn, he's smooth as fuck.

Savannah and Chelsea both look over at me with wide eyes and I realize I didn't speak at all during that encounter. Just as I suspected, I'm shit at this.

"He was flirting with you, that's how you seduce someone. Next time he comes back, say something, anything," Savannah says.

I turn on my stool so I'm facing her. "Like what? Hi Mr. Hot bartender, you look like you were sent here from the planet Krypton to save the universe in the form of giving an orgasm to every woman who looks at your handsome face?"

Savannah shrugs, and her face scrunches into a frown that says maybe that wasn't too bad. I hold my drink up to my lips taking a sip as I conjure up something better than comparing him to Superman. Nothing else comes to mind.

"I'm no good at this, maybe I should download some apps or something," I say, noticing the drink he made tastes way better than the last round.

"Apps aren't a bad idea, but you have a guy right in front of you, who was totally looking at your tits and complimenting you. Plus, he looks like he fucks well. It doesn't hurt that he seems age appropriate either, not that I would judge you if you wanted to be a cougar for a little bit. Those young ones have stamina."

I blink at my friend before shooting back the rest of the cocktail. Maybe some liquid courage is what I need. Or maybe it will make things worse.

But what's the worst that could happen? I make a complete fool out of myself and we just can't drink here anymore? Those odds aren't bad, and I need to practice. If I want to actually live like I've been telling myself, then I need to make a change. I need to take the first steps.

I wince as the alcohol trickles down my throat and hits my blood stream faster than I thought it would. My body feels hot, my limbs are loose, and I'm absolutely one hundred percent going to at least attempt to flirt with this man. Even if it ends in yet another form of rejection, at least I can say that I tried.

I'm not letting my failed marriage hang over my head another day. It's finally real, stamped on paper. I already got all the paperwork together to change my name back. I'm no longer someone's wife. I'm an attractive woman who's ready to take life by the balls, literally and figuratively.

I'm going to do this. I'm going to order another drink and say something cute and flick my hair and give him fuck me eyes. I'm not someone's ex-wife or professor right now. I'm a woman in her prime fucking years, who needs to do something about it or else I'll find myself another eighteen years from now filled with regrets, with no one but myself to blame.

I go to grab the martini glass, promptly knocking it over on the bar, where my hand lands.

"Ouch," I hiss and a grimace takes over my face when I glance down at where a shard of glass pierced my palm.

"Oh, shit, Kate. Are you okay?" Chelsea asks, waving down the bartender.

I'm embarrassed as I go to pick up the shards of glass, even while my palm is bleeding and pain is radiating up my forearm. A large hand wraps around my wrist stopping me.

"I've got a first aid kit in the office. Leo, can you get this cleaned up?" the too hot for his own good bartender asks a fellow employee.

He grabs a clean towel and holds it against my hand before walking around the bar.

"What do I do?" I ask my friends in a sharp whisper.

"Do whatever he tells you to," Savannah says.

The idea appeals to me more than she would ever know. It's always been something I craved, but never received. I think I'd have no problem listening to whatever he told me to do; in fact, I know I'd get off on it.

"At the very least, let him check on your hand," Chelsea says.

I nod as he comes to stand before me. He's tall and I have to crane my neck to look at him, even while sitting on the stool. I'm holding the towel against my hand as he lightly grabs my elbow.

"Follow me," he says, his voice sounds like a caress and I wish I could bottle his confidence up and drink even just a drop.

His hand is calloused and warm as he leads me up the stairs, unlocking an office door while I stare at his broad back and wonder what he looks like shirtless.

My mind is in the gutter, despite my hand bleeding. All I want to do is get a glimpse of more of his skin, because even if I get just that, I know he'll be featured in my fantasies for the foreseeable future.

Gavin

Divorced Women Are the Best Lays

I WAS in the office when Troy said he needed to leave early for a family emergency. It's Saturday night, and we were already short staffed, so I filled in at the bar. It's not an uncommon place for me to wind up. Ben and I fill in wherever we're needed for any of our businesses.

A boat captain out sick? We'll drive the boat.

Chef called out? We're tossing on an apron.

Our plan a few years back was to open a club, but then this space became available and it had everything we wanted. A place to dock our party boats, the perfect bay side views, and additional space that was nearly done that would play live music and feel like a club.

It was never our plan to set permanent roots in Tampa Bay, but we're both glad we did. With Lincoln and Penny popping out kids and our parents getting older, it made sense to stay close and accept that what we want in life can shift.

We still have our fun, more than our fair share, but we've become legitimate business owners and though we don't talk about it much, I know we are proud of what we've accomplished.

It's weird, understanding our older brothers more and more with each year that passes by. I get why our oldest brother Aiden is so proud to have his own business, and why our middle brother feels accomplished taking over our father's business.

Ben and I expanded this small little empire to what it is now. Granted, we couldn't have done this without the first boat our father gifted us, or the lack of pressure from our parents because our older brothers were so grossly motivated.

But looking at what we built, the responsibility we have, I don't hate it.

Our clientele for Carlson's Bar and Marina were typically more refined, accomplished with money, and that's how we liked it. It's also how we can charge eighteen dollars a cocktail and nobody bats an eye. The party boat business fits more into a younger crowd and it's an accomplishment hitting both markets.

It's a typical night at Carlson's; we have a guy in the corner on guitar singing covers and a mix of older men in boat shoes and women in cocktail dresses and high heels filling the warmly lit space.

Women are my favorite customers. They tip well, and even though I pass those along to the staff, it always gives me an ego boost.

Tonight's no different. No, tonight is even better.

I'd spotted the trio as soon as I took over for Troy. He let me know what they were drinking, along with his other customers' orders, before he hightailed it out of the bar with a somber expression on his face.

I could tell from across the bar that they were professional women, well off, put together.

But there was something about the dark-haired woman with the bright blue eyes that itched my curiosity. While her two friends spoke animatedly and with wide smiles, she seemed to be staring at the bottom of her martini glass, looking for answers.

It wasn't that it was a unique experience. Lots of people came here and used alcohol or a crowd as a vice for whatever they were going through. Yet, something about her intrigued me.

Maybe she was the type of beautiful that forced you to pay attention. It was effortless, like she was a genetic anomaly. Thick dark hair framed her face and was beginning to curl with the night's humidity, whipping off the bay. Her lashes and brows were dark, framing crystalline blue eyes. Her skin in high contrast, she must wear SPF 100 everywhere she goes to stay unblemished.

Her clothes gave the indication she was a professional, somewhere with a dress code. Maybe it was the thing that had her wound up so tight.

But something told me she wanted to untie that pretty white bow around her collar and let loose. I wasn't sure what it was about her, but it was there. Maybe it had been too long since I'd been to Avalon—a sex club I was adamant on never joining, yet now held a monthly membership—or maybe it was the fact I'd been so busy I hadn't fucked anyone in a while.

But she had my attention, and I unreasonably wanted to attract hers as well. I walk up to their party, while she's staring down an empty glass.

"Another?" I ask, her bright blue eyes glancing up at me analytically, though a word doesn't slip from her lips.

"We'd all like another. We're celebrating," her bubbly blonde friend says.

"Oh? What are we celebrating tonight?" I'm genuinely

curious, it isn't some ploy that bartenders often use to get heavy tips and repeat customers. I want to know what was going on in her pretty little head.

"Our friend Kate here is finally divorced," the brunette friend said, and I glance down at Kate, who still hasn't responded while I made the women their drinks.

Divorce is usually such a dirty word, but I've been in the divorce party business long enough that I know that isn't what people wanted to hear. "Well, you'll have to let me know his name, so if he ever comes in, I can give him a free drink for the misfortune of losing you."

Kate looks up at me like she's overthinking something, unconsciously licking the vodka off her plush bottom lip. Instead of lingering, I nod, and help the next patrons at the bar.

I overhear Kate and her friends talking about my looks, and it takes everything in me to hold back the smug smile off my face. I know how I look. Ben and I have no issues getting women. Doesn't mean I'll ever get sick of hearing it though.

My plan was to buy their next round, maybe flirt with Kate more and see if she'd actually speak to me, when fate intervened and the sweet divorcée broke a martini glass on the bar top.

She goes to pick up the glass in an embarrassed hurry as I grab her wrist. I shouldn't think about the fact that my thumb could leave a perfect bruise on the body part, but I do. I grab a clean rag and hand it to her.

It doesn't look bad, but I'm an opportunistic asshole and divorcées are my favorite flavor.

"I've got a first aid kit in the office. Leo, can you get this cleaned up?" I ask the bar back as I round the bar and come to stand before the three women.

Kate is tiny, probably five foot four in heels, as I grab her by the elbow.

"Follow me." I direct her up the stairs and to my office and flick on the light. I can feel her gaze boring into my back the whole way and realize she still hasn't spoken a single word to me, but followed me anyway.

I head over to the cabinet on the left, grabbing the first aid kit, before tapping the long desk that faces the water and houses two chairs, one for me and one for my twin brother, Benjamin.

Too short, I grab her waist and help her up onto the table, making her clear her throat, but she doesn't say anything else.

"You know, I don't usually have an issue getting women to talk to me," I joke, as I pull back the rag and take a look at her hand. I use the flashlight on my phone to get a better look to see if there's any glass stuck in her flesh. It's hard to see with the blood and I know I'll have to get her cleaned up first. I open up the first aid kit and hope that she decides to speak to me while I bandage her up.

"I'm sure you don't, looking like that," she says. Her voice is raspy and sultry. It's not what I expected, in a good way.

Her eyes go wide as she says it, but I smile, taking her in. She's beyond pretty, and I notice a scar that's clearly old on her neck that fades into her collarbone. I'm intrigued, while at the same time find it charming and unique.

"I mean, you have to know you're handsome."

"It never gets old hearing it. As I'm sure you would know," I reply.

I clean off her wound with alcohol and a cotton swab. She hisses in discomfort, but doesn't stop me as I make sure her palm is clean and there's no glass embedded in her skin.

"No. I wouldn't."

"A little cliché having a dickhead ex-husband who didn't appreciate what he had in front of him," I say as I apply ointment to her skin and wrap her hand up.

She blushes beautifully and I kinda like the fact she must not spend a ton of time in the sun. It helps you see when she's flushed.

"Do you usually bring recent divorcées into your boss's office after plying them with cocktails and then charm them into submission?" she says, before looking up at the ceiling. Clearly, the alcohol did remove some of her filter.

I don't correct her and tell her that this is my office, that I'm the boss, and that no, I haven't actually brought a woman here. Usually I fuck women at the sex club I pay for to avoid the need for courting. But every now and then when the mood strikes and the night feels right, I do sometimes treat myself to an unplanned drunken night of fuckery.

"Actually, divorcées are my favorite," I say with a grin, her lush lips parting in shock at my words.

"What?" she asks, confusion written in her furrowed brows.

"Divorced women are the best lays," I say plainly, placing a band-aid over her palm.

"How do you figure?" she asks, like she thought less of herself for ending a relationship that was consummated with the government. Like people don't break up all the time, no one thinks less of them.

"Well, they're usually so sexually frustrated it takes very little effort to make them come. Plus, they aren't looking for anything serious. I don't do serious, I do casual. Very casual."

She blinks at me, her dark long lashes shutting over the top of her calculating eyes.

"Casual?" she asks, a woman of very few words.

"Yes. No girlfriends, the occasional hookup, and other arrangements," I say vaguely, not wanting to spook her.

She licks her lips, glancing down at her bandaged palm. She could leave now, go back to her friends and the night would be over and we'd both go home unsatisfied. Either way, the ball is in her court as to where this evening should go.

Though it doesn't seem like she grasps the memo. Maybe she needs continued outright bluntness, which I can more than handle.

"Would you like me to take you back downstairs to your friends? Or would you like me to bend you over my boss's desk and prove to you why I love to fuck divorced women?"

She opens her mouth to say something, and then abruptly shuts it. Her eyes meeting mine head on, no shyness, just analysis.

"Do you have a condom?" she asks.

"I do," I say, tugging at that sweet pretentious bow wrapped around her neck and tugging. "Are you sure, Kate?"

"Yes, I'm sure. It's uh...it's been a while for me."

"Do you want me to promise to be gentle? Or do you want me to give you a memorable fuck that you can go back downstairs on wobbly legs and tell your friends about?"

Her throat bobs as my fingers trail along her collarbone, non-avoidant of the aged scar there. Kate's eyes search mine for a moment, and she doesn't respond with words.

Instead, she fists my dress shirt, dragging me down and capturing my lips against hers. At first her kiss is messy, unsure, and unpracticed. But as I tangle my hand in her curling hair and direct the kiss, she melts into the touch.

Soft whimpers and pants slipping out of her mouth.

I don't kiss the women I fuck very often, but as I kiss Kate, I wonder why. I find this enjoyable, erotic, even. Maybe I should change my stance on the act. While enjoyable and hot, I don't find it attaching me to this woman I just met. It just makes me want to fuck her even more.

We break apart from the kiss, both of us breathing heavily.

"All right sweetheart, take off your dress and turn around," I order her, and she immediately follows directions.

It has my dick hard as she grabs the hem of her dress, removing the garment completely, showcasing a mismatched set of black panties and a white bra.

I forgot how alluring it can be when a woman wasn't expecting to get fucked that night.

Kate

What Do You Want?

MY FIRST THOUGHT when he asked me to take off my dress should have been about the fact I hadn't shaved my vagina in god knows how long. While I haven't let it get full-blown 1974 down there, it was indeed not waxed or shaven to any extent.

I'm sure this super hot bartender, who I don't even know the name of, is used to pristine pussy. The kind that's devoid of razor bumps, or ingrown hairs.

But when he told me what to do, I obeyed immediately. It's like he cracked me open, seeing all the secrets of what I did to myself and what I watched in the dark.

It's like he knew I wanted to listen, that I wanted to shut my brain down for a single second and have a man take control.

His lips press against my neck and my nails attempt to dig against the resin table.

"Relax, Kate," he tells me, his voice smooth as velvet as his hard cock presses against my backside and his hands slide up my torso.

For fuck's sake. I didn't even wear matching underwear today.

He doesn't seem to mind as his hands explore, palming my breasts as his body presses harder against me.

There's a massive window in front of us, but the window faces the water, so it's unlikely that anyone can see inside. Having people watch isn't necessarily something I fantasize about, but I don't think I'm against it.

Seeing the reflection of how he's looking at my ass in the glass, however, is something that's going to be replayed in my fantasies for the foreseeable future.

He looks raw and excited.

His focus is on me, and I can't remember the last time I felt like I was the center of attention.

The hot bartender presses down the cups of my bra, exposing my breasts and playing with my nipples. I swallow thickly as his one hand glides down my torso, nervous that he'll be turned off.

But when his fingers slide against my mound, rubbing against my pubic hair, his lips suck against my skin and he grinds harder against my ass. Does it turn him on?

"Do you come easily, Kate?"

Part of me wants to lie, be amenable and say yes, *"but of course I'll come as soon as you touch my clit"*. But what's the point? I'm going to fuck this guy once and nothing more. There's no reason to lie, no reason to fake my enjoyment.

"No, I usually don't," I tell him honestly.

He hums against my ear.

"How do you usually make yourself come?" he asks, no uncomfortableness between us.

I couldn't tell the only man I've been with my fantasies, but something about the low-stakes impromptu fuck has me wanting to lay some of my cards on the table, just not enough to leave me completely raw.

"A toy inside of me and a vibrator on my clit."

"Do you skip all the lower settings, Kate? Do you just go to the highest one?" he asks.

It should be embarrassing, but if anything, it has my core clenching and I feel myself getting wetter with his questions.

"Yes."

"How quickly can you make yourself come?" he asks.

His fingertips are dancing around my clit, not touching me where I want him to, but it's making me want to beg. Something I've never done, but it's something I've wanted to do.

The sex I've had for the last five or so years has been clinical, an obligation. One where I rarely got off and waited till Will was asleep or in the shower and I raced time, cracking open my nightstand and using a toy to get myself off when he was none the wiser.

"A few minutes," I say, lying slightly. In a pinch, I could make myself come even quicker if I was worked up enough, or drunk enough, watching the right porn could do wonders.

"I can work with that," he says, sliding his fingers between my lips, pinching my clit between them, making me jolt against the desk, digging into my hips.

"Fuck," I grit out.

He keeps stroking my clit, not pressing inside of me. He's leisurely with it, like he isn't in a rush, like he doesn't have to get back to work and like he actually cares if I finish or not.

I'd have been fine if he slipped the condom on and fucked me. At least I'd taken the first step in the right direction on taking my life into my own hands.

Instead, he kisses my neck and continues grinding against my ass while he toys with me.

I know I'm drenching his fingers. He knows it too. "You're so wet. This pussy was meant to be fucked. You want it so bad, don't you? God, I know you want it so bad," he says, nibbling on my ear, and smelling my hair?

When he pushes two fingers inside of me, I gasp at the sensation of having someone else touch me this way and how good it feels. I can hear how wet I am, and he likes it, so do I.

His other hand leaves my bra, sliding up to my neck, before shifting back down. I want to grab his wrist and bring his hand back, but I'm barely holding myself up on the table.

His touch is gone, except his fingers pressing inside of me as he opens a drawer next to us, grabbing a condom.

"Are you sure you don't take all the girls up here to fuck in your boss's office?" I ask again.

He laughs behind me. It's deep and sensual.

"Only the special ones," he says, his fingers slipping out of me and I nearly whine.

The leather of his belt sliding through his pant loops, and the click of his buckle has my back arching. The rip of the foil packet of the condom has me licking my lips in anticipation. I have no idea how big he is, no idea how good he looks sliding the condom over his cock, but in my imagination he looks sexy and assured.

No matter how badly I want to see it in person, I don't turn around in fear that I'll completely lose my nerve.

He grabs the waistband of my panties, pressing them down my thighs, the head of his cock pressing against my entrance. He's big. I knew he would be. You don't walk around with that much confidence unless you have the dick to match, and he presses forward.

I'm so wet that I can feel the evidence of my arousal on my thighs.

He pushes inside of me, not in a hurry. One of his hands lands on my hip as the other wraps around my waist, his talented fingers back on my clit.

His breath fans against the nape of my neck as he stretches me. He's bigger than the toy I use and I'm biting my lip, adjusting to his width.

"That's good, Kate," he says, and a shiver rips out of me against my will.

How bad have I wanted this? Someone to talk me through it?

He moans lightly against my ear, pushing more of himself deep inside of me.

"You feel so good. Made to be fucked. So wet. So tight."

He's sliding my clit between his two fingers, applying more pressure as he bottoms out, his hips flush with my ass.

"Good?" he asks.

"Mmmhmm. G-ood. So fucking good, don't stop," I tell him, I might combust if he doesn't start moving again.

I thought feelings were the part of sex that made it good. I'd had hoped I was wrong, and thankfully this well endowed, ridiculously hot masterpiece behind me was blowing my fucking mind.

Because this felt right.

There weren't any feelings, just consideration for wanting to make each other feel good mixed with unrelenting hormones and need.

"What do you want, Kate?"

God, the way he keeps saying my name is going to give me a complex. It sounds sultry and has me feeling needy and overeager to please. As badly as I want to come and walk away from this experience with a new person, I want him to remember me too.

He could have brought me in here, bent me over this table, and rutted me until he filled the condom and sent me on my way. I'm not sure why he cares so much about what I want, but I won't look a gift horse in the mouth.

He's my divorce present, I decide, and that makes a smile take over my face.

"What do I want?" I respond as he pulls out and slowly pushes back inside of me.

"Yes, tell me how you want it."

I want a lot of things that I've never said out loud. A lot of things that aren't easy to explain while his dick is already inside of me. I could say I want to come, which is a cop-out, a given response.

But what do I want? What do I want to walk away with from this one-night stand?

"I want...I want you to be rough," I tell him, almost in a whisper.

How many times did I ask for something simple, a small fraction of what I wanted from Will, and he wouldn't provide it? What if he's more of the same and thinks there's something wrong with me for what I like?

"Can I spank your ass?" he asks and I swallow thickly.

"Yes."

His fingertips against my clit retreat, as he holds on to my hip with a bruising grip. As his hand smacks the top of my ass in a downward trajectory. I can feel my pussy clenching as he does it.

"Was that okay? Too hard?"

"Harder," I say.

I've simulated impact play on my own a few times, but nothing compares to how this feels. He takes my direction and does it again in the same spot, making a pathetic moan slip from my lips. I'm so fucking wet each time his cock slips out of me, our sticky flesh makes a salacious sucking noise.

It's a turn on I didn't know I had.

"More?" he asks.

"Please, don't stop."

His hand comes down again on my tender flesh, and my thighs quake. His large hand grips the spot that I know is flushed pink, kneading my ass cheek.

"You should see how pretty your ass looks right now," he says, his hand giving me one more solid smack before wrapping around my waist, back on my clit.

"I'm going to fuck you hard. You tell me to stop if it's too much," he says and I nod. His hips thrust powerfully, pounding against my ass. "Words, Kate."

"Yes, I-I understand."

"Good. I'm going to fuck this sweet little pussy and you're going to come all over my cock and fingers, because it's what you were made for."

As soon as the last word slips off his tongue, he does exactly what he promises. His hips slapping against my reddened ass while his fingers strum my clit like he's practiced in how my body works.

He doesn't hold back, a simultaneous effort of reaching his own climax while giving me mine. His cock is so deep that it borders on pain, and I yearn for it.

I'm so close, so so close, and he knows it as he adds more pressure on to my clit.

"I told you this pussy was meant to be fucked. Your pussy gripping my cock is driving me fucking crazy. You're such a good girl, Kate," he whispers between rushed pants in my ear, thrusting deep.

I shatter completely, nearly collapsing on the table and I can't decide if it's more from the angle his cock is pressing deep inside of me or his filthy words. He doesn't coddle me during my orgasm. He presses me against the table, my breasts and cheek against the cold surface as a strong hand between my shoulder blades keeps me in place.

He loses himself fucking me, taking what he wants while wringing me dry of any coherent thoughts. It feels like it lasts forever, like his dick is hitting just the right spot and it will never end.

He smacks my ass one more time, before grabbing both of my hips and thrusting hard, his length jerking inside of me as he finishes.

My thighs are shaking and my breath is leaving condensation against the table as we catch our breath and bask in the moment.

He doesn't slip out of me right away, just kneading my ass as he begins to soften inside me. He drags a hand down my spine before finally sliding out of me, a wet suctioning sound follows as his body leaves mine.

I'm still bent over the table as I collect my thoughts and reel from what just happened. I expect some shame or confusion, but all I'm left with is clarity.

I grin against the table as a trashcan lid closes and the stranger who just rocked my fucking world comes back over to the table.

"You okay?" he asks, his hand on my back, rubbing soft circles.

"More than okay, thank you," I say.

He laughs.

"What?" I ask, as he helps me stand up. My legs are like a newborn fawn's as I wobble and lean my sore ass against the edge of the table.

"Thanking me for sex, when it was definitely my pleasure," he says, his cock put away in his pants. My biggest regret was not getting a good look at it. He gets down on a knee and helps me slide my panties back on.

It's sweet and unexpected, making me blush. He just spanked me, but this small act of kindness is what has me clamming up.

He grabs my dress and helps me put it back on.

I catalog his handsome face, knowing I'll never forget him. Even when I'm sixty with eighteen cats, because at this rate that's how many I'll have, I'll think fondly back on the man who eased my pain. The man who made me feel like I wasn't a freak for the things I wanted. He made me feel alive when I needed it the most.

Feeling bold, maybe reckless, I grab his chin and plant a soft kiss against his lips.

"Thank you," I say again, kissing his cheek, and I walk out of the office, not saying another word as I feel him watching me walk away and I do my best not to fall down the stairs and make a complete spectacle of myself.

I'm patting down my dress, hoping that I don't look like I've just been fucked within an inch of my life, as I meet up with Chelsea and Savannah. Both of their mouths drop as they stand up from their barstools.

You would have thought I told them I won the Nobel Prize and not my back blown out the way they both squeal with excitement and clap their hands together.

"Kate is back, baby!" Savannah shouts.

"So fucking back," Chelsea adds in.

"Now tell us every single detail of what happened in the hot bartender's office. Look at you, you aren't even walking straight. He fucks good, doesn't he? I knew he would," Savannah rambles on.

"I will tell you everything if we leave right now and never

come back," I say, taking one last glance back toward the stairwell to the office.

His large frame is leaned up against the wall, a smirk on his face. I take in his appearance one last time, making sure I save it in my memory forever.

He gave me more than a one-night stand. He gave me everything and he doesn't even have a clue.

4 months later

"PLEASE, I need more stories of the whore chronicles of Kate," Chelsea says, drinking her mimosa. This is the third time we've done brunch this week alone.

It's summer and with no summer courses, Chelsea and I have too much time on our hands.

"Savannah really fucked up teaching courses this summer," I say to Chelsea who nods in agreement.

Four months have changed a lot of things for me, to be honest, I almost feel like a new person. I'm down to only one therapy session a month. I'm enjoying living alone more than I ever thought I would, and I feel lighter. So much fucking lighter.

I'm no longer hoarding secrets of myself, all those pieces I gave away to my ex-husband. I've been slowly finding them and piecing them together to build who I am today.

It took me time to realize that I'm not trying to go back in time and be the Kate I was at twenty-five. No, I'm living happily as a single woman in her thirties and it's more fulfilling than I thought it would ever be.

I hang out with my friends. I've adopted way too many cats. I go to the movies by myself and out to eat and there's no shame behind it. I've gone on some dates, but with the same end goal in mind, get laid and ticking everything off of my list.

There have been the good and then the outright terrible.

I've made a decision about how to move forward and I'm not sure how Chelsea will take it, but I'm going to tell her anyway.

"I'm done with the apps," I tell her and she gasps.

"But the lore, the endless entertainment we get from you being on apps," she complains and I give her a glare. "You're right, this isn't about me."

"I'm not looking to date, and while a lot of guys on there aren't either, so many of them suck," I complain.

They suck at sex, just looking to bust their load and dip, no interest in exploring kink or power dynamics. Others are looking to date and see me as someone who's biological clock is ticking while I clearly state in my profile that I don't want children. Which leads me to believe half of these motherfuckers can't read.

"I figure I can use money to solve the problem," I tell her and she looks at me wide-eyed.

"A prostitute?" she says, grabbing the stem of the champagne flute like a high society housewife would clutch their pearls.

"No, dumbass. I'm signing up for a sex club."

"Those are a real thing?" Chelsea asks, and I nod.

"Yes, it's a real thing. I found one I think will be a good fit. I think it will take a lot of the burden away from what I want, you know?"

"Kate, I mean this with all my heart, no. I don't know. Explain it to me."

Chelsea is happily married with a husband who gets her. They're all over each other like horny teenagers, and she doesn't have similar interests behind closed doors as I do.

"When I meet these guys on apps, they're usually a complete disappointment."

"Like Justin," she says, and we both wince.

Justin looked good on paper, normal job, nice enough guy. But he wasn't packing and didn't know how to overcompensate with his hands or his mouth. When I didn't finish, he called me a slut and said he wasn't interested in me anyway.

"I'm on an exploration to find what I like and I've seen glimpses of it. But the club will be a place where men have the same ideas minus the mental labor of fielding them out through apps and continually being disappointed."

All of my hook ups weren't bad, I actually enjoyed some of them. Though, when I found myself comparing them to the stranger at the marina, they couldn't hold a candle. Maybe I'd built up that memory in my mind, but deep down I know I didn't. He was the standard I wanted for myself, and the apps weren't providing it.

"I know to engage in the things I want to do there needs to be some sort of trust in there, which is hard when I don't want a boyfriend and I don't want to take chances on these online encounters anymore," I reiterate and Chelsea nods her head, seeming to understand.

"I'm picturing a sex dungeon or like the red room," Chelsea says and I laugh into my glass.

"Of course you would. It's actually very classy. I took a tour yesterday and filled out all the paperwork."

"So how much are we talking monthly?" she asks.

I hide myself behind my glass as I mumble the number.

"What was that?"

"Five thousand."

"A month? Kate! Do you think your Aunt Helene would've predicted your trust fund would go to supporting a sex club membership?"

I wince and grab a piece of calamari as my best friend blinks at me. A typical associate art professor wouldn't be able to afford it, but my situation of where my money comes from is unique and equally complicated.

Chelsea whistles. "If you think about the return on investment and how much each orgasm costs, damn," she says, her economics brain doing overtime.

"It's not just about that," I tell her and she nods.

She gets it, but she doesn't.

If it was just about coming, I'd continue what I've been doing. I have no issue bringing myself to orgasm, it's just I wanted more. So so much more.

She tips back her drink and her eyes go wide.

"Oh, fuck," she hisses, and my brows furrow as she looks at me. "Kate, I'm so sorry," she says.

A stroller pushes past us and I look down, only to glance up and see my ex-husband, his fiancée—sorry, new wife—and their child, age unclear.

"Kate," Will says, glancing between me and Chelsea.

I say nothing.

"Chelsea, did you hear something?" I ask, and she laughs.

"Uh, maybe I heard an adulterous motherfucker trying to speak?"

"Kate," he says in a more stern voice and I glance over at him and his new wife, who's a decade his junior.

I still hate her, hate him, and honestly, as much as it pains me, I hate their stupid baby, too. It isn't its fault that it was created during my marriage, and I wouldn't ever be purposefully mean to a child, but it's my right to loathe them all.

I'm glad to not be married to him. My life is honestly better. Doesn't mean I don't hold space to hate him and his new family. He could have ended things with me before cheating, especially before getting someone pregnant.

"Why don't you take Danger to the table, baby," he says to his wife.

I have to suck my lips into my mouth before belting with laughter. Chelsea doesn't help the situation as her mouth gapes open like a fish.

He named his kid Danger.

"Kate, I was hoping we could talk about the shares," he says. "My lawyer has been trying to contact you."

Yes, he has, and I've promptly told him to fuck himself in every way possible. I even pulled out my Synonym Finder from college so that every response was different enough, but packed just the right amount of punch.

"Come on, you still can't be bitter," he says.

Bitter.

The word makes me want to throat punch him and then pull his wife's hair. Instead, I blink at him, not saying a word, turning back to Chelsea.

"Hey, Chels?"

"Yes, Kate?"

"Do you remember that time I used a big chunk of my trust fund to start my ex-husband's business and my lawyer wisely advised me to hold on to fifty-five percent of the company when doing so in case anything were to happen? Like, I don't know, he went through a midlife crisis and got his young side piece pregnant?"

Chelsea holds up a finger. "You know, I do remember that. Well, if you got divorced, it would really suck for him that you wisely also had him sign a prenup. You could single-handedly ruin his company."

Was I petty and ruthless for holding these shares over his head? Absolutely, and I got enjoyment out of it.

Especially when he looked down at me red faced and pissed off.

"Kate, this isn't fucking funny anymore. I have a family now."

Well, that felt like my stomach plummeting to the fucking ground. At one point, Will was the only family I had, and he knew that. He knew how important his family was to me, and now they no longer existed in my life. The moment Will was done with me, so was his family. It was a low blow, and he wanted it to hurt.

I always thought that if I ended up divorced, I'd be mature and civil. I was absolutely wrong. I kinda wanted to ruin his life. I could be over him, want nothing to do with him, while also wanting to make him suffer. My therapist didn't quite agree, but Janet wasn't the end all be all of morality.

"I think you should really watch how you speak to the majority shareholder of Dennis Commercial," Chelsea says, pointing a perfectly manicured nail in his direction.

"Please, Kate. You got the house. Please let me buy my shares back."

"It was my aunt's house. It was always my house. I suggest you go have lunch with your wife and kid and leave me the fuck alone," I tell him.

He glares at me, and it feels good. As he storms over to the table, his wife looks hurt and confused. I don't hate her as much as I hate him, she's young and stupid, and shackled with his kid. But she had to know he was married, and she didn't give a shit. But Will is truly the only one to blame. He made me a promise, and he's the one that broke it. Not his doe-eyed new wife who, according to her LinkedIn, took a long break from work. I'm sure Will loves having her stay home, making his lunches, and never asking more of him.

Cheating wasn't the only problem, and I know that now. Neither of us were giving each other what we wanted. Will wanted a traditional wife. He told me he was fine not having kids, but that was clearly a lie. He didn't understand why I wanted to be a professor, why I didn't stop after my masters and needed a doctorate in fine arts. He thought it was stupid, that adding additional degrees was frivolous.

He wanted me to cook more; he wanted simple, and I wasn't a simple woman and I never would be. I was complicated, messy, something he loved but at some point that changed. Just like I wanted someone who was attentive, open, and not as stringent.

We grew too much. We're different people now, honestly I don't recognize him anymore, which is sad as it is eye opening. He isn't the boy who pieced my heart together when I moved to Tampa. He isn't the man who was there when my aunt died and he became my everything. Nor am I that broken girl anymore.

Part of me wonders if he lost interest when he realized there was nothing left of me to fix. When he realized I didn't need him. Part of me wanted him, wanted to make our marriage work, but that died a long time ago.

"Wow." Chelsea breaks my thought process as she tips back her mimosa.

We're going to need to get an Uber back to my place after this.

"So, do you have some maniacal plan of what you're going to do with his company?" she asks.

I shrug. I didn't know what I was going to do with the shares. They were rightfully mine. I invested a lot into Will and his business. My aunt would have rolled around in her grave if she knew what I did with my money. But I think she'd be incredibly satisfied with how I'm using it now.

I smile to myself. She would have loved the idea of me being free and finding myself.

"I'm not sure yet. For now, I'm holding on to it to torture him a little," I admit.

Chelsea grins at me, which I return.

"I think this is the best version of you," she says, refilling our glasses with champagne and a splash of orange juice. We clink our glasses and I realize, I agree.

I'm kinda in love with this version of me too.

Benjamin

Bad Shit

"WHERE'S GAVIN?" Penny, my cousin slash sister-in-law, asks. Though they've been married for five years, it's truly time to stop giving them grief for that shit, but I think I will till the day I die.

"He drew the short stick. He's driving a bachelorette party boat tonight," I reply, and Penny rolls her bright blue eyes.

"I'm sure he's devastated. Here, take Brynn," she says, handing me my three year old niece as she holds their one year old, Hudson. They really took the Carlson tradition of names ending in 'n' very seriously.

I hold my niece as she pinches my cheek. "Uncle Benny, snacks?" she says.

It's my job as the funnest uncle to give this child whatever she wants, especially if it makes my older brother Lincoln's life harder.

"Of course, my precious little angel, that I get to return to my cousin-sister-in-law."

"I swear to fuck Ben. If you teach her that I'll kill you."

"Kill you," Brynn repeats, nodding her head.

"I'm not the one teaching her bad shit."

"Bad shit," Brynn repeats with another nod.

Penny glares at me as the baby cries, so I take mercy on her and carry Brynn outside of my parent's house. I grab the largest chocolate chip cookie, hand it to my niece, and plant her on the outdoor furniture overlooking the lake.

I'm still not sure how to keep a three year old entertained. I love her, and my nephew, but the best part is the fact that I get to return them when it gets to be too much. Lincoln and Penny are endlessly happy in their marriage and being parents. I'm beyond happy for them, though I can't imagine it for myself.

I like to be able to pack a bag and go wherever I want on whim; I like my walls not smeared with finger print marks, and I definitely enjoy not having the heavy weight of someone's life on my shoulders.

While me and my twin's life are indefinitely intertwined, it's how we like it. He's my lifelong companion, in a sense, and I don't see the need for a serious relationship or marriage. I'm content, beyond content, really.

We have our businesses, ones we thoroughly enjoy running. We have the club, and we have pockets of fun with whatever woman we want to. Sometimes we share and other times we have our own flings.

Life is graciously uncomplicated and enjoyable. Honestly, it's a miracle we're happy here in Tampa, sticking close to our family and figuring out what direction we want.

"Oh my goodness, Brynny, you're a mess," my mother Maggie says as she comes outside. "It's almost dinner time, you gave her a cookie?" she scolds and I shrug my shoulders.

"It's what she wanted."

My mother sighs, like I'm exhausting. In fact, I think she thinks we're all exhausting, maybe not Aiden, my older brother. He was kind of perfect in every sense; I guess minus the fact he also doesn't plan to give her grandchildren. Sometimes I wonder if Lincoln knew that by giving my mother grandchildren the whole adopted cousin fucking thing would be swept under the rug.

By the way my mother looks at the chocolate-covered menace of a child, that theory would be correct. I can't deny that she's cute, favoring Penny more in looks with her bright blonde hair and baby blue eyes. But even as cute as she is, I don't want my own.

"Where's your brother?"

"Going to have to be more specific. I do have three of them."

"The one that you shared a womb with and they had to cut the two of you out of my body, making sure I never had any more children again," she says, wiping the chocolate off Brynn's face. Though I notice she doesn't take the cookie away from her either.

"Working."

"But it's Sunday," she says, like we don't have dinner with the family every goddamn Sunday like clockwork.

"You know, you could have sons who you never see, versus ones you see at a minimum once a week."

My mom glares at me, picking up Brynn, wiping her hands and holding her on her hip. Part of me wants to reach out and take her so my mother doesn't hurt herself, but I know she won't appreciate that.

"Let's go eat," she says in a baby voice to Brynn, and I follow them to the dining table.

The rest of the family is there, minus my twin. My parents, Maggie and Jeff. My aunt and uncle, Holly and Tim. My oldest brother, Aiden, and his wife Jessa. Lincoln and Penny, and their two children.

There are four empty chairs as I approach, one for me and

Gavin, and the two empty ones I believe are left vacant by my mother, manifesting that we will each find someone and settle down.

It's best that my parents don't know the intricacies of our lifestyle. We've never brought women here for family dinner and I suspect we never will. I can't see either of us ever being that interested in someone enough to shake up the life long dynamic that we have. Maybe we're too codependent on one another, but it works.

We're happy; it's enough for us, so it will have to be enough for my mother.

My brothers and Penny know how we operate, and they don't seem to care.

When I sit down and look over at Lincoln, he looks pissed. Not that it is uncommon for my dickish brother, but since he settled down with Penny, he's become a lot nicer.

"What crawled up your ass?" I ask, and he glares at me.

"Dennis Commercial giving you more shit again?" my dad asks him.

I'm thankful Lincoln took over the family business, because I don't want to touch it with a ten-foot pole, but he seems to thrive under the pressure.

"Something is up with their board. They're lowballing us on every project and winning. I'm not sure what's going on, but I'm going to get to the bottom of it," he says.

I basically tune out the conversation, eating my mashed potatoes, asparagus, and roast.

The sooner I get out of this dinner, the sooner I get to have some fun. Depending on how late Gavin's charter takes, he might come too, but I doubt it.

We were against going to Avalon, but since Lincoln doesn't go anymore and Aiden and Jessa only go from time to time on specific nights, it turns out to be a safe place for us. It makes things easier.

There are no expectations of a relationship. It's all to have fun and live out fantasies in a safe environment. I mean, god knows we paid a premium price for that peace of mind.

"Oh, Benjamin, do you know who I ran into?" my mother asks and I already know it's going to be some plot to set me up with a woman. "Do you remember my friend Deborah?"

My brows furrow. "From the Yacht club?"

"Yes! She has a daughter your age, a teacher I think, she's single."

"That's nice, mom."

"She gave me her number to pass along."

"Aunt Maggie, this roast is especially good tonight. Just look how much Hudson loves it," Penny says, forcing everyone to look at her precious little baby.

She gives me a conspiratorial wink and I smile back at her. Penny's definitely my favorite family member right now.

I just have to get out of this house without my mom trying to set me up with some random woman she ran into.

"Oh, Ben. I have the designs for the shirts for you to add to the marina. I'll email them over to you and Gavin tonight," Jessa says in a soft voice, my brother's arm tossed around her shoulder.

"Don't send them shit until they pay the invoice," Aiden complains, and I put a hand over my heart.

"Do you really believe I would stiff my sister-in-law like that? How rude," I say, whispering the word Daddy at him, causing him to glare right back at me. I learned that little secret a long time ago during a very confusing family vacation, and I fear I won't let it die. What's life worth if I can't make fun of my brothers at every opportunity?

"Don't fret, we'll get the invoice paid. Along with my very

gracious older brother printing them for us with his awesome sports supply company."

"Fine," Aiden says, and I give him a wide smile.

I look down at my non-existent watch. "I've got to get going. I'll see you next Sunday," I say, slapping my brothers on the shoulder, giving Jessa and Penny hugs, and touching my niece's and nephew's heads to stay away from their grubby little hands. When I get to my mother, she squeezes me tight.

"I'll text you her number."

I sigh, but agree, or else there's no way I'm getting out of this fucking house.

"Okay. Love you, Mom."

🪶 🪶 🪶

AVALON IS CLASSY, the front of the establishment is sophisticated with black and golds, reminiscent of a five-star hotel lobby. In the back is where all the salacious shit happens.

I'd been in a fair share of rooms and situations within Avalon's walls, and at thirty-five I have a pretty good grasp on what I like and what I don't like. It's easier to start my evening at the front of the house and work my way back, the women I like are surprisingly easy to spot.

I'm not much of a voyeur except for certain situations, so sometimes going to the bar in the back feels uncomfortable. I'm not much of an exhibitionist either; despite being a part of a sex club, the idea of being watched doesn't appeal to me.

I'm not into public humiliation, honestly degradation as a whole isn't my thing. What I like is hard to pinpoint exactly, maybe because I've only gotten little pieces here and there from previous partners of what I truly want.

I don't enjoy sharing unless it's with Gavin. So, needless to say, I like what I like and dislike what I don't and not many women are into what I wanted, and that's where my brother came into play. At least here, I wouldn't be judged or shut down. If you aren't into the same things as someone else you can politely decline and walk away; I can't say the same for picking up a stranger at a bar.

That's the beauty of Avalon. No strings, no judgment, while still getting what I need.

Cassandra is here, but she's talking to Henry. Nicole is here, but she's talking to George. So I make myself comfortable at the stool as Tex pours me a gin and tonic and slides it across the glowing bar.

"Thanks, Tex," I say, the dude has been working here for god knows how long, but he must get paid well enough to keep dealing with all of us deviants.

The stool next to me pulls out. The woman is tiny, dark hair, pale skin, wearing a red silk dress that showcases her full breasts. I notice a prominent scar along her neck and collarbone, but it doesn't detract from her beauty, if anything it makes her more interesting.

"Can I have a gimlet, please?" she says to Tex.

He gives her a once over, clearly not recognizing her.

"Can I have your membership number to start a tab?" he asks.

Ah, fresh meat. Tex knows every single one of us perverts who comes in and out of this place, but he doesn't know her.

She pulls out her black membership card, handing it to Tex, and he enters her information before handing her back the card. Her nails are perfectly manicured and I wonder what she's doing here. What's she into? Why's she here alone?

Not to stereotype, but a woman that looks like that, who obviously has money, typically comes here with a partner.

She must feel me staring at the side of her face as Tex

hands her her drink. She goes to take a sip, but her lips part on a gasp as she looks at me.

"It's you," she says, and my eyebrows furrow. Her cheeks heat a delicious pink and she clears her throat. "Oh. Um, Kate. A few months back at Carlson's Marina and Bar," she says.

A wicked smile takes over my lips as I hold out my hand. "Of course," I say, shaking her hand.

"I...uh...I never got your name."

"Benjamin Carlson, but you can call me Ben."

Gavin is absolutely going to fucking kill me.

Kate

Kismet and Negotiations

TWO THOUGHTS FILTER through me at once.

First, I'm not memorable; he didn't place who I am right away and isn't that a major fucking hit to my ego? Here I am comparing all the men I've slept with over the last four months to him, and he doesn't seem to recognize me. Exactly how many women does this man fuck? I mean, I guess it's not surprising with how he looks, and it also isn't a deal breaker for me either. I'm not looking for a man who wants more than my body. If he can be this detached, maybe that's a good thing.

Second, he's the owner of the bar, not the bartender. All that talk about bending me over his boss's desk, and he was the fucking boss. The realization makes me blush, but it also intrigues me.

So maybe he doesn't remember me, but he's here, and he's the best I'd ever had. Not that I'd tell him that, unless under serious duress.

"So, divorcées in your office aren't enough. You also come to Avalon?" I ask.

The smirk he gives me is devastating, and it's the exact

reason I let him fuck me from behind without knowing his name a few months ago.

But now that I know his name, Benjamin Carlson, I realize it fits, his name sounds as expensive as he looks. He's dressed similarly to the night we met, except his button down is dark blue, which makes his eyes look more blue than green. I knew I was right about them changing color.

"Would it make you feel special if I told you that night was an exception to the rule?" he asks with a wink, taking a sip of his drink.

Oh, this motherfucker is good.

His throat bobs with his swallow and I can't help but feel like this is kismet.

I was more nervous about coming here tonight than I'd ever admit. The amount of research I've done on sex club etiquette and the amount of time I spent on Avalon's membership portal was borderline neurotic. But I wanted to be prepared, I needed this to be a good experience.

I even went in with the mindset that I wouldn't leave the front of the room today, that maybe I'd just meet some like-minded people and chat.

And here *he* is, sitting at the barstool next to me.

The man who has no clue the drastic impact he's had in my life. He made me realize that I so desperately wanted to explore this suppressed sexual side of myself, and I'm not even sure he remembers that night at all.

"Maybe a little special," I say. My flirting has increased tenfold since that night. Which doesn't say much, because I still might be kinda shit at it.

"Is this your first night at Avalon, Kate?" he says my name in the same tone he did when we had our tryst, but somehow it seems like he's saying it for the first time.

"What gave me away?" I ask, taking a sip of the drink, grateful that it isn't too strong.

"Tex knows everyone who comes here. The needing to see your membership card was kind of a giveaway."

"That would do it."

He shifts his body so he's facing me, his long strong legs spread on the stool. He's effortless with his movements, someone who's endlessly confident and knows what a wet dream he is.

"What delicacies are you looking for tonight?" he asks and I swallow thickly.

I did come in here with a goal in mind. An insane goal at that.

"I have a list."

"A list?" he says and I nod. "Can I see?" he asks.

There's this clawing feeling of judgment that wraps around my throat, but this place is one filled with open-minded people, so I choke it down. He pays the same membership fee I do. People don't do that unless there's something they want to get out of this place. The marketing even called it a judgment-free zone.

Just treat him like he isn't the gorgeous one night stand that convinced you to explore your sexuality, show him the list, maybe he'll offer to help.

"Alright," I oblige, opening my clutch and unfolding the paper and handing it to him. His fingertips lightly brush mine as he takes it in hand.

He doesn't even read the first part as he glances up at me. "Doctor Katherine Morley?"

I blush and point to the top. "PhD in fine art. I'm a professor over at Tampa U."

His cute little dimple in his chin shows as he glances back

down at my paper. His face gives nothing away. I can't tell if he's turned on or disgusted.

"What do these numbers mean on the side?" he asks.

"If I've done it, I rate it on a system on if I would do it again."

"Spanking. Ten," he says with a smirk. Maybe he does remember. "This anal score is low."

I nearly choke on the gimlet, making its way down my throat. "Yes, but...that was, uh...more so to do with that one time. I would try it again."

He shrugs and keeps going and I wonder if anything on my list is freaking him out.

> Threesome with two men.
> Orgy? (I'd need to see how the threesome went to see if that would be something I'd enjoy.)
> Bondage
> Pegging (At least once to see what it's about)
> Cum play
> Wax play
> Power dynamic switching
> Edging (I don't know if I'm strong enough for this)
> Dirty talk ✓ 10/10

Dirty talk is checked off with a ten next to it. Does he have any idea that he's the one to receive the perfect score?

A few other things are on the list, and others are crossed off.

Degradation isn't my thing I've learned. Not after my Tinder date called me a dirty fucking slut who was only good to use as a hole. I asked him to stop, and he did immediately, but I couldn't finish after because the words felt like lead in my stomach. I could do slightly mean, but there needs to be an edge of kindness around it.

Gagging is also crossed off the list when I nearly threw up multiple times when a guy I slept with a handful of times tried to do it to me. It was something he loved, and it made us realize we weren't compatible sexually.

Primal play is also easily crossed off the list. I let a man chase me around my house and wound up slipping on the carpet of my foyer and he had to take me to emergency care when my nose started bleeding. Thankfully it wasn't broken.

All this to say, most things I'm willing to try twice, but for some, once was enough. The best part of it all is I'm slowly figuring out everything I like.

"You've been busy, Kate," he says with a smile. At first I take offence, wondering if this man is slut shaming me, but then he grabs the back of my chair leaning into my space. "Which item on this list were you hoping to grade this evening?"

He's playful about it, and I bite my bottom lip. I feel like he's fucking with me, and I kinda want to play back.

He was so in charge that night at the bar and I loved every second, but lately I've been wondering what it would feel like to take control? What would it feel like to have a man twice my size doing what I say and at my mercy? There's a good chance a man like Ben wouldn't be into it. For a lot of people it's one way or the other, or somewhere in the middle. But what would it be like to completely switch roles whenever it feels right?

"Power dynamics," I say and Ben gives me a lust-filled look, his thumb reaching out to my shoulder to make contact and I lean into it.

He almost sounds devious when he responds. "Did you not like it when I was in charge, Kate?"

Goosebumps cover my skin as I meet his eyes. "No, I liked it a lot. I'm just curious what it feels like to be on the other side, what it feels like to be the one in charge."

"Alright," he says easily.

"Alright?"

"Yes, alright. We can get a private room, and you can do with me what you please. Minus the pegging. I can't give it all away on the first night," he says and I blink at him.

"The second night," I remind him, and he nods. "You'd really be open to that? To me taking control?"

He doesn't seem the type. Well, that night he didn't seem like the type. Tonight, he almost seems like he would do whatever I want as long as it pleases me.

It makes me feel powerful, confident, and sexy.

My ridiculous amount of research into, well, everything, comes to mind as I place a hand on his thigh.

"Are there any limits of yours I should be aware of?" I ask.

He looks proud of me, and I nearly can't stand the sincerity of it. "Well, I'm okay with bondage, touching you wherever you want, being told what to do. You can talk to me however you want. Pain is a mid-level point for me."

"What do you mean?" I ask, trying to remember every single word he says and commit it to memory.

His hand is rubbing my back and mine is on his thigh and it feels more natural than I ever imagined tonight going.

"I'm not looking for a ball-busting dominatrix. Scratches on my back, light biting, hickeys. All of those things are fine."

I can't help but laugh, picturing myself in a latex suit with a whip in hand with a high heel pressing against his balls. That isn't me, and it never will be. For me, it's the idea of controlling the situation and having a man who's happy to listen and comfortable enough in his masculinity to do so.

"Ooh, what about financial domination?" I joke, lightening the mood. See, my flirting skills are getting better.

He smiles and shakes his head. "If you're here, paying for this membership, I highly doubt you need someone paying you to control and spend their finances."

"It could be fun. Maybe I'll add it to the list."

"Do you have any limits for tonight that I should know about?" My brows furrow at the question and he kneads the flesh of my thigh, his thumb now directly on my bare skin. "Just because you'll be calling the shots doesn't mean I shouldn't know anything that would upset you."

"You saw everything on my list. Anything that's crossed off is a no-go. I'm sure there will be other things crossed off, but I haven't experienced them yet to know if I like them or not."

"Should we have a safe word?" he asks, and I feel like it's for me and not him. "How about Marina?" he suggests

It makes me wonder if he truly will be able to give up control, but he's offering, willing, and I want it to be him.

God, the idea of telling the guy I've been fantasizing about for months what to do, to bring him to his knees? It has me feeling so turned on. Being in charge is one of those things I mentally sorted into my maybe column of enjoying it.

But with him?

He's probably going to get another 10/10 and not even realize it.

"Marina works for me. Should we head back?" I ask, hoping that I'm not blushing too much.

He leans forward and I expect him to kiss me, but he places a gentle press of his lips on my collarbone.

"Is that what you want me to do?"

"Yes, that's what I want," I tell him confidently and he

pulls his stool back standing to his full height; how did I forget how tall he is?

He holds out his hand for me to take and his palm swallows mine as we walk past the other patrons sitting at the bar, none of them really paying us any mind as we reach the entrance to the back of the club.

He uses his membership card for entrance and my breath hitches as I take in what goes on in the true heart of Avalon. I don't know how I know it, but just like at the bar, I know I'm walking in as one person and leaving a totally changed woman.

Benjamin

Sex Club Heaven

GAVIN IS DEFINITELY GOING to fucking kill me. I mean, we did this shit on far too many occasions as kids, our mom got called to the school at least five times for us swapping places and our teachers being none the wiser until one of us slipped up.

I don't know why I did it. Why didn't I say, "oh sorry, the man you're looking for is my twin brother who's so like me but also completely different from me in so many ways?"

I considered coming clean so many times, and then this pretty woman handed me that damn list and, like the bastard I am, I lost the ability to think coherently. I want this woman who's half my size, figuring out what she likes to use me as her little boy toy to see if she likes being in charge.

She fit the bill with her looks, but the list? The list is going to fucking kill me. If I hadn't seen so many overlapping interests, maybe I would have come clean. If she was only looking for someone to top her, Gavin would be the guy for her. But sweet little doctorate in fine arts, Kate, wants to try so many things that also align with what I want.

I'm a greedy little fuck, but at least I'll make this good for her.

That's the only reason I can have this on my conscience. Kate doesn't seem like the type that wants a man to be completely submissive. She's testing out her kinky little wings, and for whatever reason, I'm deluded enough to think I can give her that.

And maybe, maybe a small piece of me that shares everything with Gavin wants my own taste of Kate. We share pretty much everything our entire lives, and maybe the spoiled part of me wants to prove that I can be the other half of the coin she needs.

I do briefly remember my brother coming home a few months ago, telling me he christened our new office. Maybe the ten point score she gave spanking was for Gavin, and that makes me want to be on my best behavior.

Her hand is in mine as we work our way through the open space of Avalon. This room is for the voyeurs and exhibitionists. There's a stage to the left where demonstrations are held from time to time. Her eyes are wide, not with shock, just taking everything in. I keep a slower pace to make up for her short legs and high heels.

There are more rooms in Avalon, private ones you can rent with specific kinks in mind, along with smaller rooms for groups and intimate get togethers.

Once we reach the hostess stand to be directed to a specific room, I go to speak, and Kate puts a hand on my chest.

"We'd like a private room, please," Kate says, and the hostess smiles at her.

"Of course, we have three rooms available. Two are standard private suites, and then we have the spanking bench."

"One of the private suites would be great."

"You can head down to room four. Mr. B Carlson and..." she asks and I wince.

Is she going to notice the fact that they have to use my first initial because there are multiple Carlson's who come to Avalon?

"Morley," Kate says easily, and the hostess nods her head.

"Enjoy," the hostess says, marking the room as in use as Kate now leads me down the hall, looking at the numbers as we walk down the corridor, finding number four.

She opens the door and an anticipatory quiet takes over. There's no soft music or the cover of other people talking when we're in this private room and I wonder if it's going to spook her, or if she'll thrive in the new environment.

The private rooms are simple, a bed at the center, that isn't a mattress, it's made of the same material gymnasts and wrestlers use for hygiene, but it's covered with luxe, black sheets. The lighting in the space is dim, only present in the crown molding of the ceiling. There's one long table. The top of it has condoms, lube, and a few other small items. There's a mini fridge beneath that houses water bottles. Across the way there's a simple bathroom, decorated in black and gold. The feel is similar to a high end hotel, just like the front of Avalon is. Simple, but it works.

I give her space to figure out what she wants, not rushing her.

She takes in the room. I'm sure she's seen all of Avalon before, except empty, during her new membership tour. She's contemplating her next move as she glances over at me.

Is she going to change her mind? Or is she going to impress me and put her nerves aside and tell me what she wants? Either way, I'll be happy to oblige.

"Take off your suit and sit at the edge of the bed," she says with more sternness in her tone than I expected. It has my cock stirring, and a need to please rising in my chest.

She watches me as I slowly unbutton my dress shirt, sliding my arms out, and placing it on the nearby table. Her gaze is analytical, while still being fully present. She swallows as I undo my belt. A small sigh slips from her lips at the sound of me unzipping my pants and letting them fall to the floor.

I semi-fold them and place them next to my shirt; the only piece of clothing on my body is my underwear.

She clears her throat. "Those too," she says.

The corner of my lip turns up as I grab the waistband of my boxer briefs, my cock springing free as the material drops down to my ankles. I grab it and place it with my clothes before sitting on the bed as directed.

I don't touch myself, no matter how badly I want to. She's in charge tonight, and now is certainly not the time to push boundaries unless she wants me to.

Maybe another time.

Her gaze eats me up and I savor every single moment of her admiring my body. She doesn't approach me, instead she leans her ass against the table at the end of the bed and watches. She's still fully clothed in her sexy red dress, and white heels, while I sit here, completely at her disposal.

"Your body. It's a bit of a work of art," she says.

I tilt my head at her as she really looks at me, even more analytical than before. "Almost like a Jacques-Louis David painting." Her eyes are tender and I try to remember that name to make sure he's not famous for painting wild shit or men with small penises, even though I know there's no way she means that, right? "It's a good thing," she says with a lopsided grin. "You know, my only regret from that one night was that I didn't get to see you when you got to see me."

I swallow thickly, guilt shimmying its way through my rib cage.

"Can you...can you touch yourself?" she asks, and my lips part as I swallow back a moan, doing what she says, gripping the base of my cock, and stroking slowly.

She watches me like she wants to savor the moment. I can't remember the last time a woman wanted me to touch myself while she just watched fully dressed. I want to see her undress; I want to touch her, but if all she wants tonight is a show, that's okay, too.

"Slower," she says softly, and I do just that.

I rub my thumb over the tip, swiping the pre-cum down my length, slightly twisting my wrist with each stroke.

She nibbles on her lip, like she's contemplating what she wants to do with me, and the sensation has me wanting to come all over my stomach right now.

But good things always come to those who wait.

Her heels click against the floor as she stands between my legs. My hands automatically go to her hips and she clicks her tongue.

"I didn't tell you to stop," she says, her voice raspy and gentle.

"My mistake," I say, placing my hand on my cock.

"You like me telling you what to do?" she asks.

I can only imagine what her night with Gavin was like, surely nothing like this.

"I like a lot of things. A strong, sexy woman having her way with me is damn near the top of the list."

"And what's at the top?" she asks, her finger sliding tenderly across my collarbone. A near whimper escapes me and her bright blue eyes are burning with desire.

Fuck. So fucking fucked.

"A gentleman doesn't tell all his secrets right away."

She smirks. "I suppose not." She turns around, giving me her back, as she grabs her dark hair, placing it over one shoulder. Her ass is pert in her dress and every part of me wants to grab and knead the perky globes. "Help me with my dress."

I abandon my cock as I grab the small zipper, slowly pulling down, my knuckles dragging against the smooth, warm skin of her back.

Her underwear matches, the same color as her dress as she pushes the shoulders off to each side and it slips to the floor. Kate steps out of the material, grabbing the dress off the floor and placing her clothes with mine.

"God, you're beautiful," I say, and she blushes, even though she was the one who asked me to jerk off in front of her.

She appraises my body, the bed, the room, like she's trying to figure out what she wants next.

She takes a few steps, her hand on my sternum as her thumb tenderly rubs my skin, before she looks up at me.

Our height difference is staggering, and it makes the dynamic an even bigger turn on for me. That we both know if I wanted to, I could pick her up and toss her on the bed and have my way with her, but I don't want to.

I want to please this small woman. I want a 10 next to power dynamics, and I'll be damned if I don't get a perfect grade.

"Be good and lie on the bed," she says, leaning forward and placing a kiss on my pec.

I take a deep breath, looking up at the ceiling, before doing as she asks, my head on the pillow, my naked body on display as she follows suit, cautiously straddling my abdomen.

"Can I touch?" I ask, feeling needy as fuck. Thankfully, she seems to enjoy me this way.

"My hips," she says, and my hands are automatically there,

touching and squeezing the junction where her legs meet her ass. "You like pleasing me?"

I nod, taking a moment to take in her body. How good the deep red looks against her pale skin, and the stark contrast of her dark hair.

"You need to make me come before you, don't you, beautiful boy?"

A rattled breath slips out of me, and she smiles. How can she be so fucking good at this for her first try? She must be god's gift to switches, using what she likes when someone else is in charge of me, and I'm eating up every second.

"More than anything," I say, her eyes hazily shutting before her nails lightly drag against my chest. It's not hard enough to even leave sexual trails against my skin. But it's soft enough to have my balls aching, and my dick weeping pathetically.

"Should I ride your face, Ben? Do you think you'll earn me riding your cock if I come in your mouth first?"

I've died and gone to sex club heaven.

Kate

A Very Good Boy

BEING the dominant one is more fun than I expected. I more than enjoy being the one who's told what to do, talked through it. Really, I just wanted to get a taste of what it was like to be on the other side of things. I just didn't realize it would be this sweet.

Sure, I wasn't as aggressive as some of the men I've been with, but I like that Ben listens, that he wants to please me, and he does so eagerly.

I'm almost shocked that it's the same man who talked me through the first sexual encounter I ever had with someone besides my ex, but it makes calling the shots just a little more pleasurable.

He could throw me around, no problem. Physically, I have no chance when it comes to how big he is. Truly, my fantasies don't even do him justice.

But size doesn't matter in this dynamic. It's me in charge, and him wanting to please me, which excites me.

His eyes nearly glazed over when I told him he had to earn

it. I know exactly how he feels right now, and I enjoy making him feel this way. Almost as much as I'm soaking up every command he follows so beautifully.

I feel sexy, empowered, and so fucking aroused.

I'm soaking wet as I shift my body further up his chest, my hands resting on the wall as my thighs rest against each side of his head. His fingers dig into the side of my hips as I adjust my center against his lips.

He licks over my panties, and a sharp breath escapes me as I watch him. This position is a complete representation of how much I relish being in charge right now. His body is completely out of my purview and all that I can see is his handsome face, his mouth working to please me.

Ben swipes his tongue against the lace, my panties drenched with a mixture of my arousal and his saliva.

"Can I move your panties?" he asks, placing a kiss against my mound.

"You've been so sweet. I'll do it for you," I tell him.

I can feel him shifting beneath me as his breath hitches and I slide the undergarment to the side, granting him full access. He moans as he grabs my hips so hard that he might actually leave fingerprint-shaped bruises.

His eyes shut as he licks and sucks on my clit, like he's savoring me, clearly enjoying himself.

With one hand against the wall for balance, I drag another through his thick dark hair, my nails delicately scraping against his scalp.

"That feels so good, right there."

He moans, his tongue licking as his lips suck on my clit, making my hips shift against his mouth.

"Don't stop. Right there."

His hands roam against my rib cage, pushing my pussy

harder against his mouth. I'm nearly riding his face at this point as my hips shift and he sucks and laps up every drop of my arousal.

"Fuck. You're gonna make me come," I slur, forcing myself to not throw my head back in ecstasy, but watch his reaction instead.

He doesn't disappoint, as he glances up at me with heavy-lidded eyes, devouring my cunt while soaking up every single second of having my full attention.

My grip on his hair tightens as that delicious pull tingles in my abdomen, my cunt clenching around nothing as I stare down at his eager gaze.

"Is this how you want me to ride your cock? Show me how good you can be with your tongue and I'll give it to you."

His fingers dig into my hips as he eats me out with a new ferocity, like he's starving and I'm the only thing that could satiate him. Ben wants to please me more than anything, and it has me moaning out my release. My hips are unsteady and uncontrolled as I ride out my orgasm over his face and he licks up every drop of ecstasy.

My chest is rising and falling rapidly, and my wrist hurts from the way I was pressing it against the wall.

I catch my breath, shifting down his body, admiring how good looking he is. The sheen of my orgasm glistening around his lips has me licking my own. I don't know why I do it, only that I know I want to, and if I was in his place, I'd love it too. I bring my thumb to his mouth, tracing the evidence of my release on his lips. His chest is rising and falling harshly underneath me, as he stares at me, before I push my thumb into his mouth.

He sucks on the finger eagerly and I'm ready to come again, ready to make him feel good too.

Maybe having experienced being submissive helps make you a better top? I wasn't thinking too much into it, I was just following what my body and mind wanted.

Right now I want to feel good and I want to be in control of every moment.

Slowly, I adjust my body so that I'm straddling his hips, my hand on his chin as I bring him in for a kiss. He wraps his arms around my back, holding me close as we slowly taste one another.

I've found that I've always liked this. Kissing my partner after oral, there's something about tasting myself or having them taste themselves that's incredibly sexy and intimate.

"I think you earned it," I say with a smile against his lips.

"Thank fuck," he strains out, making me smile even wider.

"Condom or no condom?" I ask him.

A requirement of Avalon is vehement STI testing. It's required monthly and if you've been intimate outside of Avalon. Of course, pregnancy is another factor. "I have an IUD," I tell him.

"Please let me feel you without a condom," he says.

Still holding his chin, I bring his lips back to mine. "Take my panties off," I whisper against his mouth, and he doesn't hesitate. His hands quickly sliding down my back before his thumbs dig into the waistband of my panties and he drags them down my thighs and I lightly shuffle them off my legs.

The power is getting to my head. The way he's so fucking eager to listen, to let me touch, to let me direct everything that we do.

My legs are spread wide and his length is situated between the lips of my pussy as I move back and forth, coating his cock in my release. I'm so fucking wet that the friction is slippery and seamless.

I kiss his collarbone, quite obsessed with that particular

spot, and he seems to have a similar reaction as his hold on me tightens.

"You need it so bad, don't you?" I ask, kissing up the column of his throat, loving the strong tendons and muscles there.

"So fucking bad, Kate. Please fuck me, please."

"You beg for me so well."

I smile against his throat as I slide my hand between us, finally touching his cock for the first time with my hands. He shivers beneath me as I press the tip against my entrance and reposition myself so that my palms are resting on the side of his face as I lift my hips, slowly taking him inch by inch.

His hands slide up and down the sides of my body, his gaze flicking between my breasts, face, and where we're connected.

I keep one hand pressed against the bed as I use the other to push my breasts out of my bra. I'm glad I went with the dreaded underwire tonight, because I can't deny that they look amazing pressed up and exposed like this.

"Fucking hell," Ben whispers, glancing at my tits as I take my free hand, cradling the back of his head and bringing him to my chest.

He doesn't hesitate for a second, his hands squeezing them while his tongue tastes my nipples before his lips wrap around the hardened bud, sucking harder than I'm used to, but I love it.

It has me writhing on top of him. My clit rubs against his pubic hair with every pass of my hips, and I know I'm going to come soon.

"You feel so good," I tell him. "Fuck. I'm not going to last."

He makes undignified voices against my breasts as his legs bend. He doesn't thrust from below, but the adjusted angle is hitting all the right spots.

I slow down, circling my hips slowly around his shaft,

drawing it out. The expanse of his chest is heaving with each breath and he doesn't avoid eye contact.

The only time Ben isn't looking at me are the moments he's staring at where we're connected.

"You're so fucking beautiful," he says.

"So are you," I agree, sliding my hand over the stubble on his face. "Are you going to come pretty for me too?" He groans, his fingers digging into my hips as I pick up speed. "I think I want to watch you fall apart for me."

"God. I'm going to come. Please let me come inside you," he begs.

It's ridiculously hot having him ask for permission and seek my approval. It has me leaning forward, my clit hitting just the right spot until I know I'm close.

"Oh, fuck. Come for me. I want to feel it," I say in rushed breaths as a tingling sensation rips through me and my cunt grips him, milking his cock. He feels like he's harder inside of me, and my clit feels so oversensitive that any shifting over our bodies has me shivering.

He groans out, his thighs shaking beneath me as my forearms give out and I plant my front against his, riding out the aftershocks of my second release.

With my ear nestled close to his heart, I smirk, knowing I'm the reason it's beating so fast.

"Jesus Christ, Kate," he says, his large arms wrapped around my back, making me feel small.

Silence hangs in the air for a moment, but it doesn't feel uncomfortable. With some of my other hookups it was like post-nut clarity hit immediately and we both put our clothes on as quickly as possible and called it a night.

But this feels nice, it feels needed after the trust he gave me, and it's honestly quite comforting being held for a change.

I kiss his collarbone before moving upward, his dick falling out of me. His abdomen clenches and he winces, and I bite my lip.

"Was that all okay?" I ask, and he has a dopey grin on his face. He's too fucking charming for his own good.

"Was that okay? More than okay, Kate. That was...thank you."

I swallow thickly at his gratitude and nod. "Is there anything I can do for you? A drink, something to eat, do you want me to move?"

"I like you just where you are," he says, accentuating with a soft squeeze of my ass. "What about you? Do you need anything, was it okay for you?"

"I enjoyed it more than I expected to. I don't think I could ask for someone better to try this with," I say honestly.

"I've gotta know, what number are you going to be putting on your list?" he asks and I laugh, resting on the large expanse of his chest.

"Ben, are you asking me what grade you got?"

"You're going to give me professor fantasies. I've gotta know how well I did, Dr. Morley."

I grab his chin, placing a soft kiss against his lips. "You were a very good boy, Mr. Carlson," I say, before climbing off the bed, not glancing back, and heading for the shower.

He follows me into the bathroom like a massive overexcited puppy and I can't help but look over my shoulder at him. His large cock is semi-flacid as I look him up and down.

"Well, are you going to come clean up your mess so we can do it all over again?" I ask.

The shower is barely on before he's on his knees doing just that before filling me up again.

MY HAIR IS WET, and my panties are missing. I make a note to take a ride share the next time I come to Avalon. Driving after a long fucking session is not ideal.

Ben looks like a hot, disheveled mess as we stand in the parking garage.

"You know, I think I can help you tick more things off your list, along with doing your favorites," he suggests.

"Are you just wanting to see my list again so you know what grade you got?" I tease.

"Am I that transparent?"

"It's cute."

"So, does that mean you're open to seeing me again at Avalon?"

"Yes, and maybe if you're really good, I'll show you my revised list."

He clutches his heart and leans down, kissing me softly. He watches me get into my car and doesn't head to his own until I'm out of the parking garage.

I feel boneless, satisfied, and a bunch of other words that I'm not sure encompass exactly how tonight went.

I loved it, definitely a 10/10, though I think I'll hold on to that secret for a while. It's a bit jarring of how much I loved it even though I also really love being on the opposite side too.

Can I both yearn for control and love when it's out of my hands? Is it really possible to enjoy being in both positions so much? Granted, when I'm the more submissive one I'm open to more roughness, but I'm not sure that I could do that to someone like Ben.

What we had was the perfect medium, and it has me more excited to explore even more things at Avalon. Especially with Ben.

Safe, non-complicated sex where I can figure out what I

want with no strings attached. It's the perfect situation and I can't help but to feel like I made the right call going to Avalon.

I'm finally living for me, and even as the high from tonight wanes, I feel happiness for the direction my life is taking.

For the first time in a long time, I'm not living for anyone but myself, and it feels like the best years are in front of me, not behind me.

Gavin

Monozygotic Nightmare

ALL I DID WAS HEEL my shoes off before plopping on the couch.

Tonight was an absolute shit show. We truly need to get some more dependable boat captains. Frank has called out at least once a month for the past three months, and it's usually Ben or myself who has to pick up the slack.

I rarely mind, but tonight's bachelorette party went off the absolute fucking rails. Had women throwing up off the side of the boat, and two of the women had to be pulled off one another during a drunken fight.

I won't say I'm getting too old for this shit, because I refuse. Thirty-five is the new twenty-five and I stand by that. However, I'm exhausted and that one spot on my lower back has been killing me lately. I'll have to book a massage and get that knot taken care of in these next two weeks.

Not having the desire to get up and make my way to my room, I grab the remote and put on a background show and shut my eyes. Just a quick nap, once Ben gets home I'll wake up and crawl my ass into the shower and get to bed.

When I glance at my phone, I notice he hasn't messaged me and it's pretty late. Maybe he found something fun to do tonight at Avalon—lucky bastard.

It feels like we've been working so hard these past six months to make the businesses work. Getting the club set up has been a massive undertaking. I thought I'd hate the responsibility, but I've actually loved it, even if I am bone ass fucking tired right now. It's all worth it, being able to work with my brother and have our own thing. I'm sure it's not what our parents envisioned for us, but they still seem proud. Their approval isn't something I personally seek, but I know that it's important to Ben.

My eyes slowly shut, my phone resting on top of my chest as the front door opens. I blink lazily as Ben comes into the living room. He doesn't take a seat, and he just paces over by the TV. He looks a little manic, and his hair seems like it's wet, which is unusual, it wasn't raining outside.

"I thought we gave up coke after you nearly drowned," I say, and he stops moving and glances down at me, his hand rubbing the back of his neck.

"I'm not on anything."

"Then why are you frantically pacing all over the place?"

"Do you remember a woman named Kate? She came to the bar a couple of months ago?"

I sit up on the edge of the couch, looking at my brother, the clear as day guilt written all over his face. I can nearly feel it radiating off of him.

"What did you do?" I ask with an arched brow, instead of answering his question.

Of course I remember Kate. The way she melted against my touch and listened so sweetly. The way I wanted to do more, go further, but didn't because it wasn't appropriate. I also know she hasn't been back to the bar since that night.

"She was at Avalon tonight."

"Okay?" I say, holding out my hands in confusion.

"Do you remember back in school when we used to switch places? How funny we thought it was that people couldn't tell us a part. Like that one time you went and took my AP Spanish test for me and I took your AP Bio test for you?" He licks his lips and shoves his hands in his pockets.

"Ben. What did you do?" I scold him, but do my best to not raise my voice. Ben is pacing back and forth

"I maybe, sort of, possibly didn't correct her when she assumed I was the man she hooked up with at the bar a few months ago," he says and I blink at him.

"You did what?"

"She was just so pretty. You've seen her, you know what she looks like. Both of our fucking types," he says, pacing again. "She mentioned the fact that we—well, you—hooked up a few months ago, and I didn't correct her. I was going to and then she took out this list of all the things she wants to do."

I rub the meat of my palms against my eyes, my vision going splotchy.

My brows furrow, my brain trying to catch up with everything that Ben is saying. "She likes what you like?" I question.

I'm not sure why that's the first question I ask after he's basically admitted to lying to this woman and using my experience with her in the process.

Ben clears his throat. "Yeah, and she was fucking good at it, Gav. Like, fuck. I can't remember the last time it was that good, like we were in sync with what we both wanted from the night. She wasn't trying to degrade me or make me small. I know I shouldn't have done it. I know that it's fucked up and I'm sorry for not setting the record straight, but it happened fast and then I was caught up in everything and she was so happy at the end of the night and so was I, and I just...I fucked up."

I take a deep breath, looking at my brother while he's spiraling. It's harder for him than it is for me.

Finding women who want to be submissive, who are willing to do what I tell them, is fairly easy. Ben has a harder time finding what he's looking for. When we have sex with women together, it's easier because I call the shots. I can direct the situation so that we both enjoy ourselves.

It's stupid, really. I'm only two minutes older than Ben, but it's always felt like it's my job to protect him. I would never say it out loud to anyone in my family, but he's the person I love more than anyone in the world. I know you're supposed to say you love your siblings equally. But Ben and I? We shared a womb. We are our parents' worst monozygotic nightmare, the same genetic material tying us together for life. Every stage of life we've had, we've walked it together. Our brothers were also always so much older than us, it's really only been the last decade that we've gotten really close.

Ben is my person beyond anyone else, and as irritated as I may be about him not telling Kate the truth, I'm more worried about him.

"She wants to see you at Avalon again?" I ask.

He nods, his face that's an exact mirror of mine, looking to me for answers.

"What about when she asks you to take control, Ben? What if she wants to do other things on her list that aren't what you're into?"

His Adam's apple bobs, and it's clear he hadn't thought that far, only considered how I was going to react to his deception.

"You know how I am. You have some idea of what happened that night. There's a good chance she's going to want that side of you—us—whatever the fuck, at some point."

"Fuck," he hisses, coming to sit next to me on the couch. "Do you remember her?"

I contemplate my answer, and in an effort to protect my brother, I do something we never do between one another; I lie.

"Maybe? Only because it wasn't at Avalon," I say, right through my teeth.

I remember her well. Unpracticed, eager to try new things, excited to please me while still asking for what she wanted. Maybe I could see her being with my brother after all. Maybe these months since her divorce she's been able to find her voice. Good for her.

"This isn't like when we were in school, Ben. You've gotta come clean or else this is going to eat you up, and it isn't fair to her, either."

"Fuck. I know, I know you're right. I don't know why I lied. Fuck," he says again, flinging his back against the couch and grabbing a pillow against his stomach.

"We can go together. We'll explain everything. If she wants nothing to do with either of us, then so be it. There will be other women."

"She was just," he says, shaking his head. "Nevermind, it doesn't matter. You're right. I have to come clean before we sleep together again. I'm not even sure I could get hard with this weight on my conscience."

"I mean, you did it the first time," I joke.

"I deserve that. That was before I knew how good it was," he says, resting his head and looking at me.

"How was Sunday dinner?" I ask, trying to change the topic and let myself process everything.

"Ugh. The usual. Mom's trying to pimp me out to some woman again. Jessa finished our shirt design. It's in our email. Lincoln was cranky per usual, and our niece reminded me why I never want to have kids."

"Indeed, the usual."

"You know, I thought you were going to be more pissed than this," he says, and I shrug.

"She's just a woman. You're my brother. I just want you to be okay."

"You'll really come with me?"

"Of course, but the next three captains that cancel, you're covering their shifts," I say, pushing his shoulder, shoving him into the corner of the couch. "I'm going to bed, we'll figure out a game plan later."

Ben gives me a small smile, but doesn't get off the couch as I make my way over to my bedroom. Alone in my room, I'm allowed to let myself feel the frustration of what my brother did. Here I'm allowed to have the selfish thoughts I wouldn't tell him.

Like most things, I'll let this go.

It's easier to not dwell on shit, to not let it get to you. Because when you let things get under your skin, you're no longer the one in control.

I'm always in control.

I'll get it sorted, just like I always do.

Kate

No Crying in a Sex Club

SINCE MY DIVORCE, I've been curating my life around my wants and it's been freeing. The only person I have to worry about is me, along with the only person I need to please.

For the first time in my life, the decor in my house is everything I like.

The nude Maria Szanth painting I purchased five years ago is now proudly on display in my foyer. My books are on shelves, on the floor, on my nightstand, truly wherever the fuck I want them to be.

Hell, I even have a cat room. Will was allergic to cats, and now I have four: Frida, Berthe, Edvard, and Michelangelo.

I have a good job, one that I love and I'm passionate about.

Then, there's the copious amount of free time I have.

Usually, I consider it a blessing. I can go out with my friends when I want, read till my eyes can't form a word on a page anymore, or binge watch an entire season of a show in a day.

Maybe it's the heat of the summer or the fact that all my friends have been busy doing various things. But for the first time since my divorce, I feel lonely. Not in the sense that I want a relationship or need someone by my side twenty-four seven, I just need some human interaction.

During the school year, this isn't a problem. I spend so much time at the university, lecturing, talking, and just being around people. I wouldn't consider myself an extrovert, but I'm not completely introverted either. I love my alone time, but I also really enjoy talking and having fun with others.

As much as I love escaping into a good book or a good show, nothing seems to shake this feeling, so I'm going to push myself to be brave.

Being consciously single shouldn't mean that I need other people to do things. Hell, I went to a sex club by myself and look how that turned out? Amazingly.

I've constantly replayed both of my nights with Ben, flip flopping between scenes based on my mood. If I can be brave enough in my own sexual liberation, I can absolutely go to a sushi restaurant and sit confidently by myself and interact with people, or maybe not. Maybe I just eat, drink, and observe.

I dress for myself in a dark blue sundress that makes me feel pretty and drive to my favorite spot. I haven't been here since Will and I split up, because it was *our* place. But I miss it, and if he got a new wife and kid out of the divorce, I should absolutely win our sushi spot. Plus, I've tried other places and none of them compare.

It's a Wednesday night, and not busy at all. I get seated at the bar right away, a small glass of sake in front of me as I make my dinner selection. Pop hits are bumping through the restaurant and three TVs are showing the news and various shows behind the bar. Even if I don't strike up a conversation with someone, this is enough.

I got out of the house, showered, and I'm around human

life. I consider it a win as I order my sushi and sit back and people watch.

There's a couple clearly on an awkward first date, a few men who just finished an evening of golf, some women meeting up for drinks, and the other occasional patrons I can't place.

The salmon sashimi melts like butter against my tongue and I hum in happiness, annoyed with myself that I avoided my favorite place for so long.

"It's good to see you again," Botan, my favorite bartender, says.

"I'm glad to be back. Please tell the chef that this is insanely good," I say, accenting my words with my chopsticks as I grab another piece of fish and enjoy every single bite.

I don't know why I was so scared to come here alone, there was nothing to worry about.

Then it happens.

They walk through the door, and I feel my heart sink. Is there no sacred fucking dining establishment in Tampa where I won't run into my ex-husband and his new family?

When Will sees me, he doesn't seem surprised, and I find it odd. Did he know I was going to be here tonight?

He kisses the side of his wife's head and she glares at me with her deep set brown eyes. She has on a heavy winged eyeliner that makes her look older and the glare she's giving me is more severe. I just stare at her blankly.

I wonder to myself if she worries about Will's fidelity, clearly he had no issues cheating on me with her. Could she possibly feel insecure over the idea he'd turn around and do the same thing to her?

It would be karma, and as much as I might hate Will and his wife, even I wouldn't wish that on her. Now small inconveniences, yes, I hope Karoline shits her pants in the car when she's running late for something. Sure, maybe I wish she leans too close to a candle and all her hair catches fire. But having the man you care about most in the world breaking your trust, and hurting you as deeply as he did me, even I can't wish that on this bitch.

Will approaches me, and I groan, throwing back the rest of my sake, and pushing it away from me, indicating that I want more.

"Kate," he says, his tone far less shitty than it was the last time we ran into one another.

"What do you want, Will?" I ask, even though I know what he wants.

"You know what I want. What is it going to take for you to sell me those shares?" he asks.

His brown eyes that I used to find charming lock onto mine and I tilt my head.

"Do you even have the money to buy me out?" I ask, digging my claws in ever so slightly.

It only seems fair. Money was always a point of contention in our relationship, mostly because I had it and Will didn't. I send up a silent prayer to my Aunt Helene, thanking her for forcing me to get a prenup before we got married.

Back then, Will fought me on it. He didn't understand why we needed a prenup when we were going to spend the rest of our lives together. Genuinely, I thought the same. But Aunt Helene? She was the smartest woman I ever knew, and she made it easier by telling me she would leave all her money to an animal shelter like the woman in *Aristocats* if I didn't protect myself before getting married.

I miss her so much, her wisdom, her laugh, all the times we had together. Thinking about her makes me feel even more alone than I did earlier. I've been an orphan for a long time, but right now, besides Savannah and Chelsea, I don't feel like I have a family at all. The only other person I had strong ties to is standing in front of me, looking at me like we didn't share nearly two decades of our lives together.

It makes me hate Will even more. The shares are the only thing I have control over. He took my youth, my sense of family, my pride. He took small pieces of me without me even noticing, and he's delusional if he thinks I'll bend and give him what he wants now.

"Yes, I have the funds secured," he says, and I arch an eyebrow at him.

His wording is strange, meaning maybe it's not his money or maybe the company was doing better than I thought. I'm not surprised, Dennis Commercial has been in the red these past few years. It's one of the many things he blamed his infidelity on. He was struggling at work; I didn't understand; I wasn't there for him enough.

"I have no interest in selling at this time," I say, as the bartender slides the refill of sake toward me. He's clearly keeping a close eye on the altercation between me and Will.

He grabs my arm, squeezing it just to the point of it being uncomfortable, but not enough to truly hurt.

"Listen, I appreciate the fact that you gave me the capital to start my business and I'm sorry things didn't work out between us. I'm offering to give you more than what you put into it, but it's my company, Kate."

"Yes, you're technically the CEO. Your last name is on the sign, but I do own fifty-five percent. Which is a fact that didn't bother you our entire marriage. You never offered to buy me out then. Give me one good reason why I should sell now?"

"Goddamn it, Kate, this isn't a fucking joke. This is my life. Sell the fucking shares and be rid of me completely. That's what you want, isn't it?"

"My lawyer and business manager handle everything. I'm not involved in Dennis Commercial. Truly, there's no reason for us to ever have to see each other, besides the fact you keep showing up places where I just so happen to be. Now, I'd like to finish my meal in peace," I say, trying to turn my body.

His grip on my arm tightens more, and I swallow thickly.

"Sir, I think it's best you take a step away," Botan says, glancing at Will and then back at me.

"I'm going to make you regret this," Will whispers low in my ear, and I try to keep a neutral face as he storms off with a petulant walk over to his new wife, who's still glaring at me.

I refuse to let him dig his way under my skin and make me feel like a scared little girl. But even with my best attempt, a sense of worry fills me.

Will wasn't physically abusive. There was just one time things got out of hand, and we worked through it. But the fact is, he is capable of hurting me. Just because it was one time doesn't mean that it couldn't happen again, especially now that there aren't romantic feelings between us.

I feel anxious and out of control, and all I want to do is dissociate. I want to forget what happened tonight, but I also don't want to go home and be left with my thoughts, this loneliness consuming me even further.

I get a to-go box for the rest of my sushi, even though I probably won't eat the other half in the fear that it's no longer safe to eat, but not getting the food to-go makes me feel like an asshole. I pay my check, and when I'm leaving the restaurant, I can feel eyes on me, but I don't look back. There's no way in hell I'm going to let him know that his words bothered me or that I'm scared of him.

Tomorrow, I'll call my lawyer, Carl, and see what he suggests. A restraining order seems severe, but his words have me on edge.

When I pull out of the parking lot, I don't have a place in mind. I just know I'm not ready to go home. Why does Will have to ruin everything? I just wanted to enjoy a night out by myself and eat at my favorite place. Why does it feel like I'm constantly the one being punished for his mistakes?

My grip on the steering wheel is tight, as I take deep breaths in and out, trying to figure out how I can calm down after the altercation tonight. I want someone to hold me, to take care of me and to take this horrible feeling of fear away from me. I'm not sure if it's my subconscience or a desperate need for a safe space, but I make a decision, turning left instead of right. It only takes about ten minutes until I'm parking in Avalon's garage.

My dress is probably too casual, and I don't have much makeup on, but I still meet the required dress code. At least I didn't cry on the car ride over here, I won't deny that I thought about it. But hasn't Will stolen enough of my tears already?

I know who I came here for, which is ridiculous. I barely know the man and I consider him a source of comfort?

There's a good chance Ben isn't even here tonight, and I'll have to cross that bridge if that's the case. It's not that I'm not open to being with another man, because I am, I think. It's just that I know how he can switch roles, just like me.

Right now I could absolutely use the relief of having decisions taken away from me. I need him to be the guy that took control and bent me over his desk all those months ago.

Most of all, I need out of my own fucking head. I give myself a once over in the mirror, adding some more chapstick, before I get out of my car and head to the entrance where I swipe my membership card.

I take a deep breath in. The club always seems to smell like a mix of clove and vanilla as I glance around the bar searching for the handsome face that seems to haunt me. The place is busy tonight, sharp dressed men, and women in short dresses. It takes a few moments, I'm almost to the point where I believe that he isn't here, when I finally spot him. I take a relieving breath, until I notice that he's smiling and talking to another woman.

Fuck, what's the protocol at a sex club? Are men first come first serve? Do I even have the balls to walk over there and say something? Would he even want me to?

Sure, the last time we were together he said he was interested in a repeat, but what if he only wants a repeat where I'm topping him? Right now, tonight? I'm not capable of it.

Joining Avalon was supposed to take the stress out of fucking, but right now I feel completely on edge. Honestly, I feel like crying out of frustration, but I won't do that. I'll just slowly back out of Avalon, get back into my car, stop at a liquor store on the way home, and masturbate all night long.

Truly, that should've been plan A instead of coming here. I feel so stupid.

I'm slowly trying to make my escape, when eyes that look more green today meet mine. For whatever reason they don't seem happy to see me, and that just wrecks my confidence.

God, Kate, there's no crying in a sex club.

Gavin

Handcuffed Guilt

TAMARA IS CHATTING AWAY, as I sip my scotch, waiting for Ben to get here. As promised, he's on coverage duty of anyone who calls out, and sure enough, another captain called out.

It will probably take him over an hour to get here, and we don't even know if Kate will show up here or not. We've been coming here nearly every night hoping that she'll show up and we can set everything straight.

I still don't think I've truly let myself come to terms with what Ben did. He's been beating himself up so much; I don't see the point in adding to his guilt. We'll get this all sorted and we'll move on.

Kate will either be so outraged that she never speaks to us again, or maybe she'll somehow be able to forgive my brother's lie and have some interest in still seeing him, or maybe even me too?

It's wishful fucking thinking. No one wants to be lied to, especially with what we're doing here. We might not know each other, be romantic in any way, but there's still a level of trust that comes with kink.

"What do you think?" Tamara's voice cuts into my thoughts.

I'd barely been paying attention. Tamara and I have played some at Avalon, but we aren't truly compatible. Tamara is a brat, and while I love being the one in control, I'm also not a fan of being disobeyed. Impact play and bondage are both things I enjoy doing to my partner, and I like them compliant and begging. Tamara likes to escape handcuffs and act out for more spankings.

I'll entertain it on occasion, but it isn't my preference. No, my preference is a woman doing what I tell her to because it pleases me. She wants me to spank her because she knows how hard it makes me and how much I like to see how wet she is when her ass is nice and pink. I want to tie her up and do what I want, and she knows she'll get what she needs because she's been good.

"Sorry?" I ask Tamara.

"Did you want to play tonight?" she asks, and I glance over at the entrance, and that's when I see her.

Still as beautiful as I remember, though she has a sad expression written on her face.

"Sorry, not tonight. If you'll excuse me," I say, knowing she'll pout about it, but there are other members who are far more suited to her needs.

Kate looks like she's trying to get the hell out of Avalon when she sees me and I wonder if she realizes the lie, or if it's something else.

Fuck, Ben isn't here and won't be here for god knows how long. I'll stall, or I'll just tell her myself. Even if the idea pisses me off, I'm not the one who lied and yet I have to take the fall.

"Kate?" I ask, lightly touching her shoulder, making her turn to face me.

Her blue eyes look nearly crystalline as they fill with tears.

"What's wrong?" I ask, placing my hand on her other shoulder, rubbing the exposed skin.

"It's been a shit night," she says, rubbing under her left eye. "I'm not even sure why I came here."

"You don't?" I ask her, hoping she will say more. It's evident she doesn't know about me and Ben. There must be something else going on in her life.

She shrugs, letting out a heavy sigh. "I guess I was hoping you'd be here and it could be more like the first time we were together. I just...I want..."

Fuck, she looks so soft and small right now, but I need her to verbalize what she wants even if I shouldn't give it to her. I should tell her everything right now, but she's already having a terrible night. What if I could make it better?

"What is it you want?"

She shrugs again, and I push her hair behind her ear, leaning down to whisper. "Be good and tell me what you want and I'll give it to you," I say, hoping that what she wants is also what I want, even though I have no right, even though I know that if I take her into the back of Avalon, I'm just as bad as my brother, probably even worse.

Yet, this yanking feeling in my chest wants to wipe that look off her face, to be the reason she isn't sad. If she's going to be crying, it should be for a good reason, like she's begging to come, or choking on my cock.

"I want to not think for a while. I want you to be in charge," she says, looking up at me so sexy and so hopeful.

I stamp my place in hell as I grab her hand and drag her to a private room. I wonder what special place is dedicated for twins who lie about their identities to innocent women.

Kate doesn't question anything and she almost seems in a daze as I deal with the hostess and bring us into a private suite.

As soon as the door shuts, she looks at me with eager, shiny eyes.

"Dress off. On your knees," I tell her, pointing to where I want her on the floor.

Her breath hitches, but she nods, complying immediately as she unzips the side of her dress and places it on the table before getting down on her knees, her palms rubbing the top of her thighs.

Her panties and bra don't match again and it has my dick twitching in my pants. Something about her not planning to have sex and still being sweet and obedient at a drop of a hat does it for me.

I walk toward her, my dress shoes clicking against the floor as I pet the top of her head. She looks up at me and I know she's in the palm of my hand.

Whatever I ask of her, she'll do it, happily. She doesn't want to think about life, or about anything. She wants to be my sweet little Kate.

"What do you say if you don't like something?" I ask her.

"Marina," she says softly and I do my best not to sigh. Ben filled me in on every single detail that happened that night. I just have to accept the safeword that was chosen.

"I'll be disappointed if you're uncomfortable or don't like something and you don't tell me, do you understand?"

"I understand, Ben," she says, and my stomach tightens. My treacherous dick doesn't feel guilt, though, still tight and hard in my pants.

"You'll call me sir tonight," I tell her, not wanting her to call me by my brother's name.

"Yes, sir," she says, her breath hitching, and her flesh pebbling with want.

I pet down her hair again, and watch as her lids go heavy, and her chest rises and falls with her deep breaths. It's almost like watching all the stress she's dealing with slowly slip out of her, and I've barely touched her.

"I'm going to be rougher than the first time we were together. Are you okay with handcuffs, blindfolds, and me spanking you?" I ask.

Her cheeks heat as she glances up at me from her lashes.

"Yes, sir."

"You sit here and you wait till I get back. No touching yourself."

I pet her head one more time before going back to the hostess and getting the items I'm planning to use for tonight.

I have more than enough time to contemplate what I'm doing. I should walk back in that room and tell Kate the truth. What does it say about me that I don't? That this urge to make her feel better overrides all of that. Which is equally a lie, because I'm also the selfish fuck that wants to do this. Saying that it's all about Kate is the lie I tell myself, so guilt doesn't consume me.

The truth?

After that night in my office, I wanted her again, but let the memory slip away. When Ben told me what he did, jealousy seeped in along with curiosity. There's never been a woman who's been so well matched for the both of us, able to fill both of our needs.

Maybe deep down I feel like I have a claim to Kate since I saw her first. Either way, I know I'm an asshole for walking back into this room. I know it's wrong.

Instead of stopping, I just dig myself in deeper, placing the black lace blindfold over her eyes, like if she can't see me. It makes a difference.

Her soft pink lips part as I lean down, placing her wrists

behind her back. These handcuffs aren't totally handcuffs, but the best option for beginners, a simple duel silicone cuff. If she wants out of them, she'll be able to do so for herself.

"Let me see your tongue."

She flattens her tongue as I unfasten my belt, slipping it through the loops before letting it clank to the floor. She doesn't close her mouth, she just waits, even though I'm taking my damn time.

There's still time to turn back, to untangle myself out of this lie, but like the sick fuck I am, I don't.

Instead, I pull my cock out of my pants and briefs, tapping the head of my cock against her tongue three times.

She has no use of her hands, with them behind her back straining her arms. I imagine by now her knees are aching from being on the hard floor, but her posture is still poised as I slink my length into her mouth.

"Keep that tongue out, Kate," I tell her, and she listens, letting me use her mouth and throat.

She doesn't try to impress me by making noises she doesn't mean, or taking control, licking all over my shaft.

She takes what she's given, like a good girl.

"I want you to wrap those pretty lips around the head and suck."

I gauge her gag reflex, moving in and out of her throat, seeing what she can take. At what point is too deep and she never pulls back.

I trail my thumb over her throat. "Is this too deep for you, baby?" I ask, pulling out, her saliva dripping off the head of my cock.

"No, sir."

"Your throat was made to be fucked too, wasn't it? Show me how good you are at sucking me off."

Kate shifts on the floor, rubbing her thighs together and I

groan as her mouth latches on to the head of my dick and she sucks, hard.

"Fuckkkk," I hiss, knowing if she keeps doing that I'll be coming in her mouth and not her pussy.

I pull out of her mouth with a pop, the suction almost too much to bear as I cup her chin and tilt her face up.

"You might be too good at that, sweet Kate."

I can't even see her eyes, but the corner of her mouth tilting is all the reassurance I need.

"I'm going to help you onto the bed. I want you on your knees, ass in the air. I'm going to spank you and finger your pussy until I've decided you've had enough."

"Yes, sir," she whispers as I grab her by the waist.

She's unsteady without her arms for balance and there's a good chance that maybe one of her legs went to sleep. Instead of guiding her to the bed, I pick her up, an arm wrapped around her back and the other around her thighs as I lie her on the bed, rolling her on to her stomach.

Without a command, she bends her knees; her face pressed against the sheets, with her ass in the air. I stare at her peachy little ass for a moment, before removing the rest of my clothes, neatly folding them and placing them on the table.

The anticipation has Kate nearly shaking on the bed. When I grip the hem of her panties to slide them down her thighs, she gasps.

"Did sucking my cock make you wet for me?" I ask.

She doesn't respond as I shift my fingers between her legs, feeling her cunt.

"Mmm. I think we can do better," I say, with a swat to her ass.

Kate moans into the bed, her wrists fighting against the restraints at the base of her spine as her fingers curl into delicate little fists.

I reel my hand back, spanking her in the same spot, and she inhales deeply.

"Do you want a bruise?" I ask, praying that the answer is yes. Hoping with everything that she wants me to leave marks on her. That tomorrow while she's sitting at home doing hot professor shit, that every time she sits on this sweet ass she thinks about *me*.

"Yes. Please," she says in that raspy tone that goes straight to my fucking cock.

I squeeze her left cheek, hard, to the point she's squirming against my touch. I rear my open palm back and hit the same spot three times in rapid succession.

Kate is panting, her knuckles are white from her fists being clenched against her back.

The spot on her ass is a bright red, a stark contrast against her creamy flesh. But it's not enough to leave a mark for more than a day. She must know it too, as the muscles in her back tighten as she awaits the next strike.

I don't give it to her right away, and she doesn't ask. She patiently waits.

She's fucking perfect.

I spank her five more times, the start of a purple splotch forming against her ass. Kate is panting against the mattress as I cup her pussy, making her jump.

"You're fucking dripping for me. You should see how good your ass looks. Fuck, Kate."

I drag my fingers through her wetness, sliding my thumb into her pussy as my fingers toy with her clit.

"You feel so good. Come for me so I can wrap that pussy around my cock."

Her moan is soft but brain rattling as she rocks back against my hand. Her essence coats my fingers and my dick is nearly weeping with need.

I lightly smack the tender spot of her ass as I finger her before fisting myself and rubbing my cock along her reddened ass. The smooth curve of her ass has my cock weeping as I smack her flesh a few times with my length like a promise of what's to come.

I don't let up with the curve of my fingers, fucking her hard and fast with my hand till she finally falls apart, her knees nearly buckling beneath her as she cries out her pleasure. I hold her hips up, not relenting my movements in the slightest as she gasps, trying to catch her breath.

When I slide my hand away from her pussy, she winces, and I'm glad she's blindfolded so she can't see my smile.

Her thighs tremble as I get off the bed and grab a condom, sheathing my cock, before lining up behind her, shifting my length through her pussy lips.

"I'm gonna take you fast and hard. You're going to take it for me, aren't you?"

"Yes," she says, nodding her head.

"Yes, what?"

"Yes, sir," she rasps out.

She's so fucking wet, there's no resistance as I slide my cock into her warm heat. She feels perfect and it might be the very moment I realized how absolutely fucked me and my brother are.

Kate

Aftercare & Butterflies

HE WASN'T LYING when he said he was going to take me hard and fast. His cock pushes so deep inside of me I think I might burst, along with every slap of his hips hitting my sore ass.

I relish in it.

My brain is completely shut out to the outside world. The only thing that matters right now is how good this feels. The way my thighs are quaking and I can barely hold my ass in the air. The stinging of the bruise that's going to be left on my cheeks, and the way I can hear how wet I am with each thrust.

This is what I needed.

Ben made it all go away.

Somehow, him taking control, using my body, making the decisions, is letting me just live in the moment and forget everything else.

Despite the odds, he makes the world quiet and I owe him for that. I feel like I'm floating and falling apart at the same time, and tears are nearly falling from my eyes at how I feel right now.

He pulls against the silicone band holding my wrists together, making my arms ache and strain.

It feels cathartic in a way, being used like this, being dominated. I get even more pleasure knowing how much he's getting off on being in control. It's a sexual quid pro quo and I'm not sure there's been a hotter transaction ever explored.

I need him to fall apart; I need him shaking with his orgasm just like he did me. My knee slips, and suddenly, my whole body is pressed against the bed, giving my legs a much needed break.

His cock slides back into me. In this position, he feels so much tighter as he pushes my ass cheeks together and fucks me from behind.

His muscular thighs are bracketing mine as he presses into me, my body shifting against the wrinkled sheets with every thrust. Large fingers squeeze my tender flesh as I moan into the sheets.

When he pulls out all the way, the head of his cock pressing in and out, I can't take it as he hits just the right spot. As badly as I want to spread my legs, I can't. His weight pins me down and it sends a rocketing sensation being at his mercy. I shock myself as I come again.

It isn't as hard and toe curling as the first, but it's there. My hands are going numb as I clench them into fists and I drool against the bed. I'm a complete fucking mess and I wouldn't have it any other way.

Ben presses deep inside me, making me nearly shout as his thrusts stall and a sexy moan rips out of his throat as he finishes. He doesn't pull out right away. His cock still inside me as he removes the handcuffs, rubbing my wrists softly, before his fingertips graze against the flesh of my ass.

The juxtaposition from hard to soft is jarring and sweet as he slowly pulls out of me. I tug the blindfold off my eyes, blinking against the warm seductive lights in the room, feeling completely satisfied.

"Be right back," he says and I blink at him, glancing down to see his length sheathed in a condom. He stands and I watch his firm ass muscles move as he heads to the bathroom, the soft sound of sink water running snaps me somewhat back to reality.

I feel boneless, and satiated.

When he comes back, I don't know what to expect, but him laying against the headboard and placing my head on his lap wasn't it. I knew he wouldn't tell me thanks for the fuck and have a safe drive home, but he's tender as he pets my hair as I stretch out my arms and legs, knowing I'll be feeling him tomorrow.

"Does anything hurt?" he asks.

"Only in a good way."

"Was anything too much?"

"No. But I might change my mind tomorrow when I can't sit down comfortably."

He laughs, his fingers still petting down my fly away hairs and I wonder how much I should share with him, if we should talk about anything personal. Logically, I know what he's doing right now is the standard for anyone who was in our position, making sure that I'm okay. That's the whole point of Avalon, having sex with no strings attached, or coming here with your partner.

"Can I ask you something?"

"Hmm?" he says, his eyes closed as he rests his head on the headboard, giving me a glimpse of his strong jaw and Adam's apple. His dark hair is messy. He truly looks like a painting.

It's been nearly two years since I stepped foot into my own studio, but as I look at him now, I see it. I envision the composition, the colors I'd use and what I have in mind. The idea of painting him has butterflies flapping in my stomach and I'm not sure how to feel about it.

"What was your question?" Ben asks, glancing down at me. His eyes that look more green pinning me, making me feel raw.

"How are you able to switch it on and off?" I ask him, and his throat bobs when he licks his lips.

"I don't know, how do you turn it on and off?" he asks with a smirk.

I smile back at him, knowing he has a point. Though, I don't feel like there are two sides of myself like I feel like there is with Ben. Every time we're together, it's almost like I'm with a different person. Maybe he's just special, because I don't know many men who can switch from top to bottom so effortlessly.

"I'm not sure. Last time we were together was the first time I did something like that. I really enjoyed it, but I also loved this too."

Honesty is good. Exploring your sexuality is all about the harsh truths and not being ashamed.

He doesn't say anything for a long time, and I almost consider getting up and getting re-dressed when he finally speaks.

"You looked upset when you came here tonight. Do you want to talk about it?" he asks, surprising me.

Instead of looking into his too-handsome-for-this-world face, I stare at the dark hair on his massive thigh. Wasn't I just thinking about what the line of sex club etiquette and getting too personal is?

"You remember how I told you I just got divorced when we met at your bar?"

"Yeah," he says, because he knows I won't look at him to see if he's nodding.

"I ran into him today, him and his new wife. He got her

pregnant while we were still married. I mean, we had problems well before then, but it was a knife in the back. That's not the point, but back when he was starting the business, I was his biggest investor, and still am. He's been hounding at me every turn to sell my portion of the company back. I keep refusing, mostly to get under his skin, I think, but tonight was different."

"Why?" he asks, no longer petting my hair, but resting his hand on my waist.

"It felt like he was threatening me if I didn't comply. Part of me thinks I should just sell him the shares so that there's no link between us. But the other part of me is just so angry. I gave him everything. Without me, he wouldn't have that company, so why shouldn't I keep them? I paid for them not only with money but my entire youth. Hell, he's been the only man I'd ever been with until that night at your bar."

His body stiffens, and I wince.

Fuck, I was really going to take that to the grave.

"What?"

I pop off from his lap and blink at him. I worry that he'll be turned off, but it mostly seems like surprise, and maybe some guilt?

"Please don't make it weird," I say, and he shakes his head.

"I'm not making it weird."

"You look like you're making it weird," I say, pointing at his confused face.

He raises his hands in surrender before grabbing my face and bringing me in for a soft kiss. I realize then that it's the first time he's kissed me tonight.

"I was just thinking that you're extraordinarily lucky to have me fuck you first post-divorce. So many women don't find good dick till the fifth or tenth guy," he says and I shove his chest.

"Oh, great, so you're also full of yourself."

"You were also full of me, too, not even twenty minutes ago," he says.

I can't help it as I laugh. Even after sex, I still feel lighter. He made it happen; he got me out of my head and let me enjoy myself.

"I should probably head home," I say. He swallows, but nods in agreement.

"Yeah, you probably have to get back home and check some things off your list."

"If you think I'm telling you your grades, you have another thing coming."

"Oh, sweet Kate, I don't need to see your list to know what grades I've received," he says, so much more assured of himself tonight than he was the last time.

"Just like I said, full of yourself."

"Let me walk you to your car?" he asks, petting down my hair one last time as I collect my panties and my clothes.

Ben takes my hand and squeezes it as we walk through the club, but people are far too involved in their own sexual conquests to notice us. It's a throng of people in the act of seduction or currently preoccupied in some sexual act. A few years ago, maybe I would have been scandalized to be at a place like this, or maybe I would have longed to see what it was like.

But as we walk through the darkened hallway, I realize that in its own way what happens at Avalon is an art itself and everyone's tastes and desires are different.

"You okay?" he checks in and I nod as the door creaks open to the garage. He walks me over to my vehicle and he stalls. "Kate...we should probably talk some more about what's happened at Avalon these past two nights," he says.

My brows furrow. "Was it too much, did you not want to be in control tonight?" I ask, feeling insecure.

"Fuck no. Tonight was perfect. You were perfect," he says, his eyes searching mine. He parts his lips and then closes them, giving me a soft smile as he rubs his hands over my arms. "You were perfect. We can talk more next time?" he suggests.

I take that to mean he wants more of this, and maybe I'm a hopeful idiot but I want more too. "I'd like that. I'll see you around."

"Yeah"—he smiles, leaning down to kiss my hair—"I'll see you around."

I get into my car, and he watches me go. I don't know how but I feel exhausted and amped up the whole drive home. It's almost like my body is on autopilot to get me home safe. I definitely need to stop driving myself to Avalon.

When I get home I feed the cats and step foot in my studio for the first time in forever and I paint.

I stay up till four in the morning, mixing acrylics and getting it out of my system. Art has been a passion of mine in so many ways. Early in my education, I wondered if I could do it professionally, but realized the monetization part of it all was too crippling. Instead, I pursued education, and being able to teach about fine art, creating was a hobby, an outlet.

One that I'd long forgotten, and I almost wanted to berate myself for letting this slip away from me.

But as I look at the base layer of the painting, there's a deep satisfaction that fills me.

It has a long ways to go. But I look at the man, one side of him with eyes closed, face to the sky in pleasure. The other half looking down with hooded eyes seeking approval.

I'm not sure what I'll call it just yet, but I go to bed feeling sore and satisfied.

Maybe I'm going to be okay.

I SLEEP till nearly two in the afternoon, with short bursts of disruption as different cats curl up on my side and others bat me, seeking attention. I'm not sure why I do this today, just that I know it's been far too long since I've had a chat with my aunt.

I drive to Rest Haven Memorial Park and walk to her headstone, standing there with a massive sun hat as the sun beats down on my back.

"Hey Aunt Helene," I say, and thankfully no one answers or I'd really need to go back to therapy immediately. "It's hot as fuck today. You'd hate it," I tell her, looking around and wondering why she ever set roots in Florida when she hated the sun, a firm hatred she instilled in me.

According to Aunt Helene, SPF was a religion and the sun was the antichrist of that said religion.

"So, I joined a sex club and started painting again. I know you're very proud of me," I joke, smiling down at her headstone. "Will wants me to sell back his shares, and I don't know what to do. What would you do?" I ask.

But I know the answer. My Aunt Helene was the embodiment of a feminist icon. She never married, but had many lovers. Education was her life, another trait she passed down to me. When I came to live with her at fifteen, I was no longer a kid; I was an adult. Aunt Helene treated me as such, and I'm grateful for it. She took me to museums; we traveled together; she taught me about life and art, and all the richest things the world had to offer.

She died when I was finishing my doctorate program, and I feel like that was the exact time I latched on to Will and his family for dear life.

My Aunt was my last living relative, the person who guided me through life, and even though it's been so long, sometimes her death feels super fresh.

It makes me feel guilty that I miss her more than my own

parents, but she was pivotal in turning my life around and being who I am today. I owe her everything, including my exorbitant lifestyle.

"You're right, fuck 'em," I say, hearing it in her rich voice. She hated Will, and she wasn't quiet about it, but she knew I loved him.

Part of me wonders if I should've listened to her, and never married him. What would my life look like then? Then another part of me feels like my life was supposed to end up this way, that I'm exactly where I need to be.

"I miss you, and don't worry, your crape myrtles are thriving," I tell her.

When I renovated her home, I made sure the exterior all stayed the same; it was her pride and joy. I smile down at the ground, knowing that I'm talking to the ether, but maybe...just maybe she knows I'm thinking of her.

Benjamin

Entanglements and Family Matters

WE GENUINELY NEED to find a better system for our party boats as soon as possible. It's not that I hate running them, honestly I love being on the water. But spraying sticky cocktails off a vessel and blotting rum punch off my shirt isn't how I planned to spend my evening.

Including a string of text messages that have me concerned.

David is tying us up at the marina as I finally scroll through them all.

GAVIN

No sign of her yet.

Are you still coming?

Tamara cornered me. How do I politely tell her that unless she wants to take my dick all the way back in her throat so she can't talk, I'm not interested?

I shake my head and laugh at him until I see his last text.

I fucked up.

It's later than I thought as I look at the time and instead of texting him back, I call him while spraying the deck.

"Hello?" he answers.

"What? Did you wind up taking Tamara back to a private room? She mouthed off so much you lost your boner?" I joke.

"Ben," he sighs my name, and it's then I know.

He did the same fucking thing I did, and I can't even be mad at him.

"She showed up?"

"Yeah, she showed up, looking sad and shit, asking for me to make it all go away. What was I supposed to do?"

Part of me wants to tell him that he should've kept his dick in his pants or told her the truth, but that would be unfair of me. I'm the one who got us into this mess, and Gavin is the man she hooked up with at Carlson's. I'm the one who lied, and in turn I've put my brother in a shitty situation.

The worst part is, I don't regret it. I think about that night with Kate often, and I know it's wrong, but what makes it worse is I'd probably lie again to end up in the same position.

"I think this might be the most fucked up thing we've ever done."

"You're not wrong. How much longer will you be at the marina?"

"Probably another forty-five minutes."

"Alright, well, I think we can both agree that neither one of us can do this again. We only go to Avalon together from here on out so we can tell her the truth, okay?"

I don't deserve my brother, I really don't. I started this mess, and yet, he's taking the blame and not letting me face Kate alone.

"Deal."

"I'll see you at home," he says, and I hang up, and go back to cleaning off the bar tops.

How in the fuck did we end up here?

a a a

"PLEASE, BEN," Penny begs me on the phone. "Lincoln had to go in and deal with some cluster fuck at work and these kids are driving me crazy. The weather is shit and they want to go swimming."

"Fine," I groan over the phone, looking at the time. Too damn early for my sister-cousin to be calling me, begging for a helping hand at the pool with my nieces and nephews.

Aiden and Jessa are using the Bahamas house this weekend and Gavin is overseeing construction for the club.

"Meet you there in twenty?"

"Yeah. Yeah."

I put my bathing suit on and grab a T-shirt and a change of clothes, along with a protein bar and a bottle of water as I head over to the gym.

I scan my pass and head right over to the pool, where Penny has one kid on each hip.

"Uncle Benny," Brynn says, holding out her tiny little arms that I seem to be weak for.

I climb into the pool and take her from my cousin's arms. Penny gives me a soft look.

"Thanks for coming to help."

"Why didn't you just go to Aiden's?" I ask.

"They're having some maintenance done while they're on vacation. Plus, there aren't any other kids at Aiden's."

I glance around the gym pool. There is a kiddie section where multiple mom's are hanging out playing with their toddlers.

"So why aren't you in that section?"

Penny grimaces. "Brynn may or may not have said F-U-C-

K really loud when we first got here, and the glares I got were borderline lethal. So I'm going to need this set of stuck up bitches to roll out and a new crop of moms to roll in."

"Bitches," Brynn repeats, splashing at the water.

Meanwhile, Hudson is in Penny's arms trying to fist and swallow down the overly chlorine filled drops he catches.

"You should probably stop cursing in front of your little foul-mouthed clone here."

Penny spins Hudson around in the water, making him giggle, and she looks over at me.

"Speaking of clones, how's Gavin?"

I wince, covering Brynn's ears, which she thinks is hilarious as she kicks her feet in the water.

"We might sort of be fucking the same woman and she thinks we're one person."

Penny's mouth gapes open, wet tendrils of her blonde hair sticking to her face.

"Say that again?"

I sigh, swinging Brynn in the water so fast that all she can do is laugh and not pay attention to all the horrible words slipping out of my mouth.

"Gavin hooked up with her months ago. She ran into me at Avalon and assumed I was him. I didn't correct her. I was going to tell her the truth and then she ran into Gavin and well, you can imagine what happened. So, yeah. We're basically horrible deviants and we made a promise to only go to Avalon together from here on out so the next time we see her we can tell her the truth."

Penny blinks at me, until she belts out a laugh that I swear ricochets against the indoor pool walls. She gets glares from the mommy group, but she just rolls her eyes.

"Well. It's official. You and Gavin are the most twisted of all of us."

"Hey now. Don't go that far. Aiden married his dead best friend's estranged daughter, who calls him daddy. Don't even get me started on your situation," I say, glaring at her and her nostrils flare.

"At least Lincoln and I weren't lying to each other. It was circumstantial how we started. Fate if you will."

I cover Brynn's ears again.

"Did you really just say that fucking your adopted cousin in a glory hole was fate?"

"Okay, you know what? We're not talking about me right now. We're talking about you and your freak of a twin, and how you're going to get yourselves out of this mess. I mean, you guys go through women like socks, is it really that big of a deal?"

I can feel my cheeks heat and Penny gapes at me. "No? No?" she repeats it twice like the fact that I care so much is unbelievable. "There must be something in the Carlson genes, maybe your frontal lobes don't develop until you're thirty-five instead of twenty-five."

I glare at her. "It's just. I mean, of course, I don't want anything outside of the physical. But she's perfect for me and Gavin. I want to keep seeing her at Avalon, but I'm not sure if that will be on the table when she knows the truth."

She moves the baby around and I realize she knows too much, considering she isn't questioning what that means.

"What did Lincoln tell you?" I ask, and she shrugs, kissing the baby on the cheeks, and he grins.

"Don't use your baby as a shield. What did that grumpy fuck tell you?"

"Fuck, fuck, fuck, fuck," Brynn says, almost like she's a motor engine.

"Look what you did," Penny says, grabbing Brynn and

handing me Hudson, who's far more content to just be held and splash in the water.

This part of the pool is dedicated to swimming. The spot next to us has an aerobics class where geriatrics are using pool noodles for exercise and then the rest are lanes dedicated for swimmers.

I take Hudson in my hands and pretend he's a shark as we swim over to the edge where Penny is obviously hiding from me and trying to get Brynn to hold the edge and kick her feet.

"Tell your mommy to spill the beans," I tell Hudson, who splashes his fat little hands against the water.

Oh, to be an infant again, with not a single fucking care in the world. Hudson just worries about playing, eating, and sleeping. He's truly living the dream.

A flash of black catches my attention, and I put Hudson on my hip as I look over to my right.

It's a wide-eyed Kate in a black bathing suit, slipping over the edge, staring at me like she'd like to blow my head off with a laser.

"Kate?"

She looks at me, the baby I'm holding, and then Penny.

"You're her?" Penny says in a shocked tone, which just has Kate scooting the hell out of the pool even faster, not even looking in my direction.

"Fuck," I hiss, keeping my hold of Hudson as I make my way over to the stairs and chase her.

She's nearly at the women's locker room when I grab her arm.

When she turns around, she looks pissed as hell.

Kate

You Are Not The Father

I'M REGRETTING MY 'NEW ME' mindset around my tenth lap in the pool. I swam in high school; I loved it, but it's clear my body isn't the same as it used to be. I'm going to need to keep coming back if I want my muscles to not ache every time I get out of the pool.

Even though my arms feel like they might fall off, I feel accomplished as I grab the edge of the pool and toss off my swimming cap. The ache feels good, granted, not as good as the remnants of the giant bruise on my ass from the other night. I'm contemplating going back to Avalon tonight, but wonder if that would make me seem too needy.

Truly, someone needs to write a book on sex club etiquette, cause it feels like I have no clue what I'm doing. We're not dating, we don't owe each other our time, but it's also so fucking good. Part of me almost wants to bypass the club itself. Not a full-blown relationship, but an agreement of sorts.

It would be so much easier if I could text him and ask him if he wanted to fuck and get an idea of what type of night it would be. Am I going to get bossy in charge Ben? Or am I going to get soft and sweet, compliant Ben? It's unreal how he can be whatever I need him to be, and I wonder if he feels the same about me.

God, now I sound like a girl with a crush, and I'm not a girl with a crush.

I'm a woman who's getting the best sex of her life, and I won't let feelings get in the mix. Nope, it's simple, an agreement between our bodies and nothing else. Of course, there's a level of trust in what we do, and small talk will happen, but friends small talk all the time.

Ben is my hot, very fucking hot, sex club friend, that's it.

If I go to Avalon and he's not there, am I willing to hook up with someone else? I'm honestly not sure. It would be the smart thing to do. We aren't exclusive. Far from it, it would probably be a good idea to go and fuck someone else.

Yeah, I'll do that. I'll go to Avalon and see what else the club has to offer.

There's splashing to my right and a cute toddler is kicking her feet in the water.

"Mommy won't let go of you, just keep kicking your feet," the pretty blonde woman says to her toddler. I smile as I watch the sweet moment, until I glance next to them and I feel my heart sink into my ass.

It's Ben.

It's Ben holding a baby that looks exactly like him, and when I glance at the little girl, she doesn't look too far off, either. She probably favors her mother.

Guilt drips through me, which is replaced by absolute rage.

Does his wife have any idea what he does at night? What he does at the bar he owns?

I lift myself over the edge, hating myself, hating men even more.

Why? Why do they have to look so good when they're all

fucking evil? How can he have that at home, a wife and two kids, and do what we did behind closed doors at Avalon?

There's a chance they have an agreement, but I doubt it. He fucked me without a condom and then went home to his wife, his devastatingly beautiful wife.

Why couldn't I be into women? I tried. Really, I gave it my best, but it just goes to prove that sexuality isn't a choice. Cause as of right now, I want to swear off men. I thought going to Avalon would be a safe place to find like-minded people. That it was a sure thing, that I wouldn't get hurt or have to deal with the ordeal of having feelings.

Well, I'm having feelings, big ones, and I fucking hate it.

He's just some guy I fucked. I shouldn't care. It's not like I knew he had a wife. God, that poor woman. I know what that pain feels like and even if I was ignorant of what he was doing, this motherfucker made me cause harm.

I'm trying to get out of the pool so he doesn't see me.

"Kate?"

Looks like I literally have zero luck.

"You're her?" his wife asks in a shocked tone, making me shimmy out of the pool faster.

Did his wife find out what he's been doing late at night, or do they have some sort of open relationship? Either way, I don't like being lied to, and that's how I feel right now.

"Fuck," Ben hisses as I briskly walk to the locker room.

I'm about three feet from the door when a hand wraps around my bicep.

"Kate, give me a second," he says, and I turn around to see a chunky, precious baby on his hip.

It isn't that I didn't like kids. In fact, I find them honest and sweet. It's that I don't have the desire to be a mother for many reasons. Seeing him hold his son makes me feel things, though.

It makes me feel lied to. It makes me feel silly for romanticizing the nights we had together.

I feel used again, and I hate that I let someone do that to me again.

"He's my nephew. That's my niece, and that's my sister-in-law," he says quickly.

My cheeks are flaming fire engine red; I feel like an asshole jumping to the worst-case scenario.

"You're not the father?" I ask.

"Definitely not. Lincoln and my brothers all look pretty similar. That's why this guy is so handsome," he says, bouncing the baby on his hip.

I wrap my arms around my waist, feeling like a complete idiot

"I'm sorry—"

"Hey, don't apologize. I don't blame you for thinking that. My brother had a work emergency, and Penny asked me to join so she had a helping hand."

Great, so I assumed he was a married cheating asshole, and he's the kind of guy who wakes up early to help his sister-in-law with the kids in the pool.

"I think we're going to the diner after this. Do you want to come?" he asks.

His gaze is hopeful, and after being such a judgy jerk, I feel like I have no other choice but to agree. Which is probably equally stupid.

This man left a palm shaped bruise on my ass, and I'm about to park that same ass in a booth and eat pancakes with his family?

"Please, Kate. Let me buy you breakfast."

I tilt my head at him and he grabs the baby's fist and waves it at me as he speaks in the wildest baby voice ever. "Please,

Kate. Take mercy on my Uncle Benny. Have pancakes with us."

"That's just...wrong."

Ben grins at me. "So, is that a yes?"

"Fine. Let me shower. I'll meet you all there. Posey's?" I confirm, with it being the next block over from the gym, I knew that was likely where they were going.

"That's the one. Let me go tell Penny, and we'll head that way. You won't regret it," he says, like he can read my mind and knows I'm already second guessing having said yes.

I go back into the locker room and get into the shower, rinsing the chlorine off and trying to get my wits about me. It honestly feels like I'm being haunted everywhere I go in Tampa lately.

If it's not my ex I'm bumping into, it's my sex club buddy.

Maybe this is a sign to never leave my house again.

I scrub the shit out of my hair, maybe hoping that I'll grow a single brain cell in the process. When that doesn't work, I step out of the shower and dry myself off. I blot my hair with a towel and detangle it with a brush, knowing it's going to look like an absolute disaster, so, instead, I toss it into a messy bun.

I didn't bring any makeup, and I blink into the mirror taking in my simple shorts and T-shirt. Well, this is as good as it's going to get.

What the fuck are you doing, Kate? Going to get breakfast with the guy who started your sexual revelation, along with his niece and nephew. Christ.

Instead of going home like a normal ass person with common sense and self preservation, I walk over to the diner.

As soon as I reach the entrance, Ben's waiting—alone.

I glance around and Ben laughs.

"Penny thought it would be too much for her and the kids to tag along. I hope that's okay?" he asks.

Now I feel really bad for thinking she was his wife.

"Yeah, more than okay," I say. Relief fills me immediately as we walk inside and take a booth by the window.

The server, with very large hair tucked behind a headband and over dramatic eyeliner, takes a rag and wipes down the linoleum countertop before handing us menus that are way too big for this kind of establishment.

"Can I get y'all something to drink?" she says, taking out the pad and paper.

"Coffee, with cream please," I say.

"I'll do the same."

"Great, I'll be back to take your order in a minute," she says, walking away in her Keds.

I flip open the menu, even though I don't need to look through it, knowing exactly what I want. Ben doesn't open his, just plants his elbow on the table and rests his head on his hand.

So it looks like I have sweet Ben today. I'm not sure which side of Ben is more appealing to me. Both have me absolutely fucked up.

"You already know what you want?" I ask him.

"I'm in no rush," he says, taking out his phone and shooting off a text, placing it face down on the table.

"I'm sorry that I assumed you were married with kids and a piece of shit," I say, hiding my face with the menu I'm currently not reading. It's at least useful as an emotional shield right now.

"I don't blame you. I can see how it might have looked. I would imagine with your history, it would have been triggering."

"The idea of being lied to is a soft spot for me," I say, glancing over the menu and he swallows thickly, his eyes flicking back down at his phone.

Our server comes back and we place our orders, my figurative shield being carried away with her, but at least I have coffee now. I add two packets of sugar and a splash of cream.

Ben just adds cream as we both take sips, staring at each other on opposite sides of the table.

Okay, so, I can tell him what to do when we're naked and he can blindfold and spank me, but we can't have a normal conversation.

"How has your summer been so far? Do you have any trips planned?" he asks.

"It's been good. I've spent time with friends. I started painting again," I say, but don't mention that he was the muse for the piece I've been working on. "As far as travel goes, not really. I usually wind up tired and with a stomach ache," I say. I'm relatively independent, though the idea of traveling alone scares me. Will never wanted to go to the places I wanted to, either. "What about you? Any trips?"

"I'll probably head down to the Bahamas once or twice. My family has a place down there. But getting the club up and running has been a lot lately, so not much time for much else."

"Do you have a timeframe on when it'll be done?"

"Hoping for mid-August. When do you go back to work?"

"August twentieth."

"Are you looking forward to it? Do you like teaching?"

I smile, taking a sip of my coffee. "I actually really enjoy it. Having tenure and only working at one university makes it more enjoyable."

"People teach at multiple? Sorry, I got through three semesters and realized it wasn't for me."

He seems shy or embarrassed by telling me that, and I just shake my head.

"Yeah, a lot of teachers are adjunct, making shit money and working their asses off. Others are staff professors and are working their way to tenure or headed in another direction."

"So, what exactly do you teach?" His neck is blushing red.

"I don't teach the process of creation. Like my friend Savannah, she's in the photography department. I teach the study of art, the social and cultural impact of art throughout history. I have a few classes I teach that start from the Renaissance to the twentieth century, another that is solely contemporary art. I also teach a class about women in art starting from the sixteenth century and beyond."

"You love what you do," he says softly. It's not a question.

"I do. I love my students. Besides the few classes that meet the art requirement to graduate, they're all very passionate."

"Did you always know this is what you wanted to do?" he asks.

I take another sip of coffee and think over my answer. "Not always. When I moved here to live with my aunt, it became clear. She was brilliant, a research professor in biochemistry. She had so many patents, she made a ton of money, but more than anything, she was passionate. She showed me art, introduced me to a world beyond my own. I'm sure she would have preferred if I became a scientist, but if she was disappointed, she never showed it. When she saw art was my passion, she fed it. She was my greatest teacher, and I wanted to be just like her," I say, my eyes watering slightly and I blot them with a napkin.

Ben looks down at his phone, his brows furrowing, before looking back up at me.

"She sounds like she was pretty amazing."

"She was. What about you? Did you always want to be an entrepreneur?"

He smiles, that cute little dimple in his chin deepening.

"Honestly, yeah. I always knew I wanted to work with my

brother. I knew I didn't want a boss, that I wanted something that was mine. The marina wasn't in the plans, but it worked. I'm glad we stayed in Tampa to be around family. Do you have any family in the area?" he asks, as his phone buzzes frantically on the table. "I'm so sorry. Let me take this."

He picks up the phone and I drink my coffee, loving that the conversation is going easier than I imagined. But I almost fear that it's crossing a boundary. Blurring the lines between fuck friends and real friends. Does there need to be a line between the two?

"Fuck, are you okay? You need to go to the hospital? Fuck. Okay, okay. I can be there in twenty minutes. You're sure you're okay?" he says, his eyes going wide.

He ends the call, grabbing some cash out of his wallet and placing it on the table.

"I'm so sorry. My brother was in a car accident. I have to go...fuck. I've got to go," he says frantically.

"Do you want me to drive you?" I ask him and he swallows, shaking his head.

"Sorry to run out on you like this. I'll see you around," he says in a rush, as he rushes out of the restaurant.

I feel like I have whiplash from the encounter and I realize I don't have his number to check on him later and see how his brother is doing.

Shit.

Kate

Drag & Dragged

DRAG SHOW brunch was a socially acceptable excuse to get wasted in the middle of the day and there wasn't anything anyone could say about it.

Savannah was finally on the tenure track, and we were celebrating. Hard. So hard I knew I'd regret it come tomorrow morning.

Twatzilla was doing her set to the song Get Ur Freak On by Missy Elliot. The drag queen was currently shaking her ass on a bald, nondescript white man while I was on number who knew how many mimosas of the afternoon.

I felt lighter than I had in a long time, my lips as loose as my wallet as I held out a twenty dollar bill. Twatzilla, the icon that she was, shoved my hand down her cleavage as she shimmied her ass to the beat and pretended to spit in my mouth along with the song.

The three of us could barely stop laughing as they announced it was intermission and to help ourselves to more food before it was gone. The french toast, berries, and bacon did nothing to soak up the alcohol in my system.

Chelsea holds up her champagne glass, and me and Savannah did the same. "To Sav! We're so proud of you, sweetie."

"We really are. This is incredible. You're incredible," I nearly slurred.

But she was incredible. My friends were the most beautiful and perfect women in the world and I wanted to sob into my champagne with a splash of orange juice over the fact they were the most perfect angel babies on the planet.

"I want to do something awesome. Something big. I was thinking—a sexy photoshoot," Savannah says, wiggling her eyebrows.

"Why are you looking at me like that?"

"You've let me take pictures of you before. You're perfect. You could be my model along with some hot ass stud we find," Savannah says, giving me puppy dog eyes.

"I'm not getting naked in front of students."

"No, something tasteful, like leotards, or maybe that panty set you bought last year at Cline's."

"I'll think about it," I tell her, not wanting to make a drunken promise.

"Have you been fucking any hotties who might be interested?" she says, talking with her hands, the drink spilling over her knuckles.

I try to take a sip of my glass and ignore her question, but Chelsea points a manicured finger at me.

"What happened at the sex club, Dr. Morely?"

Savannah puts her drink down and rests her hand on her palm. "Yeah, what happened? In very explicit detail."

"Do you remember the night we went out to the marina bar?"

"Carlson's?" Chelsea so helpfully adds. "The very fucking hot bartender who popped your divorced lady cherry."

I glare at her, but then nod. "Yeah, that one. He also has a membership."

"He must make a lot of tips. I mean, he's ridiculously good looking, but even so," Savannah says.

"He owns the place."

"Holy shit. What's his name? Aiden? No, that's the baseball player one. God, have you seen him?" Chelsea slurs, pulling out her phone and typing this man's name all wrong, but finally some images pull up. "Look at that tight little ass in those baseball shorts. But he has to be what? Forty-five now?"

"Ben is mid thirties, that must be his older brother. I wonder if he's the one who got in the car accident."

Savannah and Chelsea both squint at me in confusion, like they're trying to follow my story that is making little sense.

"Alright, let me start from the beginning."

⁂

FIVE SALACIOUS DRAG SHOW PERFORMANCES, too much alcohol, and my current sexual history later...

"Why are you paying so much money when all you want to do is fuck this one guy? He sounds perfect, your little freak match," Savannah says with a hiccup.

"You really went there every night this week to see if his brother is alright, and didn't take up any of the other guys offering their willing dick on a platter?" Chelsea says, her eyes completely glazed over.

"I don't have his number, and I felt bad. And okay, yeah, I wasn't interested in anyone else there, just him."

Savannah boops my nose. "You little sweet fucking perfect idiot. You know where he works."

Chelsea snaps her fingers. "Right! You should just go there, check on how his brother's doing and maybe I don't know, peg him and come back and tell me what it's like. Alex gets weird even if I grab a butt cheek," she says, wrinkling her nose.

"Who would have thought our little Kate would wind up being the least innocent out of all of us? I agree. Go to his job and find out what's going on. At least you won't be going to that club all night just waiting around."

"Isn't that crossing some sort of boundary?" I ask, nibbling on my lip.

Maybe it's the champagne sloshing around in my brain like a ship in Drake's Passage, but this idea has some merit to it.

"I'll think about it," I say and Savannah looks irritated but nods, anyway.

"Are you sure you don't want Alex to drive you home?" Chelsea asks as I sign our check and we walk out of the restaurant.

"That's okay. I'm on the other side of town. I'll see you guys next weekend. This was fun. I really am so proud of you, Sav," I say, hugging her, and we both sway and nearly fall over as Chelsea's husband, Alex, pulls up to the curb.

"Oh, boy, I see we all had lots of fun at drag show brunch," he says with a smile.

"So much fun. Play your cards right, mister, and you might get a BJ," Chelsea says, making Savannah and I both snicker like we're twelve.

Alex shakes his head and clears his throat. "Are you sure you don't need a ride, Kate? It's not a big deal."

I wave him off. "Nah, you guys head home. I'm putting in for a ride right now."

"Text me as soon as you get home," Chelsea says in her mom voice.

"Of course I will," I say, holding up the phone, showing that my ride will be here in one minute.

Alex is herding Chelsea and Savannah into the backseat of

his car as the silver Honda pulls up and I note that the license plate matches.

"Kate?" he asks, and either he's my driver or he's a clairvoyant serial killer.

I'm going to go with driver. "That's me," I say, sliding into the backseat.

"Cherry Hill Lane?" he says and I squint again.

I could just drop by...I mean, I'm not going to want to leave the house when I get back home tonight. There's no way I can go to Avalon. I'll just go, say hi, make sure his brother is okay, and then I'll leave. It's not a big deal. I mean, we had breakfast together, we're friends, kinda.

"Actually, how far away is Carlson's Marina and Bar?"

Jo searches and I squint at his phone, seeing it's basically the same distance to my house, about ten minutes.

"Let's go there instead."

"You sure?" he checks in.

"Yeah I'm sure."

What's the worst that could happen?

JO DROPS me off at Carlson's Bar and Marina; it's only two on a Friday, but the place is still pretty busy. As soon as I shut the car door, Jo was off, not even giving me a second glance. Maybe I chatted too much in the backseat, whatever.

I tug my dress down my thighs and pull out my phone and fix my makeup really quick before walking into the bar.

A quick look around and I don't see him anywhere, so I decide to sit at the bar and grab another cocktail, probably not my best decision.

When the bartender comes back with my drink, I lean forward.

"Hey, is the owner in today?"

"Which one?" he asks. He's cute but far too young for my tastes.

"Ben," I say easily.

"Yeah, I think so," he says nothing else, and I find that annoyingly unhelpful.

So I sip my drink. I sip and I wait.

The longer I sit here, the more pathetic I feel. What the actual hell am I doing? Coming to the place he works, like a stalker, to see what's going on with his life.

Big decisions such as these should not be made after drag show brunch. I leave the bartender a large tip, grab my clutch, and walk on wobbly legs out of the bar. The sun is still too damn harsh even as we trickle into the evening hours.

I'm stumbling over the sidewalk as I try to order a new ride, and I see Ben walking toward me. No wait, I see two Bens walking toward me.

My brother in Christ, how much did I drink?

"Kate?" his rich voice asks and I blink a few times, trying to combine the two Bens into one. It doesn't work, cause one is wearing light blue, and the other is wearing white.

Not to mention the other one has a heavily bruised cheek and a soft cast on his wrist.

"There are two of you, right?" I ask, pointing between the two of them and hold up my hand in front of my face. Only one hand. "I'm not seeing double am I?"

"Shit. Kate. We didn't want you to find out like this," one of them says.

I blink rapidly, holding my hand over my eyes to block the sun and really get a good look at the two of them.

"Find out what? This is your brother who was in the accident. I came to see how he was and that you were alright," I say easily and watch both of their faces fall.

"Do you think we could go inside and talk?" the one in the white shirt says, and I assume that's Ben?

"We'd really like to sit down and explain everything," blue shirt chimes in.

I glance between the two of them. They're identical in nearly every way, minus the one that's injured. What could they possibly both want to talk about?

It takes my drunken mind a few moments to piece it all together. They're both talking to me like they know me. They both want to sit down and talk. There would be no reason for that, seeing as I was under the impression I only knew one of them.

How many times did I wonder why each time with him felt different? How fascinating it was that a man could switch from being a Dom to being so beautifully submissive, so effortlessly.

The first night at the club, he didn't seem to recognize me...

It hits me like a slap in the face.

The dream man who's been checking off my erotic bucket list isn't a man at all. It's this set of twins.

These lying, handsome ass motherfuckers have been toying with me. I take a few steps backward and one of them reaches out for me.

"Kate, please let us explain."

"Explain what?" I snap, feeling a deep simmering anger build up in my throat. It's either anger or vomit, and the last thing I need is to toss my cookies on the front step of their bar, even if they deserve it.

"Can we just go up to the office and talk this through?" the injured one asks.

"Were you the one who fucked me over the desk, or was it you?" I point at blue shirt, who looks like he might throw up too.

"That was me," blue shirt admits. "Gavin," he says.

"So you're the one responsible for the faded bruise on my ass, and you?" I cross my arms, staring up at the other twin. "I'm guessing we got breakfast and you got off on me telling you what a fucking good boy you are? Well, I take it back!" I nearly shout.

I turn on my heel, stomping on the pavement. My heel hits a divot and I go tumbling down in what feels like slow motion. The palms of my hands and knees eating concrete as I hit the hard surface and wince.

"Ouch. Fuck," I hiss, turning to sit on my ass.

I look up at the sun and curse every man who's ever breathed near me as two identical faces block the fierce light.

"Come on, let's get you cleaned up," Gavin says and I glare at him, pulling my arm back.

"Fuck you. You two rats in a trench coat sex club parent-trapped me. Do you know how fucked up that is?"

Ben winces and goes to hold out his arm again. "Kate, your knees are bleeding. You've clearly been drinking. Let us get you cleaned up and home safely."

"Oh, I've clearly been drinking, huh? Don't touch me," I snap as he goes to grab my arm.

"Do you have someone that you can call to come and pick you up?" Gavin asks, his tone irritated.

Oh, he's irritated? The man who lied to me? I understand we weren't in a relationship, but trust and honesty are huge pillars of kink. What is it about me that's a magnet for liars?

God, I'm tired, my knee stings, and so do my palms. And maybe tears are welling in my eyes and there's nothing I can do about it. Except to set the record straight.

"I'm not crying because you're assholes who tricked me. I'm crying because my knees and hands hurt, just so you know," I say, even though nobody asks.

"Alright, fuck," Gavin says, scooping me up over his shoulder like a limp doll.

"Put me down," I say weakly, my head feeling fuzzy.

Deep, vast regret over the amount I've drunk today hits me as my stomach sloshes and my head pounds.

There's a chirp of a car lock as I'm laid down in the backseat. I don't know which twin drives and the other sits in the passenger's seat. I just know they ask for my address and I stupidly give it.

Maybe I cry in the backseat. I can't confirm or deny.

Hopefully, the blood on my knees stains the tan leather of the backseat. Maybe I rub it in a little, I also can't confirm or deny that either. I also, maybe consider sliding my fingers down my throat to throw up in their backseat, but decide against it.

Maybe I need to talk about my petty streak the next time in therapy.

My head is pounding and all I want to do is take a hot shower, cry some more, and re-watch an unrealistic romance show.

Instead, one of these assholes is digging through my clutch, taking out my house keys, and carrying me inside.

I'm placed on my kitchen counter, and I glare at the man in front of me.

"Where's your first aid kit?" he asks.

I point to the cabinet on top of the fridge, and he grabs it. The other twin takes a paper towel and cleans off my palms and my banged up knees. I hiss when he does and he whispers a hushed sorry.

"What exactly are you sorry for?" I ask, glaring down at where he's at on his knees.

"Everything. For lying, for not coming clean sooner."

I use the back of my hand to wipe my face. I just don't have it in me to hear his explanation right now.

Frida, my calico cat, comes sauntering into the kitchen and hisses at the two men.

"She hates men," I say plainly.

Maybe I should be more like Frida and write men, sex, relationships, all of it off. It's done nothing but hurt me.

For fuck's sake, the entire point of Avalon was no strings attached, and yet somehow I managed to find two men who made a very complicated web of bullshit before me.

"I can bandage up my knees. I'd like for both of you to leave," I say, not looking at either of them.

"Can we talk when you're feeling better?" Ben asks, and I just stare at him, not giving him an answer.

I wince as I slide off the counter and usher them out of my house, Frida hot on my heels like she can't wait for the testosterone to get the fuck out either.

I'm about to slam the door and hit them on the ass on the way out as Gavin places his good hand against the door. "For what it's worth, neither of us went into this with the intention of lying or hurting you. We're sorry. I hope you feel better tomorrow," he says.

He doesn't wait for me to reply, and I shut the door.

As soon as they're gone, I take a very cathartic tear-filled shower and finally allow myself to throw up.

Gavin

We Fucked Up

OH, we fucked up.

We fucked up bad.

I knew it the moment the realization hit her. Kate's a smart woman, and even as inebriated as she is, she pieced two and two together—literally.

Not only was she visibly angry, but the fact she hurt herself trying to get away from us has a lead weight sitting on my stomach.

It's the exact reason Ben and I are sitting in her driveway. She's a responsible grown ass woman, but a sense of duty and guilt has us sitting in her driveway making sure she's alright.

Her house is larger than I expected it to be and sits on more land than typical for this neighborhood. The exterior is a cottage style house, with white shingle siding and wooden accents. Large trees frame the property and her silver Audi sits in her driveway, blocked in by our car.

"What do we do?" Ben asks, his knee bouncing as we stare at her house.

"We make sure she's okay and then we give her space."

Ben looks at me like he hates that answer, but Kate owes us nothing. We had no reason to lie, and with her divorce being so fresh, her reaction is valid.

He'd texted me last week that he ran into her at the gym with Penny and to meet them at the diner. I was headed there, ready to set the record straight, even though coming clean was the last thing either of us wanted to do. Taking responsibility over a shitty action sucks, but we were going to do it. It was the perfect opportunity to calmly explain the situation and hope for her forgiveness.

In my haste to get there as quickly as possible, I rear-ended a man in a four-way intersection. He was fine. The damage done to the cars isn't bad. But I smacked my face and sprained my wrist.

We were going to go back to Avalon as soon as my wrist felt better and this shiner was completely gone. We were going to do the right thing, and then it all fell to shit.

It's not Kate's fault, and if anything, it makes me feel like a bigger piece of shit. She came to the bar to make sure that I was okay. Granted, it clearly took her a lot of liquid courage, but she's just kind like that.

She's kind, and beautiful, and going through it, and we just made it worse.

"I feel like there's more we need to do," Ben says.

"How do you apologize for...What did she call it? Parent-trapping her at a sex club. Hey, so sorry that we pretended to be one person so we could both fuck you. Here's a bouquet of flowers?"

I glare at my brother, and he aims his narrowed gaze right back.

"She just deserves a better explanation."

"Do you really think she's open to hearing what we have to say anytime soon?"

Ben inhales and exhales loudly as we stare at the house. We've been sitting out here for god knows how long. Kate's front door swings open and she looks pissed. She's out of the dress she was wearing earlier. All she's wearing is a worn FSU T-shirt and sandals. Her hair is in a messy bun, and large glasses sit on her face as she storms down the brick walkway and roughly bangs her fist against the passenger-side window. I roll it down, even though I know her words aren't going to be kind.

Her arms are crossed over her chest as she glares at me for a long moment.

"Well, what are you two doing sitting in my driveway creepily staring at my house after telling me you two were pretending to be the same person?" she says, extremely bluntly.

"We wanted to make sure that you were alright."

She blinks a few times; her lashes nearly hitting her glasses.

"What did you think I'd storm off in my car in an emotional rage? I'm fine. I'm not going anywhere. You two can leave and never come back."

"Kate," Ben says pleadingly, and she shoots him a dark glare, to the point he quickly shuts his mouth.

"I'm done talking about this. Please leave," she says, without another word, turning on her heel and walking back to her house.

Knowing that she's okay—as okay as someone can be in her position—and that we aren't wanted. We leave her home, both of us feeling like the scum of the earth all the way back to our house.

"YOU DID WHAT?" my sister-in-law Jessa says, her mouth hanging wide open as she sits on my brother's lap.

It's Sunday night dinner. My siblings and I are all around the firepit drinking as Ben and I give a recap of what happened this last week.

"We were going to tell her, but he got into a fucking accident," Ben says, pointing at my face dramatically and I swat his hand away.

"I'm not sure you can come back from that," Lincoln says, unhelpfully.

"You got your adopted cousin to marry you," I snap back.

"Yeah, well, I'm better looking, richer, and she was already in love with me. You should have waited until she was in love with one of you semi-conjoined freaks."

I glare at my older brother and Penny swats at his arm.

"That's rude. She seemed really sweet in the moment I saw her at the gym," Penny says, giving me a small smile.

"You mean, when she thought you were Ben's wife, and that my children were his?" Lincoln says and I'm about to punch my brother.

"You're my least favorite brother," I say to Lincoln and he grins.

"That makes sense," my oldest brother says, and Lincoln turns his glare on him.

"So, how are you going to apologize?" Jessa says, the sweetest of anyone in the family, it's hard to be rude to her. Even if we do occasionally mortify her by knowing the little roleplay games her and Aiden like to play.

"What do you do when you fuck up?" I ask Aiden.

He shrugs. "I don't fuck up."

"Me either," Lincoln says smugly.

"Oh, be so fucking for real," Penny says, rolling her eyes.

"You were persistent as a chronic illness, trying to get me to be with you."

"Sure, but I had nothing to apologize for," Lincoln says.

"God, Penny, you could have done so much better," Ben says, and we laugh as the conversation takes a turn into Lincoln's business, which used to be our father's.

"Dennis Commercial is crushing us right now, outbidding us on everything by lowballing our estimates. This will be the fifth commercial building this year," he complains.

"How are they even making a profit?" Aiden asks.

"That's the thing, we have no fucking clue, but I'm going to see what I can figure out and hopefully these clients will realize they're making a mistake by going with them instead of us," Lincoln huffs and nods his chin. "How's the club coming along?"

"Good, should only be a few weeks before the grand opening. All of you degenerates are invited, of course."

"Good, we need a good night out," Penny says, and Lincoln's face softens for her ever so slightly.

Jessa clears her throat, clearly still locked in on the previous conversation. "What if you see her at Avalon again?" she says.

Ben and I blink at her and then look at each other.

I hadn't thought about that. But I know the idea of her walking back to a private room with another man has bile sizzling in my throat. It's a foreign feeling, and I don't like it one bit.

☙ ☙ ☙

BEN and I go to Avalon for the next four nights in a row. Kate isn't there, and no one interests us.

Kate

Chocolate Apologies

I'M A MESS.

One of my repeat shows is on, it's basically background noise at this point. Michelangelo is sitting between my legs and I stalk my DoorDash driver on my phone.

I didn't just double dash. I fucking *triple* dashed. Currently, Marvin is on his way to my house with Chicken Alfredo, Oreo cookies, and a bottle of Moscato. I haven't showered in two days, and my hair clearly shows it as I sit here and feel sorry for myself.

The only solace I can take is that my uterine lining is currently waging war against my body at the moment. It's also why I'm giving myself grace over the way I handled the whole twin switcheroo situation.

God, I was more vocally angry with them than I was when Will told me he got his mistress pregnant.

I'm absolutely blaming the mimosas and my luteal phase for my absolute freak out. Even though I feel like I had every right to be as pissed as I was, I mean, who does that? Maybe my trauma made the situation worse, but what they did was messed up.

I thought I found the guy that I could really safely experiment with. Someone I could put trust in to go further with my kink exploration and he turns out to be a literal two-faced liar.

Maybe I should have heard them out. Maybe I shouldn't care so much about the whole ordeal when we never made any promises to each other.

A bunch of what ifs won't do me shit. Right now, all I feel is sad.

There's a knock at my door and my brows furrow. I chose for the driver to leave everything at the door so he wouldn't have to see me braless or the shame of grabbing all my purchases. I did leave him a large tip for going multiple places.

When I open the door, it isn't Marvin. My stomach churns, not because I'm desperate for my alfredo, which I am, but because of who's standing on my doorstep.

It's one of the twins, the one I suspect to be Ben, based on his unblemished face. I hold the door close to my hip, not letting him see the inside of my house as he looks sheepishly down at me. Thankfully, there isn't pity in his gaze, just concern.

"I brought you this," he says, holding out a heart-shaped chocolate cake with the sparkled words 'We Fucked Up' on the top of it.

"Where's it from?"

"Publix," he says, and I hold out my hands to take the offering.

It's definitely better than the Oreos I have headed my way.

"Do you think...do you think I could come in and maybe explain what happened? I don't expect your forgiveness, but I'd like to at least tell you our side of things," he says, and he looks so charming and handsome.

The petty side of me that I'm slightly concerned about wants to slam the door in his face. The pathetic, emotional wreck that I am, however, wins, because I do want to know what happened. Plus, the cake doesn't hurt. It's better than flowers or showing up empty handed.

"My place is kind of a mess," I say as I open the door, and he follows me.

I place his peace offering on the table, fully intending on eating that entire cake on my own tonight. Even if his explanation or apology sucks, at least I'll have cake.

"You haven't been to Avalon in awhile," he says, as he glances around my house.

Stacks of books are piled everywhere. There may be a wine bottle or two on top of empty water bottles, and a bag of chips that I quickly roll up and put on the coffee table.

"I'm on my period. It has nothing to do with you or Gavin," I say, probably too sharply. His cheeks redden, but he quickly shrugs me off.

"Sorry." He clears his throat. "It's just we were hoping to see you there and explain. We didn't do anything with anyone else while we were there," he says, as I move a blanket and offer him a place to sit on the brown, contemporary sofa I'll never get rid off. It was one of Aunt Helene's most prized possessions, and now it's mine.

"It's none of my business what you and your brother do at Avalon."

He scratches the back of his neck and nods. Michaelangelo, the absolute traitor, rubs against Ben's legs and without hesitation, he pets the orange turncoat as he pieces his thoughts together.

"The whole situation is my fault," he says, clearing his throat, petting my cat as a distraction, not looking at me. "You were beautiful, and you thought I was Gavin. I was going to come clean, but then you showed me your list. It's difficult for me to find women who are into what I like. A lot of the time they want to switch it off and on, and I get that, it's easier to manage when Gavin and I share someone. They can be submissive to him and I can be submissive to them."

"You and your brother share?" I say with a swallow.

Maybe a very hot threesome pops into my head, but I'm still mad, so I very quickly diminish that fantasy. Bad Kate. We're not forgiving them or even contemplating letting them touch me again, let alone both of them. But damn, if it isn't an unreal visual.

"Yeah. It's something we do pretty often. But, like I said, it's hard for me to find women who are interested in being with just me. Some women want to be too dominant for my liking, others only like being what I want when I pay them to be. It's just rare. And there you were, small and so fucking pretty, and you wanted to be in charge. One of the biggest turn-ons for me is having a petite woman tell me what to do," he says, picking up my cat and cuddling him close to his chest.

I briefly look away from him, because that part of our dynamic is also a big turn on for me. With both of them, it had been. I liked how large he was and the fact that he was at my will. Then, on the flip side, I liked how large he was when he took control of me. Well, Gavin, I guess.

It also strikes me how brutally honest he's being, that he even mentions having ever paid for sex, beyond paying for Avalon. He's being vulnerable, and I think he's telling me the whole truth.

"When I say it's the best sex I've ever had, I'm not lying. As soon as I left Avalon, I felt so goddamn guilty and I told Gavin right away. We had a plan to tell you. He was going to tell me if you showed up at Avalon and vice versa. I don't want to speak for Gavin, but I was working a bachelorette party on one of our party boats and couldn't get there that night you were with Gav. Again, I don't want to speak for him, but he saw you were upset and thought he could make it better."

I take a deep breath, remembering how upset I was that night and how he really did make me feel so much better. Fuck, I started painting again after that night. When I glance over at him and push up my glasses, he gives me a soft smile.

"I think you look really pretty with your glasses."

"No. Don't be charming right now. Continue your story," I say, even though I'm flattered. I look like shit right now, and he seems completely nervous. He gives me a soft smirk, stroking Mikey's coat, and the cat is rubbing his head against his chest, covering him in orange fur. Ben doesn't seem to mind whatsoever.

"Right. Then I ran into you at the gym. You thought I was married to Penny, which is hilarious, but we'll get into that another time. I texted Gavin to come to the diner so that we could sit down and tell you the truth, and that's when he was in the car accident. We were waiting for him to heal up before we tried to find you at Avalon, but then you showed up and everything went to shit."

"Why should I believe anything you're telling me? How do I know this isn't something you two get off on?" I ask, because as badly as I want to believe him, I've been burned before.

He swallows and nods his head a few times, trying to articulate what he wants to say.

"You don't have to believe me, or forgive me—us. I just wanted you to know our side of things. We both feel terrible and the last thing we wanted to do was hurt you, because fuck, Kate, you're like perfect."

This time my cheeks heat. Perfect? Me? I'm an absolute disaster.

I shake my head as my phone chimes and I see that Marvin

is here with my food. I need some time to mull over what Ben said. I get up and grab the to-go bag, the non-discreet bottle of wine and my Oreos by my front door.

"No judgment," I say as I place them all on the table next to his apology cake.

"Not from me," he says, petting Mikey before placing him on the couch as he stands to his full height.

As large as he is, he's also gentle as he slides his hands in the pockets of his shorts. "I'd understand if you don't want to see me or my brother again. Thank you for listening, and if you're ever open to being friends, just know that I'd really like that," he says, giving me the sweetest dimpled smile. "Enjoy the cake."

He leaves my home without me saying another word and something loosens in my chest.

I may or may not cry while drinking the bottle of wine and half the heart cake later that night. My thoughts filled with ever confusing feelings about what I want and what I deserve.

🍪 🍪 🍪

I COULD FEEL my ass getting bigger. Between not going back to the gym again and the exorbitant amount of takeout I was devouring, I needed to make a change.

That's why my stupid ass is at Trader Joe's on a Saturday and I'm questioning every mistake I've ever made in my life. Trader Joe's is like a grocery store created in an alternate reality. No one knows how to act. The store is too small, and despite its poor design and tremendous crowd, I'm still here because their food is amazing. I'm shit in the kitchen, and they have the best freezer meals that even someone like me can't fuck up, not to mention that they're portioned to where I can usually eat all the meal in one sitting, or one half for lunch and the other for dinner.

My cart is dangerously full of food I don't need, but I rationalize that it's cheaper than getting it delivered to my house. There are a few bottles of wine and some sorbet I can't wait to eat as soon as I get home. Once the semester starts, I usually only drink on weekends. But I'm in the midst of a mid-life sad girl summer or something similarly tragic.

I've been thinking about reaching out to Ben, now that I'm no longer in a hormonal spiral, and looking to savor some good out of these last weeks of summer. Despite wanting to use my very expensive Avalon membership, I haven't bitten the bullet yet. Something is holding me back from going for it. Maybe I'm still upset that they lied or I'm worried about what would happen if I did agree to some sort of friendship with Ben or Gavin.

All I know is I'm not going to make the decision lightly. If I decide to forgive, truly forgive them, I can't hold any resentment and I'm not sure if I can do that right now.

I can barely move my cart down one of the narrow aisles as another cart hits the end of mine. I take a deep breath instead of losing my shit at the slightest inconvenience, but when I look up and see that it's Will with a full cart of food, including baby food, I consider choosing violence.

I can count on one hand the amount of times he went grocery shopping when we were married.

He doesn't look surprised to see me and I'm getting really concerned that he really is following me. This is just too many coincidences. Tampa isn't a small town. I shouldn't have to run into my ex-husband this often. It honestly feels like I'm in my own personal Truman Show hell and everyone is seeing what it's going to take to finally make me crack.

"Kate," he says, trying to act surprised when he sees me.

"Do I need to get a restraining order?" I snap back.

There are too many instances that don't make sense. Sure, the sushi place I could understand, but brunch and now Trader Joe's?

"Jesus, Kate, when did you become so paranoid?"

"Maybe when my partner of nearly two decades got someone pregnant and ruined my marriage in a blink of an eye, or something," I say, going to move my cart and his large hand clamps down on the side and he invades my space.

My spine stiffens, and my heart rate quickens. I know I'm in a public space, that he can't hurt me here, but there's still an underlying fear.

I swallow thickly, staring into brown eyes I don't recognize anymore as he sneers at me.

"Some things don't change do they? Still a lush," he says, nudging the neck of one of the wine bottles in my cart.

It makes bile rise in my throat. I didn't realize how much more I started to drink toward the end of my marriage. How I used alcohol to wash away what was a clearly failing relationship. He's all too eager to rub it in my face, and gaslight me into thinking it was all my fault.

I know that the collapse of us was a two way street, but what he did was inexcusable.

"Will, I suggest you back off." It comes out in a harsh whisper.

"Listen, I'm sick of you holding this shit over my head. We're over, been over a long fucking time. Give me my company and you'll never have to see me again."

I'm speechless as an arm wraps around my shoulders, making me flinch. When I glance to my right, it's Gavin. A slightly yellowed bruise still showing on his eyebrow.

"You get everything you need, baby?" he asks, using his body to create space between Will and I.

Patrons of the grocery store are getting pissed as we block the soup dumplings and Will looks at Gavin with distaste, but backs up out of my space. It shouldn't excite me that Gavin is taller or bigger than Will, but it does.

If there's a dick measuring contest in the frozen foods section, Gavin is winning, while Will is shriveling up due to cold temperatures.

"Is there a problem here?" Gavin says, raising his bruised eyebrow at Will, his arm sliding down my back and holding my waist.

"Think about it Kate, I'm serious."

"Are you threatening her?" Gavin says, placing me behind his large back. I have to tilt to the left to see Will's pissed off expression and it's very much worth a million dollars.

"Mind your own fucking business. What, is she doing all that freaky shit she's into so you're her lap dog now?" Will says and I nearly hold in a squeak as a seventy year old woman walks by looking absolutely astonished. Of course he had to throw that dig in there, like our sexual chemistry is the reason we got divorced and not his infidelity.

"I don't know. Are you her prick of an ex-husband who's acting like a fucking man child in the middle of Trader Joe's?" Gavin asks.

Oh god, am I going to witness a full on brawl in a grocery store because of my poor taste in men?

Will is fisting his cart so hard his knuckles are white. He looks like he's going to say something but instead curses under his breath, pushing his cart dramatically in the opposite direction, baby food jars clink against each other. I take a deep breath as he walks away, and Gavin turns to face me.

"Are you stalking me too?" I ask, and he shakes his head.

"Are you okay? How many times has he shown up somewhere you were?" he asks, looking genuinely concerned for me.

Fuck these men and them sweet talking me into forgiveness.

"It's the third time he's shown up the same place I have been in the last few months."

"Is he blocked on your phone?" Gavin asks and I shake my head. "Can I see it?"

I'm not sure why I hand him my phone, but I do, and he looks through a bunch of apps.

"You're not sharing your location with anyone. I'm not a tech wiz, but you don't seem to have any weird apps on here. I think you should still go to your provider's store to make sure he hasn't installed something on your phone. I'm not telling you what to do, but would you consider a restraining order?"

"Maybe," I whisper, not knowing how I feel about things going that far. I should just sell the damn shares, give in and get it over with.

"I put in my number. Just in case you have any issues," he says it so easily as he glances around the store. "How much more shopping do you need to do?"

"I just need to grab some cheese and cereal," I say, because I'm so dumbfounded. He popped out of nowhere, stood up for me, and most importantly he made Will back off.

"Let's go get the rest of your stuff."

"Oh, you don't have to come with me," I wave him off and he gives me a look that says it doesn't matter what I want as he holds the cart with one hand, not caring when people are clearly giving him dirty looks that he's in the way.

"So...what brings you to Trader Joe's?" I say, because what else do I say? He has a basket in his hand, but the only thing in it is a container of blueberries and two pre-made salads.

"It's my turn to do the shopping. Ben and I are a little help-less with food."

"Same," I say with a shrug.

"Ben told me he came over and explained mostly everything."

I glance up at him as he looks down at me with eyes that are more green than blue today. Why do they have to be so pretty? And kind, and fuck, am I about to forgive them? Yeah, I am.

Maybe it makes me weak, or maybe their transgressions are really worth forgiving for both my peace of mind and for saving the remainder of my summer.

"He did."

"I told him not to, that you shouldn't forgive us, but every-thing he said is true. That night we met at the marina, I had no other intention but to make you feel good and for me to take something I wanted. I'd thought about you since that night, and I would've recognized you if it really was me at Avalon. Ben started this mess, but I didn't stop it when I could've, and I'm sorry about that."

He leans down, so his lips are nearly pressed against my ear. "But it's hard to be that sorry when you were so fucking good that night. I am sorry for lying though, that we hurt you."

My lips part as I grab the cheese I want and I don't break eye contact with him.

"Are you two going to make out? Or are you going to get the fuck out of the way?" the same seventy year old woman says and Gavin and I give each other a look before walking away, both of us giggling.

He stays with me as we both check out, neither of us saying anything. He walks me to my car and places my groceries in the trunk and we both stand there under the hot summer sun for a long moment.

With his hands on his hips, a gray T-shirt stretched out against his large chest, and basketball shorts showing off his ridiculously hot calves I know that I'm definitely going to cave. When the hell would I ever have this opportunity again?

"Seriously, use my number. For anything. If your ex bothers you again, or like Ben said, if you want to be friends."

"Friends," I repeat.

"Good friends," he says with a smirk.

"I'll think about it. Thanks for helping me back there. I appreciate it."

"Make sure you get your phone checked," he says. He looks like he wants to say more, but doesn't, instead he gives me a wave. "Drive safe."

"Yeah, you too."

⚜ ⚜ ⚜

TWO HOURS LATER, while heating up my frozen Alfredo and drinking a sparkling lemonade, I finally send the text I knew I wanted to the moment I left the parking lot. Maybe I'm a fool, or maybe I'm just a horny bitch with a newfound twin fantasy. But I send it before I can change my mind.

> Maybe we can be friends.

I expect a reply, and I get one, but this time it's as a three-way group chat.

GAVIN

> A dinner between friends on Friday night?

BEN

> Hi Kate!

> Friday night sounds great.

Maybe it won't be such a sad girl summer after all. There's no revenge as sweet as forgiveness, right?

Benjamin

The Ground Rules

I'M NERVOUS, but excited as Gavin and I sit and wait at the restaurant. We're in the back of the patio, giving us enough privacy and a view of downtown as we wait for Kate to join us.

That's if she hasn't changed her mind and decided she was having a total lapse in judgment in forgiving us and starting... whatever the fuck it is we're starting tonight.

"Will you stop bouncing your leg?"

"I either bounce my leg or I go into a spiral. Which is it?" I ask Gavin, and he rolls his eyes.

"She'll come. It was her idea. You have nothing to be nervous about."

I nod, and then continue bouncing my leg, thinking about all the things I'm indeed fucking nervous about. Kate agreed after seeing Gavin at the grocery store, not after I showed up at her house. What if it's Gavin she's interested in? What if I'm far more invested in this than everyone else? I know that Gavin doesn't want a relationship, and I'm not really sure what Kate wants. From her being at Avalon, just getting out of a messy divorce, I can't imagine she wants what I secretly want. It's not something I've told Gavin, and shit, maybe it's something I haven't come to terms with myself.

Maybe it's just Kate that I feel this way about, but the idea of something more, beyond a sex club, beyond casual, it doesn't seem so scary anymore. Not with Kate, anyway.

"What're you so nervous about, anyway?" Gavin asks.

Instead of spilling my guts, instead of being honest with the one person I'm always honest with, I hold it in.

"I just want it to work out, is all."

Gavin squeezes my shoulder, kneading the muscle as Kate walks over to our table. She's wearing a pretty dark blue dress that's tight around her chest, and fans out around her knees. Her dark hair is down in slight waves and she looks pretty as ever.

Gavin and I both stand, and he slides her chair back. She slides the back of her dress down before taking a seat and giving us both a sheepish smile.

"I love this place," she says, as she grabs the drink menu. "Thank you for inviting me."

"We're glad you wanted to meet, that we could be friends," Gavin says, enunciating the word friends.

It's because he means it. He can be friends with Kate and fuck her till she can't think straight. Usually I'd be the same, but with Kate, I don't know if it will be as easy for me to not blur the lines. Obviously, I'm open to trying.

It's not like me to catch feelings like this, to care so much, I can keep it in check.

"What can I say? You're both too charming for your own good."

Our server takes our drink order and we decide that we have to get the cheese wheel pesto pasta and a few other items to share. It seems a little indicative of the future, but I don't want to get too far ahead of myself.

"Did you get your phone checked out?" Gavin asks.

"I did. Thank you for the suggestion. They didn't find anything odd on it," Kate says, taking a sip of her wine.

"I meant what I said. We're friends now. If you ever feel unsafe, either of us will be there."

Kate gives my brother a soft smile and nods. "I'll keep that in mind." She taps her finger against her wine glass a few times like she's working up the courage and then suddenly it all spills out of her. "We're all on the same page that this would be a friends with benefits situation, right? We aren't just cocktails and dinner friends?"

"Can't we be both?" I ask, and her cheeks heat at the slight innuendo.

"Of course it can be both. I'm just making sure that if we do this that we're all on the same page. That we should have ground rules and be honest with one another."

"Ground rules," my brother repeats and she nods.

"And definitely nothing but honesty," I say, feeling like I'm the one who inadvertently got us all in this tangled mess. It's important that she knows we would never betray her trust from here on out.

"Yeah, like, do we only go to Avalon? Can I text you when I'm horny at ten at night for one or...both of you to come over? Are we sleeping with other people? I think laying it all out in the open is the only way to do this sort of thing, no?"

Gavin rests his chin on his palm, looking at Kate like she's precious. It's odd. I've seen Gavin flirt with women plenty of times, or even joke with them, but he's putting in more of an effort to make this situation work and I'm wondering why.

"You like rules, Kate?"

"Yes, and I know both of you do, too. I think setting our expectations and being honest is the only way something like this can work."

"Okay, what would your ideal rules be?" Gavin asks.

"I think we shouldn't restrict ourselves to Avalon, honestly I would be fine not paying the membership any longer. I don't really have an interest in sleeping with anyone else right now, but I wouldn't put it off the table and I wouldn't expect you two to not sleep with other women if you wanted to. I do think if we are sleeping with anyone else that we need to be clear about that with using protection. I'd be comfortable coming to your house or you coming to mine. And I think we make the most of it. There are things I want to try, and I'm sure there are things the both of you are looking for. As long as the situation continues to be agreeable for everyone and we communicate, then I feel like an arrangement like this can work."

Gavin and I are both speechless for a moment. Kate isn't what we're used to.

"We can agree to those terms. We're so busy with the bar I don't see us having the time or energy to be sleeping with anyone else right now. Avalon has its moments, but I don't think we need them to facilitate anymore either. For your last point, you know I've never actually seen this physical list," Gavin says.

Just casually bringing up the part where we pretended to be one another. Kate goes to grab her purse as the server rolls up with the cheese wheel and begins making our pasta. The whole time he's talking about the age of the cheese, how many wheels they go through a week and how they clean it, I'm thinking about the list in her purse.

Did she ever grade me for our night together? Has she added more things? Are there things I'm willing to try that I might not have been before? With Kate, I find myself considering more possibilities. Things that were on her list that I haven't fully jumped into are now on the table. Maybe it's because I know Kate would make it good for me, or because I trust her, unlike the other women I've been with. Is this what it's like to consistently want to have sex with the same person? Have I been missing out on this my whole adult life? Or is it something specific about this woman?

"Are you alright, Ben?" she asks softly from across the table as our shared plates are between us.

"Yeah, more than alright," I tell her and she smiles as we eat.

The list and discussion over ground rules is forgotten as we give her updates about the club portion of our business, and she talks about the upcoming semester. It's easy, casual, just like we would talk to any friend.

The meal is delicious, and Kate's head is tilted back, her delicate throat exposed, laughing at something Gavin said. I like that she doesn't hide her scars and part of me wants to ask how she got them, but now doesn't seem like the right time or place.

Dessert is brought out, and Gavin circles the conversation back to what we were discussing before.

"Did you bring your list?" he asks.

Kate is slightly flushed from the wine and the summer air, but licks her lips and nods as she opens her purse. She pulls out the list that's clearly been folded multiple times, and hands it over to Gavin, and he angles it so I can't see. The bastard fucking knows too well; he knows I want to see what she rated our experience and if she's added anything new or god-fucking-forbid any additional ratings on there.

It's not like I have any right to be jealous if she slept with someone else, but something about the idea doesn't sit right with me. Fucking my brother? I have no problem with, but the idea of her being with another man the way she is with me? I find the idea unsettling in a very disturbing way.

Gavin taps his chin, hoarding the list like an asshole.

"We wouldn't invite anyone else to join us. Just the three of us," he says, and Kate's throat bobs.

"That works for me," she says, taking a sip of her wine. She's been nursing that second glass since we got dinner.

"Obviously me and my brother are very different with our tastes, as you can imagine."

"I think I'd like a clearer picture of what that looks like," she says, glancing between the two of us.

"I need control, and I like subservience. I don't like push back, obviously I want to know if something is too far, but I don't like a brat. You were perfect that night I was with you at Avalon, I think we could push it even further. I also like sharing with Ben, but no one else."

She accepts his answer and then turns to me. Telling her my sexual desires on an outdoor patio where anyone in downtown Tampa can hear me is something. But we're all laying our cards out on the table. She said communication was key, and I can do that.

"I like the opposite. I like being at your will, but nothing too rough. I wasn't lying when I told you that the night we had together was the best I ever had. I've been looking for a woman I felt comfortable enough to really explore the more submissive part of myself with. If I could see the damn list," I say, grabbing it out of my brother's hand.

My eyes zone in on power dynamics. She left notes.

10/10 I loved being in charge.

I can't even focus on anything else as I look over the list at her. She smiles softly at me and shrugs. I glance back down and see a star next to pegging.

"I'd be willing to try it," I say, and she doesn't even have to ask me which item I mean as she arches a dark brow at me.

"What about you, Kate? Obviously, you have this list, but what do you want?" Gavin asks.

"I want it all," she says as Gavin and I look at her like she was fucking made for us. "That is, everything on this list," she reiterates.

"We can do that," I agree happily.

"What I mean or want to reiterate is that we all agree that there are no strings attached. I've forgiven you both and I truly don't think you were out to hurt me, but I'm still healing from some things. Sex and friendship are the only things I can commit to."

"A friendly sexual agreement," Gavin says, though he doesn't explicitly say he agrees.

"You're the one in charge," I reiterate and she smirks at me before nodding her head.

"With that all cleared up. What do we do now?" Kate asks.

"We could start tonight?" Gavin asks in his forward ass tone, and I watch Kate squirm in her seat.

She clears her throat. "The three of us?"

Gavin nods, and Kate downs the rest of her wine. "Alright," she says, as Gavin waves down our server for the check. Okay, I guess we're going from her hating us to going all the way into the deep end.

It's time to sink or fucking swim.

Kate

Kate's First Threesome

OKAY. Alright. Okay.

We're doing this. We're really fucking doing this. I mean, in the back of my mind I had the thought that the night could turn into a twin sandwich, but maybe I didn't totally conceptualize the idea?

We all knew this wasn't a totally friendly water under the bridge type dinner. While they apologized to me separately, it was a dinner to discuss where we go from here, and it went better than I expected. I understood the basics of what both Gavin and Ben liked in the bedroom, but now that it's all out in the open, I wonder if it's really possible to have it all.

I'm probably about to join a very exclusive club of women who've fucked twin brothers and while I'm nervous, I'm also endlessly excited. What's it going to be like being with two people? Will it be too much? Will it be fucking awesome? I don't know, but I'm about to find out.

Not driving myself to the restaurant was the correct choice as Gavin has the valet retrieve his car. Ben and I are standing under an awning as this summer storm works its way through

Tampa. In another hour or so I'm sure the setting sun will be out and the rain will be completely forgotten. But what happens after I go through with this? It's not like a passing rain. It feels like whatever we do, it's going to stick with me forever, and shockingly, I'm not scared. This is something I want to experience.

I'm more nervous than anything.

Gavin steps under the cover, his dark hair shining with specks of rain as he grabs my chin and plants a soft kiss against my lips.

"Don't be nervous," he says. I swallow quickly and run my arms over my pebbled flesh.

When I look over at Ben, he looks so utterly confused over what just happened between Gavin and I, and I don't understand why. I'm about to ask as the valet drives like a bat out of hell, pulling Gavin's car to the curb and handing him his keys.

Do I sit in the back? Ben's far taller than me.

"Why don't you get warmed up with Ben in the back," Gavin says easily.

Ben opens my car door and I slide over to the left, behind the driver's seat. Gavin shifts his passenger seat as far up as it goes, giving Ben more leg room.

"Do you need my address?" I ask.

"Nope," Gavin replies, as Ben reaches over my shoulder and grabs my seatbelt, clicking it into place before doing his own.

Ben looks at me with the softest of looks and I can't help it as I reach out and brush back his soft hair and cup his face. He nearly melts against my touch and it spurs my confidence on. They want this just as bad as I do. Enough to agree to a somewhat of an exclusive agreement.

Not a relationship. Definitely not a relationship.

But something else.

They don't judge me. In fact, they both seem eager to help me explore what I like. I'll never get this opportunity again and I'm realistic about it. I genuinely know I'll never be with anyone the same way I am with these Carlson brothers.

So I make a choice right then and there. I'm going to fully embrace this. I won't let fear, nerves, or insecurities get in my way. If this is as good as it's ever going to get I'm going to gratefully and eagerly soak up every single minute that they're mine. Well, not mine, but the closest thing to it.

These brothers aren't the kind of men to be kept, and I don't want to belong to anyone, either. This is...whatever it is, and I'm going to savor it.

"You weren't supposed to see your grade, you know?" I joke with Ben and he bites his bottom lip, that ridiculous dimple popping up as he smiles at me.

"It's already gone to my head, I fear."

I tug his bottom lip away from his teeth and glance toward the front. Gavin's gaze rotates from being on the road and looking in his rearview mirror.

"Have you touched yourself, thinking about that night?" I ask, my heart rating picking up and the need for friction between my legs rising with every second I'm in this car.

Ben's hand slides onto my knee, his thumb rubbing soft circles against my exposed skin. His touch is always soft, reverent, and sweet. I soak it up like a needy cat basking in a ray of sun. Ben makes me feel powerful in a way I didn't know I'd ever need, that I'd ever crave.

His eyes are hooded as he looks down at me.

"All the fucking time," he says honestly.

"Show me," I say, and his eyes search mine, but he doesn't hesitate.

He removes his hand from my leg and unzips his pants, sliding down his briefs and exposing his weeping hard cock.

Part of me wants to lean down and lick the tip, but another part of me needs this to last for as long as humanly possible.

Ben fists himself at the base, his eyes locked with mine as he swipes his tongue over his lips.

"Slow," I remind him, as his wrist moves leisurely, his pressure on his cock light. It's more torturous for him than anything, but he enjoys it. I can tell by the way he looks at me and the mess he's making of himself with pre-cum leaking from the tip.

Gavin says nothing as he drives, and there's this never-ending awareness that he's there, that he's listening and watching. At the same time, Ben and I are in our own little bubble. The car windows are tinted just enough that there's no worry of some unsuspecting pedestrian seeing Ben's dick, but the optics of it have me shifting in my seat.

"What do you think about when you touch yourself?" I ask him, my hand on his face, and he's nearly nuzzling against my palm. He kisses my wrist softly.

"The way you fucking look at me, like I please you," he says, his grip tightening around his cock, and I wrap my hand around his, stilling his hand.

"You want this to last, don't you, baby?" I say, his grip loosening under mine, but I can literally feel him shiver.

"Fuck," he hisses. "Can I touch you? Can I get you off?" he nearly begs.

"You have...six minutes," Gavin says, looking at his GPS.

"Please, sweet Kate," he whispers in my ear. How exactly am I supposed to say no to that?

As a response, I spread my legs for him. His warm palm starts back at my knee, before gently sliding up my thigh and palming my pussy. I know he can feel how wet I am through the fabric.

He leans forward, tenderly kissing my collarbone, again

with no shyness around my scars. I try not to think about the times Will said they "didn't bother him." He never once kissed me there. Somehow, with Ben, it becomes an erogenous zone for me, apparently, making me spread my legs wider.

He pushes the fabric aside, the tips of his fingers gliding against my cunt.

"I think about this," he says, sliding his fingers inside of me. "How wet you were, how soft and pretty, how good you tasted."

"Show me," I say, and he pulls his face away from my neck and pulls his fingers out of me.

I nearly mourn the loss as he holds eye contact, slipping his fingers into his mouth. He sucks them hard, before sliding them out and back under my dress.

I fist the front of his shirt, taking his mouth against mine, tasting myself on his tongue. Ben moans into my mouth as we kiss and he fucks me with his fingers. His movements aren't rushed or rough, but he's hitting just the right spot as his palm rubs against my clit.

The car smells like sex, and we can all hear how wet my pussy is in the car's silence.

"I love hearing you come. I think about it all the fucking time," he groans against my lips.

Ben doesn't ever make demands, he always eagerly takes what I give him. It makes me want to reward him, to make him feel good, to know what a good job he's doing.

"Yeah? You love being good for me, don't you?" I ask him softly, my tongue licking into his mouth as the speed of his hand increases, his palm pressing harder against my clit.

I'm right there, so fucking close as the curl of his fingers changes, hitting that sweet soft spot that sends me over the edge.

He pulls away from the kiss, watching my face as I fall

apart, my skull hitting the headrest as my thighs shake and squeeze against his hand. He doesn't stop until I grab his wrist.

His eyes look more blue today as his wet hand trails against my thigh and I give him a nod. He knows exactly what I want as he puts his fingers back into his mouth, shamelessly licking up the mess I've made.

He leans forward, kissing my neck again as I run my fingers through his hair, catching my breath.

A throat clears and I look up front; Gavin's turned around in the driver's seat and points to my house.

"We're here," he says, and I can see the need and something else in his face.

He watches me and Ben with almost a look of confusion. Maybe trying to piece the version of me he gets along with the version Ben gets?

"Right," I say, kissing the side of Ben's face and whispering in his ear. "You did so good, baby. Did you like making me wet while your brother listened?"

He groans as he tucks away his still unbearably hard length, and it makes me want to relieve his ache, but that can wait till we're inside my house.

"Soon," I tell him, grabbing his chin and planting a kiss against his lips as I pet down my hair and make sure my dress is in order.

As I suspected, the rain's stopped as I get out of the car.

We're all headed to my front door as my neighbor, Pat, across the street waves.

"Oh, Katherine, dear. Who're your friends?" she says, waving and adjusting her glasses, almost like she's trying to figure out if she's seeing double.

"Hey, Pat. Hope you're doing well," I say, avoiding her nosiness.

"Oh, yeah, well, you know, Marsha down the street is being

a real piece of work. You know she's trying to oppose the speed bump. It's probably because that old bat needs her license taken away and thinks it's a personal attack on her driving. Which it honestly is. Are you having more guests over, dear?"

Gavin coughs into his fist, and Ben is trying to adjust his hard-on.

"No, Pat. Have a nice evening, okay? I'll see you at the next meeting and support the speed bump."

Her gray eyebrows furrow like she's trying to figure out what's going on. I suppose most people would be extremely judgmental if they knew what was about to happen behind closed doors. Most people wouldn't approve, but it doesn't matter what they think. It's an agreement between consenting adults, and it's not like anyone will find out besides my friends, who are endlessly supportive.

"You know, Katherine, there's been something else I wanted to talk to you about," she starts.

Pat is really bringing down my post-orgasm bliss.

"I'll stop by tomorrow, Pat. Have a good evening," I cut her off again. Pushing Ben and Gavin by their lower backs, ushering them to walk faster toward my door.

Mrs. Pat seems peeved that I wouldn't take the time to speak to her, but she lets it go as I put in the code and shut the door behind us.

Everything changes the moment we're sealed away from the world, and I'm not sure I'll ever be the same.

Gavin

Want

IT'S a relief mother-time across the street finally stopped talking and we're finally at Kate's house. I considered taking her back to ours, but figured she would be more comfortable here, and it wouldn't be as awkward when it was time to part ways and her getting home.

The last time I was here, I didn't get a good look around, but this time I see her house for what it is.

It's slightly moody on the inside, not what you would see in a typical Florida home. Her house is decorated in dark greens, woods, and blacks. Nearly three walls are filled with book-shelves, along with books stacked on the floor, and tables. There's also a ridiculous amount of cat furniture and nearly every wall is covered in different art pieces.

I listened the whole time when she was with Ben, nearly a completely different woman than the one I've been with. It's confusing, intriguing, and dangerous.

She's like a fucking magnet and Ben and I are two different metals being dragged into her force field. There's no turning back, no second guessing this. I know this agreement is probably stupid and bad for my health, but I don't give a shit.

I've never wanted a woman more, and neither has Ben. I'm not going to ruin this for us, even if this has an expiration date that isn't set in stone. We might as well enjoy it while we have it.

"Should we go to my room?" Kate asks, some of that confidence I saw in the backseat of my car diminishing when she looks at me.

Is it possible that she could be the most dynamic switch I've ever been with? Ben and I have been with plenty of women, some further on his spectrum who don't want to submit to me. Or others further on my side where I have to take control of the sexual script.

I keep in mind that while Ben and I have done this before, Kate hasn't. In fact, she's still figuring out what she likes, and what she wants sexually. This needs to be good for her, even if it's not something we do all the time. It's important that she enjoys herself and doesn't feel like she's been ripped in two between us.

She doesn't have to be one inherent thing, though I don't think she realizes how easily she shifts in between her roles with each of us.

"Lead the way," I say as an orange cat zig zags between my brother's legs. He pets it quickly as we head down the hall into the owner's suite.

This room is lighter than the living room, although the color scheme is the same. A wall with palm frond wallpaper holds a king sized bamboo framed bed. She has even more shelves with books in here and at least three cat beds that I can find. The massive TV in here is a surprise, but I find it charming as the large windows in the back face a lush private backyard.

She licks her lips, flattening out her dress and looking between the two of us.

"Dress off, edge of the bed," I tell her while rubbing my mouth.

She swallows, but immediately grabs the zipper of the side of her dress, letting it fall to the floor as she sits at the end of the bed. I motion for Ben to sit next to her, and he undresses down to his briefs and sits next to her.

Still clothed, I approach her, grabbing her chin, forcing her to look up at me. Her bright blue eyes are filled with want and I'll be damned if I don't have her legs quaking along with checking something off of her wishlist.

"What do you say if you don't like something?"

"Marina."

"What do you call me?"

She licks her lips before answering. "Sir."

I glance over at Ben. "You might be in charge of him, but I'm in charge of everything. Do you understand that, sweetheart?"

She nods with my hand still holding her jaw.

"If it's too much and you need a break, you tell me. You always tell me what you need, Katherine."

"Always," she says, her gaze heavy-lidded with the use of her full name.

"You want me to fuck you while you swallow down my brother's cock, don't you?"

Kate licks her lips as she nods against my palm.

"Tell him where you want him then," I say, nudging her face so she's looking at my twin.

"Clothes off, back against the headboard, hands flat on the bed," she tells him in a voice so starkly different from the one she speaks to me with.

It has me hard, so fucking hard that my dick is straining

against my pants and I consider being impulsive and shoving my cock down her throat. She chooses to obey me, eagerly. She could choose to give me a hard time, fuck she could decide she only wants to be on top.

But she doesn't. An equal counterpart to my need to control and Ben's need to be controlled.

It's effortless. She's perfect.

The reality of it all is hitting me right in the center of my chest, but I ignore it. Right now is all about letting these carnal urges free, nothing more.

Ben, of course, follows her orders. Removing his boxers and sitting at the head of her bed. Dark green pillows surround his back as he waits patiently and Kate looks back up to me for direction.

Fuck. I'm so fucked.

I need to rein this feeling in, whatever this feeling is. It's just sex. Mutually agreed upon, convenient sex.

"Are you wet?" I ask her.

"Yes," she rasps out.

"Show me," I say, not even worrying about Ben. He's probably getting off on the fact that he has to wait even longer.

Kate spreads her legs, the balls of her feet balancing her as her hand comes down to her pussy, pushing her panties to the side, showing me the evidence of what my brother did to her in the backseat.

She's always so wet. So fucking needy for it. It makes me want her more. I want to hear her cunt sucking in my dick; I want my crotch tacky with her juices and my cum.

Want. Want. Want.

When was the last time I wanted something this bad?

I glance over at Ben, who, as I guessed, is patiently waiting to be told what to do, before glancing back down at Kate. I could easily toss her over on the bed, slide into her with no resistance, and fuck her however I want. She'd take it, she'd like it, we'd all get off.

Yet, I find myself stalling. Wanting this all to last.

She stays quiet as I contemplate what my next move is.

"Come here."

She closes her legs and stands from the bed, giving Ben a cursory glance and he smiles at her. His hands at his side, not touching himself.

"I think I'm over dressed for the occasion."

Kate smirks at me, unbuttoning my shirt diligently, as she slides it over my shoulders. Her palms are warm, her touch gentle and sweet as she moves to my pants, using the same precision as her big blue eyes look up at me.

Her undivided attention is a turn on, just as much as sharing her is going to be.

"You like being good, don't you?" I ask.

"For you," she says, tugging down my underwear, letting my aching cock spring free.

I stare at her for a long moment. Is this side of her just for me? Does she lean more dominant, but for me she's willing to bend?

The thought has the tip of my dick weeping with want as I turn her around, so she's looking at my brother as I palm her pussy and kiss the soft spot on her neck.

"You ready for this? You want both of us?" I ask, pushing her dark hair to one side, placing more kisses against her throat.

Ben looks between Kate and me, a mixture of turned on and confusion taking over his features.

"I want both of you," she whispers as I push down her panties, and she kicks them off of her legs.

"Then go suck Ben's dick. I want that ass high in the air for when I decide to fuck you."

Her breath hitches, but she does as I ask, crawling onto the bed, dragging her nails over my brother's legs gently before placing a kiss at the tip of his dick.

"You earned my mouth on you, didn't you, sweet boy?" she says to him as he pushes her hair to one side, smiling down at her.

"I sure fucking hope I did," he jokes and her tongue swipes against the slit of his head, making him shudder.

She's soft with both of us, but with Ben, it's different. It's that dominating gentleness that I know that he craves. Yet, against my touch, she gives me the supple subservience I need too.

It's why we made this arrangement, it's why we needed her forgiveness. We work sexually. It doesn't have to be anything more than that.

Kate listened to my directions, her ass high in the air as she rests most of her weight on her elbows as she toys with my twin.

It's fucked up, but as I watch them, I can almost put myself in his shoes. I can picture him as me, with Kate's mouth wrapped around my cock. It's not jealousy that rattles through me, just more want.

Instead of holding myself back for a second longer, I join them on the bed. My hand grips her thigh as my mouth presses against her ass, placing kisses before biting the round, soft flesh.

She moans against Ben's cock and the back of his head thunks against her headboard.

My bruise on her ass is long gone and I hate it.

The barely there teeth marks will disappear in a few short hours and it doesn't feel like enough. It feels like if I don't have intangible evidence that I fucked her, that she was mine in that moment, then it isn't real.

"I'm going to mark your ass, baby," I say, the term of

endearment slipping out of my mouth against my will. I give her a moment to disagree, to protest, and she doesn't.

Perfect, sweet, acquiescent Kate.

I take the flesh of her ass back into my lips, sucking, reddening the flesh, before sinking my teeth back in. Her back arches, and her thighs quake, but she doesn't tell me to stop, nor does she stop touching Ben. She just takes what I give her, not a single protest slipping off her tongue, only blissful sounds of pleasure.

I admire my teeth marks on her ass, knowing I'll be jerking off to the imagery for the foreseeable future, just like I did when I spanked her ass red.

My fingertips grip her hips as I line myself up with her pussy. She's dripping with anticipation, ready to go completely as I thrust into her with one go.

She gags on my brother's cock and he helps pull her off, like the decent man he is, but I don't relent. Her ass bounces against my thighs and I watch as her asshole tightens as I fuck her from behind.

I want to fuck her there, too. I want to show her how good it can be, because I'll always make it good for her.

It's an effort between both Kate and Ben, keeping her mouth on his cock. He's holding her biceps, helping her keep balance as I take and take from her body.

The rhythmic bouncing of her ass is making me spiral as I collect spit on the tip of my tongue, spreading her cheeks and watch as my saliva covers her tight little hole. I don't stop fucking her as my thumb circles my spit against the spot I'm going to make mine some day.

Kate writhes under me.

My brother cherishes her while I fuck her hard.

He gives. I take.

"Look at you, so full of cock and loving it. You were made

for this. God, if you could see how pretty your cunt looks wrapped around me and how tight this little hole is," I say, pressing my thumb harder against her hole, but not penetrating.

"I'm so close," my brother rasps out and the sound of Kate suckling the tip of him has me throwing my head back, trying to not come. Not yet. She pulls away from his dick, stroking him slowly with her fist.

"Not yet, I need you to wait for me. You can do that can't you?" she asks Ben.

"Yeah, I can do that for you," he says, pushing her hair away from her face.

"Of course you can, you're always so good for me."

I can't help myself as I grip her hips and thrust as hard as I can, my balls pressing against her entrance. Her cunt clenches around my length and she moans, her thighs quaking as I reel back and fuck her harder.

She swallows my brother back down, her moans garbled around his dick as I fuck her harder to listen to her muffled cries of pleasure.

"Are you going to come on my cock? I want to feel it," I tell her.

"I'm close," she pants.

"I'm not going to last, not with your mouth on me like that baby," Ben says, and it's clear he's doing everything he possibly can to not finish until she gives him the okay.

"You did so well waiting. I want you to come on my tits," she tells him, her hand stroking him even as her body rocks back and forth from the pace of my thrusts.

"You want to be covered in cum?" I ask in panted breaths, my orgasm nearly taking over.

"Please," she says to me, or Ben, but I'm going to imagine it's me.

"Fuck," Ben hisses, his throat bobbing as he moans and Kate jerks him off, covering her chest in cum.

"Christ," I groan, wrapping a hand around her hips, toying with her clit. "Give it to me. Come on, baby. Come on my dick like a good girl and I'll cover this sweet ass. Give. It. To. Me."

I enunciate every word with a hard thrust of my hips, my fingers strumming through her sopping wet cunt.

My brother is watching her cum-covered tits bounce as she finally hits her peak. Her pussy gripping me so hard, milking my cock. I shudder, as I hold back for as long as I can. My hand leaving her clit, as I pull out and fist my shaft, spreading her ass cheeks as I come all over the the reddened mark on her ass and that hole I want so fucking bad.

She's panting, her back arching as she tries to catch her breath. My brother's stroking her hair, checking on her, while I stare at the streaks of my release covering her ass, along with the bite mark.

I immediately know this is dangerous, that I don't usually feel this possessive, this consumed with a person. I push the feeling down as I squeeze her hip.

"Stay right there. I'll go get something to clean you up," I say.

She glances back at me with pink cheeks, and her hair clinging to her face. She looks beautiful and confident as she rests her face against Ben's thigh as I escape to the bathroom for a moment of sanity.

I turn on the tap, rinsing my dick off before warming the wash cloth and wringing it out. When I glance at myself in the mirror, it feels like I'm looking at a different man. I'm just not sure what he wants.

Benjamin

Caution

I'M PETTING Kate's hair, my length now flaccid, but getting ideas about going again. I'd never come on someone like that before. Didn't think that I'd ever like it, but with Kate? With her telling me that's what she wanted? Watching as ropes of my release splattered against her bouncing tits?

Yeah, I liked it.

"You okay?" I ask her, and she kisses my thigh before pushing herself up more, cautious about not making a bigger mess of her bed.

"More than okay," she says with a dreamy sigh. "I didn't know how it would work, if it would've worked. I wasn't as vocal as before. Was that okay for you?" she asks.

Shit. I'm already so enamored of her, and then she asks me how I am. If she was enough for me.

"Your hands and mouth were all over me, and you let me come on you. I'd say I'm better than okay."

"It's just, I know you like—"

I cut her off, leaning down and kissing her forehead.

"It was good for me. Very good for me. It doesn't have to be the same script every time. When you're with just Gavin, it will be different than when you're just with me, just like it will be different when you're with both of us. It's different, not any less. Trust me, you...this was everything I needed."

She nods as Gavin comes in with a warm washcloth, wiping over her chest, before moving to her ass. He's methodical, quiet, and I know that I'm not alone in this feeling, in this fucking madness.

Once he's wiped her down enough, he plops on one side of the bed, putting Kate between us. His chest to her back, and her eyes meeting mine as our legs tangle and she pets down my hair.

Gavin's hand is wrapped around her waist and we just lie there. This isn't standard protocol. There's always some level of aftercare and checking in at Avalon, and if I'm being brutally honest, if we were with a woman we met at a bar, we'd already be halfway home right now.

This is different, and I'm not sure any of us know how to cope or what to say.

Thankfully, my cat friend decides to help make it unawkward as he jumps on the bed, chirping as he holds a toy in his mouth, placing it between Kate and me as he nearly hollers for attention.

"Mikey, you know you're still my man," she coos, petting his chin.

"How many cats do you have?" Gavin asks conversationally, though I can tell more is on his mind. He pets the cat along with me and Kate, and the small orange prince seems to love all the attention.

"Four," she whispers. "In all fairness, I got Frida and Berth together, since they were a bonded pair. But then they didn't like each other, so I thought they needed more friends and I got Michelangelo and Edvard. They all get along minus Frida.

Berth hides most of the time. Mikey and Edvard are my two cuddle bugs."

"You don't have to rationalize the amount of cats you have," Gavin says.

"I like cats," I repeat.

She's clearly somewhat embarrassed, or defensive about having four. It may have something to do with single cat lady stereotypes, but it's clear based on her home they're very well loved and cared for. If they make her happy, which I totally get as this fat guy purrs and looks at me with innocent eyes, who cares?

"Do you guys have any pets?"

"No, we've been too busy getting the business off the ground. Speaking of which, what're you doing next weekend?" Gavin says, kissing her shoulder.

It's bizarre watching my brother be so intimate with someone. This goes beyond how he normally is with the women at Avalon.

"Hmm," she says, tapping her chin. "I'll have to check my very busy calendar," she jokes.

"We're doing a soft launch for the club. Friends and family type thing. If you'd be interested in coming," I say, my brother gives me a look that says I phrased it too much like a question and I want to roll my eyes.

"I'm very interested in coming," she says with a grin, shooing the orange cat out of the room as she climbs my lap. It seems like she's trying to avoid the question of coming to the launch and I won't push her on it. If Gavin wants to press her more, he can, but that's just not me.

"And how would you like to come?"I ask her with a smile.

"Well, there are three of us, I don't think three rounds is out of the question."

"You can have whatever you want from me," I tell her.

She slides her hand between us, stroking my semi-hard cock, each swipe of her thumb over the head making me harder.

It's not long before round two becomes round three and then four.

☙ ☙ ☙

I WAKE up with something sitting on my bare chest. When I blink my eyes open, it's Kate's cat. We spent the night.

We never spend the night.

I wonder if Gavin is going to wake up and have an absolute meltdown, but when I look over, there's no one else in the bed.

"Where are they?" I mumble to the cat.

He tilts his head at me, like he doesn't have a single thought in his head. When I go to move him, he digs his claws into my bare skin and instead of pushing him off of me; I cradle him like a baby and make my way into the kitchen.

They each have a yogurt parfait in front of them and a third one sits waiting for me. I rub my eyes, and place the cat on the floor, and take a seat, glancing at my brother and then back at Kate.

"It's not a big deal," Gavin says, and Kate nods her head.

"I agree, sleepovers are fine. Friends have sleepovers all the time," she says, like she's trying to make herself believe the words coming out of her mouth.

"Okay," I say, spooning a mouthful and eating my breakfast.

"So, this weekend. You'll come?" Gavin asks, bringing up the conversation from last night that got interrupted by more sex.

Kate's cheeks blush, but she nods. "Well that's entirely up to your and Ben's stamina, isn't it?"

"I think we more than proved ourselves in the stamina department last night," Gavin says, arching a brow at her.

She lets out a breath of frustration like she wants to talk herself out of going, but nods. "Fine, I'll come."

"Good, music to my ears," Gavin says, going back to eating.

"Good," I repeat, because I truly don't know what else to say. Morning afters have never been a thing we've endured. It's not awkward per se, but I'm not really sure how to act.

Kate kicks us out after breakfast, saying she has errands to run, and when I'm alone in the car with Gavin, I finally turn and face him.

"That was a lot of kissing," I say, trying not to be too accusatory, because I'm not sure what I want out of this conversation.

Mostly I want to know that I'm not alone in this feeling, that he also feels this strange cosmic pull to this small woman, that she's sunk her hooks into both of us, and what the fuck are we going to do about it?

"I don't have an issue with kissing."

"Oh, you're so full of shit. You kissed her on the mouth at the restaurant before we were even fucking. Just kissed her to be nice. I think the last time I saw you kiss a girl because you wanted to was senior year at prom with Harley Paulson."

"She jerked us off at the same time in the limo," he says, reminiscing instead of owning up to what I'm saying.

"You kissed her. On the mouth, and everywhere else. Not to mention this whole leaving marks thing you've got going on right now."

He slides his sunglasses over his eyes, keeping his focus on the road.

"What's your point, Ben? Are you not also into Kate? We agreed to rules, it's an agreement. You're reading too much into it," he says.

All I hear is denial leaking out of his lips, and I'm not sure how I feel about it. Me and my brothers are all stubborn as hell, but Gavin might just take the cake in that regard.

"You like her," I accuse and Gavin shrugs his shoulders.

"We both do. That's the whole fucking point of this agreement. No need to go to Avalon and roll the dice on what kind of night we're going to have. She's a sure thing. There are rules in place. You're making a big deal out of this for nothing. And for the record, I'm not anti-kissing."

Fucking liar.

He turns to face me, though I can't see his eyes through his sunglasses.

"What's really bothering you? Do you like her more than a friend? Should we stop this before it even starts?"

That's the last thing that I want. I agree with him, of course I like Kate. She's easy to like in every way. It might be a physical way right now, but what happens when I get to know her? Already the little glimpses I've seen have me intrigued. I've been so dead set on never having a relationship and I'm starting to wonder why.

For the longest time, it felt like becoming serious with a woman would change my relationship with Gavin. But if we were committed to the same woman?

"No, we shouldn't stop. I just wanted to see where your head was at. Tonight seemed different," I say.

Maybe Gavin is being honest, and he doesn't see this going anywhere beyond our agreement. Or maybe he's like me and hiding what he really thinks.

All I know is that I'm not as scared of the idea of having more with Kate. What I'm scared of is being the only one who feels this way.

Either way, I'm getting way ahead of myself. We spent one night together. Albeit a very hot fucking amazing night. One that has my quads aching and I know I need to rehydrate. But it was just fucking...and a sleepover. Not to mention I think that the orange cat is imprinting on me.

It's what we agreed to. A friendship with very delicious benefits.

Kate's just providing an outlet I've been yearning for. I'm getting ahead of myself. It's physical, it's fun.

"It was different. Good different. Are you sure you're okay with this agreement?" he asks and I nod.

"Yeah, I'm just being cautious."

"Don't be. She's our friend, that we're fucking. It's simple."

Simple.

Yeah. Fucking. Right.

Kate

Dirty Dancing

SAVANNAH IS OVER, helping me choose what to wear tonight.

"You sure you don't want to come?" I ask.

"No, I have a date tonight. Plus, you'll be too busy being the center of a twin sandwich, anyway."

I glare at her as I put on the next dress. It's olive green, and semi backless, so there's no way to wear a bra.

"Yes, if you're trying to get fucked on the dance floor. They must be hot if you forgave them so easily," she says, plopping a grape into her mouth, giving me a smile.

"We weren't exclusive, and they were both very apologetic."

"Are you talking about a real apology or an apology in the form of orgasms?"

"Uh, both?" I say, grabbing the next dress.

"Wait...were they separate apologies or one big, giant apology?" she asks, clearly riveted in my sex life.

"Also both."

She gasps, clutching her metaphorical pearls. "Both? At the same time?"

My face feels like it's on fire as I nod, confirming her suspicions.

"It was a very good apology," I say as she tosses a grape at me.

"So, it's just sex?"

"Just sex," I agree, trying on the next dress. "Well, I guess friends too. They invited me to their opening night. So friends with benefits, no feelings, just sex."

"Are you totally capable of having no feelings?"

"I think I've proven over the last few months I'm capable of having sex with no feelings."

Savannah clicks her tongue. "What's the most times you've slept with the same person since your divorce?"

"There was the Scottish guy, Arran. That was three times," I say, feeling really proud of myself, because I had absolutely no feelings toward him, honestly I couldn't understand half of what he said. I was, however, really interested in being with a man who was uncircumcised, and quite enjoyed it.

"How many times have you been with each of them?" she asks, instead of high-fiving and agreeing with me that I can have sex with no strings attached.

"Well, does the other night count as once?" I ask.

Savannah's mouth drops. "How many times in one night was it?"

I bite my lip, trying to count in my head, and then there's the distinction between oral and penetration.

"It doesn't matter. We'll count it as one night. That would make three times with Gavin and twice with Ben."

"So, tonight will be night four with the hot bartender?" she asks, like number four is some magical fucking number and suddenly my heart will start pulsating between my legs.

"They don't want anything serious either."

She hums and points at my dress. "You should wear that one tonight," she says, changing the subject, and I'm grateful.

"Really? It's not too slutty?"

"Kate, you're going to the club to meet your booty calls. We're not going for subtle here. Plus, you're smoking fucking hot. Flaunt it."

This dress will also require that I go braless. It's a glittery, purplish-brown. It hugs my breasts and waist and flares out slightly at my thigh, showing off a hell of a lot of leg. I'm pretty sure I bought this one drunken sad night when I realized I was closer to thirty-five instead of twenty-five.

"You're triple sure you don't want to come tonight?"

"Don't tempt me, but I actually like the guy I'm going out with tonight."

I pause as I grab the earrings and necklace I want to wear tonight. "You like him?" Savannah may be the biggest man-eater I know. She sees them as fun little distractions, and maybe I've been basing how I've handled my divorce around her lifestyle. Suddenly, now, she likes someone?

"He's smart, generous, and oh so fucking talented," she says dreamily.

"Talented?"

"Oh yes, talented," she says, holding her fingers in a v and sticking out her tongue. "And maybe he's also an amazing photographer and maybe I have some sort of crush on his brain, too. I'm sure it won't last," she says.

I look at her curiously, but don't harp on it.

If my role model of sex with no strings attached is falling for someone, what the fuck does this mean for me?

I'M HOLDING my clutch under my armpit as I wait for my driver to arrive, he's only a few minutes away, as my neighbor, Pat, waves me down.

"Katherine, dear," she says as I mumble a whispered fuck under my breath. "Well, my goodness, where are you headed off to this evening?"

"It's a club opening for my friend," I say sweetly.

"Oh, was it one of the gentlemen who stayed the night the other night? You know, I've got to get my prescription checked. They sure looked a lot alike from over here. I noticed they drove together as well, and didn't leave until morning."

You have to love old people who have nothing better to do than stalk the neighborhood.

"Was there something you wanted to discuss?" I ask, redirecting the conversation.

"Well." She clears her throat, possibly scandalized over the fact I had two men stay the night the other day. "Yes. I've noticed this SUV in the neighborhood almost every day, and I was wondering if you knew who it was. It's black, and oh, I don't know the car labels well, but I think it has a K in the logo."

"What time are you seeing them in the neighborhood?" I ask, my pulse racing.

"Usually later in the evenings. That's why I thought it was odd. They never pull into anyone's driveway. Sometimes they drive down the street a few times and others they park right down there out of the streetlight and just lulls there. I wondered if maybe it was another guest of yours?"

Is Pat politely calling me a slut? I want to roll my eyes at this nosey woman, but I'm also thankful for her watchful gaze at this moment.

"Pat, do you think you could keep a close eye out and see if you can get the license information the next time you see the vehicle?"

She lights up, like snooping is her purpose in life. "Oh, absolutely. Is there anything I should be worried about?"

"No, I just want to be cautious," I say and she nods.

"Now, about those tall gentlemen," she says, as my ride share pulls up.

"We'll discuss another time. Thanks again, Pat."

"Have a lovely evening," she says, looking me up and down, making me feel like the town whore as I sit in the back of the car and he takes me over to the club.

Shit, could Will really be scoping out my house? Maybe Gavin was right and I truly need to consider a restraining order, or I could just get over myself and give him what he wants.

Would it be the worst thing to concede and take the high ground? Every ounce of me hates the idea, but the thought of him taking it this far has me feeling unsettled. My home is my safe space and suddenly I don't feel so safe. The locks have been changed, as well as the codes, he wouldn't take it that far would he?

I'm so wrapped up in my own thoughts, I don't even notice as we reach the club. I thank my driver, rate him five stars for his considerate silence, and send his tip.

There's a bouncer at the front of the club, and I give him my name, giving me access right away. I considered texting Ben and Gavin, but it's their opening night and I didn't want to be a distraction. There's no pretense that I'll be going home with them. Tonight I'm here as a friend, and maybe if I'm lucky, there will be some benefits at the end of the night.

The club isn't like what I remember from my very limited experience as a college student. The floors weren't covered in sticky beer; the clientele wasn't questionable in age, and while the lights were dim, it wasn't in a seedy way where you had to wonder what was happening in every dark corner of the room.

The place fits the vibe of their bar, but in a different way. While their bar is more relaxing, great for somewhere to grab a drink after work or after you get off your boat, the club is for partying, just with a more mature crowd in mind.

Though there are younger women here who make my dress look matronly, there are also women my senior here, too. In fact, most of the women here seem to be in the thirties to forties bracket, along with the male partygoers.

The space embraces the outdoors indoors with flora and fauna backlit by purple lightning. There's a long, backlit bar on the right side with barstools, along with other leisurely places to sit inside and outside of the club. Looking down at the ridiculous heels I chose, I'm pretty sure I'm going to be grateful for the ample seating at some point tonight.

It feels high end without being too in your face, while also being nostalgic in a way. I almost feel like I'm a mafia wife in Miami or something. To be honest, I'm impressed with everything they've accomplished here.

Songs I haven't heard in years are funneling through the speakers, loud enough to feel like a club, but not so loud that you have to scream to speak to the person next to you.

I make my way to the bar and order a martini as a hand grips my shoulder.

"Add it to our tab," the voice says, and when I turn around, I surmise that it's Gavin.

I haven't been around the twins much, but they have small tells. Just hearing their voice isn't enough since they sound exactly the same, but the way they say things is different. Gavin is more brazen, while Ben is more polite. Gavin smirks more than he smiles, while Ben smiles with his whole face.

They both carry themselves confidentially and share the same face. Though looking at Gavin now, he clearly got a haircut.

"You got a haircut?"

"I did," he says, with one of his smirks I can now identify. "What do you think of the place?"

"It's really amazing, Gavin. You guys really have something special here."

He takes the seat next to me and orders his own drink. "We're only open on Fridays, Saturdays, and select holidays. The bar does well enough as it is, but we wanted something new, something different in Tampa."

"I think you managed it. The place is beautiful. It doesn't remind me of the clubs I got into with my fake ID," I say with a crinkle of my nose.

"Good. You look fucking unreal tonight."

"Not too slutty?" I joke.

"The right amount," he teases back as another hand hits my shoulder from behind me and lips gently kiss my cheek.

"There you are," Ben says excitedly. "Why don't you two grab your drinks and we show you the patio," he says.

Gavin looks at his brother nervously, but nods. I hold on tightly to the stem of my martini glass and follow them out to the patio, which is even more magnificent than the inside. Fairy lights brighten the space that's filled with even more plants and plush chairs, along with another outdoor bar.

Ben leads us over to a section of people, and I have to take a deep breath as I recognize the blonde woman before me. It's his brother's wife, Penny, who I thought was Ben's wife at the gym. She's flanked by two older versions of Ben and Gavin and a small brunette woman with warm brown eyes.

Oh, my fucking god. I'm meeting their family.

I mean, it was in the invitation, wasn't it? It was a soft

opening for friends and family. I'm the friend, they're the family.

"This is Kate, be nice," Ben says, as he places an arm around my shoulder and pulls me in tight.

The three strangers watch the motion with confusion, blinking at us before Ben clears his throat.

"You met Penny, who again, is not my wife. She's Lincoln's wife, and his cousin," he says, not giving me a moment for my brain to catch up to that statement. "This geriatric over here is our oldest brother, Aiden, and his too sweet for him wife, Jessa."

"I swear to fuck if you don't stop telling people my business," Lincoln says.

"Penny was adopted, so it's alright in the eyes of god and the state of Florida, don't worry," Gavin interjects as Ben leads me to a black cushioned seat. He sits to the left of me and Gavin sits to the right.

The two couples take their seats and just stare.

I'm automatically on edge and regret coming tonight. Our agreement never extended to meeting their family, and I can't help but wonder what they're thinking, what judgment they're passing on to me as Ben has his arm around my shoulder and Gavin's pinky finger is toying with the hem of my dress.

"What is it you do, Kate?" Jessa says, her voice is soft and melodic as she gives me a warm smile. Aiden is clearly at least a decade older than her, not that he looks old by any means. He's as handsome as his brothers, but the graying edges around his ears and the soft wrinkles around his eyes give him away.

So, the oldest brother is in an age gap relationship, and the middle one married their adopted cousin? Maybe my fucking their twin brothers isn't as wild as most people would consider it to be.

"I'm a professor at UT."

"She has a PhD, she teaches fine arts, like the history and significance of it," Ben chimes in, and I can't help but to hide my blush behind my cocktail. He was listening when I was talking about my job, and he almost sounded proud?

"A PhD and you're hanging out with these two?" Lincoln says, and his wife jams her elbow into his stomach.

"What he means to say is that's really nice. Do you take the summers off?" Penny says.

"I do. It's been really nice. Though I'm excited about the new semester. What about you? What do you all do?" I ask, trying to take the conversation off of me.

"I'm a stay at home mom, Lincoln is in commercial building," Penny says. She keeps talking though all I can hear is my heartbeat. How did I not pick this up before with the name of the bar? Carlson Marina and Bar, Carlson Commercial.

Carlson Commercial has been the bane of Will's existence since he started his company. I keep that information to myself as I listen on.

"I have my own promotional products company and Aiden owns a sports supply company, though he was a professional MLB player in another life," Jessa says, holding Aiden's hand.

"So entrepreneurism kinda runs in the family?" I say, and Ben gives me a squeeze.

"I guess you could say that. Need another drink?" he asks.

I swore to myself that I was going to take it easy tonight. There's no way I'm falling on the front concrete of this property ever again, but given the current company, I cave. I need liquid courage being around these people.

"Please," I say, as he gets up and asks anyone else if they want anything before heading over to the bar.

"I'm sorry," Gavin whispers in my ear and I turn toward him.

I can still feel his family's gaze on us, even if they're trying to be discreet.

"I could've come another time if you didn't want me to meet your brothers."

Gavin's brow furrows, and he shakes his head. "I don't give a shit about that. They're just a lot to take in. When I invited you I didn't think about the fact I'd be putting you in that position. I just wanted you here." He shrugs.

He just wanted me here.

"Is it hot out here?" I say, fanning myself instead of responding. Ben comes back with drinks, and I let the cool liquid glide down my throat as the siblings joke and chat with one another, meanwhile I feel lost in my thoughts.

Savannah's words are ringing around my head from earlier. I almost want to call a car and go the fuck home right now. It feels like the more I get to know these guys, the quirks that tell them apart, these small things that make them different, the more I like them.

Sure, liking them isn't the worst thing in the world. I had to like them to some degree to commit to this agreement and to forgive them for what they did in the first place. But as they joke and banter with their brothers and as Penny looks at me like I'm some sort of mystical unicorn she's never seen before, I'm wondering if I'm making a mistake.

I made a promise to myself to not get into a relationship. I'm almost positive my ex is scoping the outside of my house periodically. The last thing I need is to fall for someone else, let alone two someone's.

I'm about to stand up, make some excuse about my stomach hurting, and go home and clear my head, when Ben smiles over at me.

"You can't come to Double Palms and not dance," he says.

"Double Palms?" I repeat.

"The club name. Come dance with us. At least for one song," Ben pleads.

"Yes! Dancing time," Penny says, dragging Lincoln to the dancefloor, where I reluctantly follow.

I'll dance. I'll get it out of my system and then I'll get the fuck out of here. When I'm in the comfort of—my possibly not being as safe as I thought—home, I'll wonder if I'm making the right choices.

In the middle of my spiral, Britney Spears comes on. Penny makes a squeal of a noise, grabbing Jessa's hand while I get bracketed between the twins. Gavin is at my back and Ben is at my front.

It feels oh so reminiscent of our night together, and I can barely stand it.

"You look so fucking hot," Ben says against my ear, his hand on one hip while his brother's hand is on the other.

I can't deny how I feel when I'm with them.

Confident, sexy, powerful.

It's addictive and I'm not sure I can give it up. At least not yet. Surely, getting to know them won't change things. I can keep things separate.

This is a physical relationship. It's all it has to be.

The way they dance is sinful. Gavin's hardening cock is grinding against my ass, his breath fanning across the side of my face. While Ben's leg is between my thighs, making my dress slide up even further.

Fully out in public in between twin brothers.

I'm not sure if Aunt Helene would be proud or mortified. I make sure to not look at anyone around us. It feels different now that we're out in public. Neither of them seem to give a shit what people think, and I wish I could be more like that.

This whole summer, the whole divorce was about finding myself, being authentic to who I want to be. But I'm still fucking hiding and I don't have a clue what I want.

"Just relax," Gavin says in my ear, his hand sliding further over my hip against my stomach, caged between mine and his brother's body. "Everyone either wants to be you or fuck you. Don't worry about anyone else," he says so confidently.

So I shut my eyes and somehow go along with the old adage of dancing like no one's watching.

I dance like we aren't on a dance floor, like Ben and Gavin don't own this club, like their goddamn brothers aren't just feet away from us. For a moment I just let my brain shut down and let my body take control.

It feels so good, getting lost in their mingling touches. The mix of soft presses of lips and rough fingertips gripping my flesh.

Beads of sweat are forming in between my breasts and I feel almost hyper aware that there are, without a doubt, eyes on us. I keep mine closed, not facing the judgment and letting myself have this one moment of peace.

Ben's fingers lightly grip my chin, and my eyes flutter open, his handsome face the only thing I can see as his lips meet mine. Ben always kisses like he belongs in a regency romance novel. He's sweet, kind, but beyond all his manners, he's a very dirty boy.

"I'm glad you're here," he whispers against the side of my face as he pulls away, his brother still dancing behind me.

Penny glances over at us, her cheeks red from dancing, and then there's the group of younger women behind her, also shamelessly staring. One of them holds their phone up, and I can see the flash, which is quickly turned off and their phone pocketed.

It's then the reality of how this looks from the outside looking in makes me feel the ignominy of the situation.

"I'm going to run to the restroom," I say really quickly, barely giving the brothers a moment to say anything, as I part myself from their arms and rush over to the bathroom. I hoped it would be a moment of reprieve, but it turns out to be even worse.

Kate

Second Guessing

THE BATHROOM IS DARKLY LIT, with the mirrors being backlit with an almost ring light quality.

I felt hot when I left the house. Even as I look at myself now, my hair curling from the humidity and a sheen of sweat on my skin, I still feel hot. But, there's this lingering doubt, this feeling of who the fuck do I think I am?

I'm a professor playing what? Young club girl who has two hot and successful club owner fuck buddies? Meanwhile, my ex-husband could potentially be staking out my house. I'm not worth this trouble, and I'm not sure if I can handle public criticism of what I do behind closed doors.

Needing a moment to get my shit together before I leave and tell the guys I need to head home, I go into a stall, grateful that they are floor to ceiling doors.

I sit on the toilet, my thumbs rubbing my temples as my fingertips cradle my forehead, taking a few deep breaths.

There's no way we can continue on the path we're headed down. It's too much. I'm not strong enough to handle this shit. Sleeping with them again is a bad idea. Savannah is right. I'm not mature enough to not catch feelings, because seeing them with their brothers only made me more curious. Every touch and conversation outside of the bedroom has me wanting to get to them on a deeper level.

My life is chaotic right now. The last thing I need is people judging me for this forbidden relationship.

The door to the bathroom hits the back wall, women laughing as they gather by the sink, the water running as I sit there and debate when to make my great escape.

"Do you think they all fuck?" one woman says with a giggle.

"I mean, did you see them? Like, I can help you upgrade," another says, and I rub my temples harder.

I haven't felt this way since high school. I was never an outcast, specifically bullied, but I was never on the inside. I was always on the skirts of popularity, and they always made me feel it. I was the girl with dead parents, a suspicious scar, who somehow caught the eye of the All State Men's Soccer goalie.

I scoff to myself, remembering how Will always made me feel it too. Little digs that let me know that he was the prize. I believed it too. Believed it so hard that I followed him and his scholarship to FSU. I got into fucking Brown and I gave that up so that I could hold on to him. Even though I don't regret it, FSU has an amazing fine arts program. What I regret is letting him run my life, for letting other people's words put me down. It's not how I want to be. Who I want to be.

I wish I cared less about what people thought of me. It's not how I want to value myself, but at this moment, I can't help but feel like that stupid young woman who followed a man because of what other people thought. Is me caring what these complete strangers think of me any different? I feel like I'm stuck in this same stupid societal game of what's expected of me and what's morally right and wrong.

I'm an adult woman, we're all consenting adults. We're allowed to decide that line for ourselves.

"Do you think there is some twincest happening there?" A snicker and a bunch of laughs bursts out and I've had enough.

It's one thing to talk about me, but talking about Ben and Gavin like that? It makes the decision easier, as I step out of the stall and go to a sink to wash my hands.

I glance into the mirror. None of the women, who are likely barely legal, look at me. Though two of them look like they're about to burst into a fit of laughter.

"It's strange wondering what complete strangers do in the bedroom. But if you must know, they love having me in the middle. Did you want to know what it's like taking two men at once? Or should I tell you about my last gynecological exam? What information would you like?" I say, not looking up as I wash my hands.

Now that I'm done, I grab a paper towel, glancing at them all, properly chastised. None of them tries to apologize or speak, and I'm not sure that I would want them to.

I toss the paper towel in the trash on my way out, not looking back as I hold my head high and make my way to Ben and Gavin. Maybe it's my small little breakdown, the need to prove to myself that I'm not crumbling because it's what other people expect, but I vow to myself to have a good night and not let myself overthink this.

TOO MANY DRINKS LATER, we're back outside and I'm fanning myself as Penny leans in, her arm clutching my forearm. Her pupils are massive. Clearly she's had just as much as me.

"Tell me again what you said to them," she says, her mouth trying to find her straw.

"Baby, leave her alone," Lincoln says.

She rolls her eyes and glances back at me. "I'm finally out of the house doing adult things. I need to know everything."

"They were talking about Ben and Gavin, and well, me too, but once they started talking about them, I couldn't stand it anymore."

"Are they still here?" Penny asks, looking around.

I shrug as I look around. "It doesn't matter."

"Damn right. Don't let people judge you. Who cares what they think anyway?" Jessa says, nodding dramatically.

"Who's judging who?" Ben says, plopping down next to me. The top few buttons of his shirt are undone, and he looks deliciously rumpled.

"Some girls in the bathroom were talking about you guys and Kate," Penny says, her filter completely gone.

"Oh, yeah?" he asks with a grin, his eyes crinkling with his smile as he rests his head on my lap. "What did they say?"

"Nothing worth repeating," I say, scratching my nails against his scalp as he looks up at me with pure happiness in his gaze.

I'm glad I didn't leave earlier, that I didn't let insecurity or fear get in the way. I'd be lying if I said it wasn't lingering in the back of my mind, but I'm working through it. I'm just refusing to let anyone, including myself, ruin my night.

"Crisis averted. Ice machine is back up and running," Gavin interrupts me, staring at his brother as he sits right next to us.

"Gotta say I thought this place was going to turn into a cum dump of an event space, but you guys really made something here," Lincoln says.

I blink wildly as a smile spreads against his face, and Gavin whacks his brother on the shoulder.

"Shut the fuck up. You knew it would be awesome," Gavin jokes.

"Maybe," Lincoln retorts.

It's interesting watching all the siblings interact. It's something I always wanted but never had. I wanted a sister so damn bad, especially when I went to live with Aunt Helene. The idea of having someone you're tied to genetically, who goes through nearly the same walk of life as you, was compelling. But alas, I was an only child, and now I feel completely void of a family. The closest thing I have to a family are Savannah and Chelsea. Watching this family interact has me wishing I had more.

"It really is impressive. It looks great. The group of women I was talking to earlier said this is exactly what Tampa needed. A club for the occasional club goer that doesn't feel like it's a teeny bopper spring break," Penny says with a very serious face.

"Thanks, Pen," Ben says in my lap.

"We're only going to be open on Fridays and Saturdays, maybe some holidays. I think making it more exclusive is the way to go instead of trying to staff this place seven days a week," Gavin says.

"Glad to see you two finally grow up," their oldest brother, Aiden, says as he ruffles Gavin's hair, an arm wrapped around Jessa's shoulder, where she holds his hand. "It's getting late and we're going to get a ride home."

"Aw, come on old man," Gavin says, but there isn't much heat to it, not when Ben is nearly falling asleep on my lap.

"Congratulations. And it was so nice to meet you, Kate," Jessa says with a smile.

"Nice meeting you all too," I say honestly. They were

welcoming; sure it was like being thrown in the deep end, but I'm glad they were here.

"I think we ought to head home, too. Brynn and Hudson aren't going to give a shit that mommy and daddy are hungover tomorrow."

"Aren't they with Mom and Dad?" Gavin asks.

Lincoln gives him a look that screams 'stop cock blocking me' as Penny leans forward, not giving a shit that Ben is on my lap as she gives me a hug.

"It was really nice to meet you officially. I hope we'll be seeing more of you," she says.

Gavin gives her a look, and she shoves him back by the forehead.

"Later, losers," she says to her cousins.

Gavin gives her the finger and Lincoln acts like he's going to bite it before they leave and it's just us three.

Well, us three and a club full of people.

"The club is very impressive," I say, as Ben straight up turns on his side, using my lap as a pillow.

Gavin rests back on the chair, looking at me softly. "No, what's impressive is meeting our family and not running for the hills. I should've warned you beforehand. They can be a lot."

"It was nice. I never had siblings. I always wanted them. It's nice to know that the hazing doesn't stop even as you age."

Gavin gives me a grin before leaning down and pressing a soft kiss against my lips. He shoves his brother's head, who grumbles.

"Everything is covered here. Should we head out?"

"Yeah," I say, though my body feels heavy, my feet hurt, and I should very well be going to my own house. I should really say thanks for having me, but I need to feed my cats, which would be a lie. Well, not if you ask them.

I'm in no shape to have a repeat of the night we all spent together, mentally or physically. My head is still a mess, only numbed by the amount of alcohol in my system, but at least if I go to Gavin and Ben's house I know I'll be safe, at least physically. As far as my heart or head goes, I have no clue. It's best to just act like nothing is going on in those regards.

I'm not catching feelings. Nope. Not me.

We're just friends, and my friends are making sure I have somewhere safe to go for the night. So, against everything I felt earlier, I get in the car with Ben and Gavin. I even remember walking into their home and marveling at how shockingly clean it is. Sure, they didn't have many personal touches, but it's nice. I even remember using a spare toothbrush and doing my best effort to wash off the makeup off my face and removing my contacts. I'm not sure which one of them loaned me a T-shirt, but it's only when I wake up the next morning that I realize I spent the night and nothing sexual happened.

I can't decide if that's a good or a bad thing.

But as lips press against my neck as the summer sun shines through the slanted blinds, I realize there are far worse ways to spend a Sunday morning.

Benjamin

Certified Simp

IT'S a unique experience waking up with a woman in my bed. Usually if this happens I'd be at a hotel room, or I'd be at their place and slowly slinking out of their bed before a single ray of sun peeked over the horizon.

But here I am, with Kate in my bed. Her dark hair is splayed all over her pillow, and she's wearing my shirt, and I like it.

I like her too much. I knew this shit was going to happen, and yet here I am, staring at her sleeping form like a besotted asshole.

Gavin offered her the guest room, but I all but dragged her to mine. I probably wouldn't admit to my twin that I kept waking up to find myself tangled up in Kate's arms and her in mine, but with no one else around, with only me awake, I don't have to lie to myself.

I never pictured a woman out with me and my family. Any time Gavin and I considered dating, it changed everything. It fucked up the dynamic we had, and maybe we're codependent assholes tethered together by the same DNA and a lifetime of togetherness, but we always agreed our relationship came before one with a woman. So, we've been endlessly single, happily so, even. I've never felt a lure to have more than sexual intimacy. What would it be like to know the ins and outs of a person and for them to choose to do the same?

It's fucking scary. It's even worse that Kate has made her intentions more than clear, she doesn't want another relationship, not after her divorce. My brother is the same way, saying he doesn't want anything beyond a sexual agreement. So that leaves me, lying in this bed with the imprint of my sheets on my cheek, staring after the woman I can't completely have. That doesn't mean I won't take what I can get.

I press a soft kiss against the scar on her neck and she stirs. Her eyes blinking open as she squints.

"Shit, I didn't bring my glasses and I must have taken my dailies out last night," she says, and I realize she doesn't do this either. She doesn't do sleepovers to where she would actively need to think about bringing another set of contacts or packing her glasses. Coming home with us wasn't something she planned, especially not staying the night.

"I'll drive you home when you're ready to go. Or if you just want to pick up your glasses and stay in bed with me all day, that would be just fine with me too," I say, placing another kiss on her collarbone.

She swallows and runs her fingers through my hair.

"Why do you always kiss me there?" she whispers.

I run my thumb against the scarred flesh. It's light, nearly the same shade of her skin, but raised enough to be noticeable.

I shrug as I meet her eyes, smiling as she squints even more at me.

"It seemed like a spot that needed attention. Plus, I find it attractive," I tell her with honesty.

I never thought I'd consider a scar a turn on, but the way

she doesn't hide them? In fact, she wears dresses that show them off, proving how strong she is.

"My ex didn't."

"I think we've established he's an idiot. Do you mind me asking how you got them?"

She shakes her head but licks her lips before speaking. "It's from a car accident. The one I lost my parents in," she says softly.

"Fuck. I'm so sorry. How old were you?"

"Fifteen. My parents were good enough parents. They worked hard, gave me a good life, but they could be absent, you know? Now that I'm an adult I get it, I can't imagine what it's like to try and keep yourself afloat while also trying to keep another human happy and alive. I could tell my mom felt guilty that they weren't always around when I needed them, so they decided we were going to take a two-week road trip and see everything worth seeing out west. We had already done Zion National Park, the Grand Canyon, and Joshua Tree. We were going to spend the rest of our trip in San Diego, but we didn't make it."

I rub the soft spot on her collarbone not knowing what to say. To be honest I've never faced much adversity in my life and I don't know what you say in these situations.

"It was a good trip. The best. I'm glad I had those last memories, even if I was a moody teenager and was calling my mom by her first name to spite her. But it's because we were having such a good trip that I was in the middle seat, chatting away to my parents. Glass was embedded in my collarbone. My parents died on impact and thankfully I was unconscious during the rescue. I woke up to my Aunt Helene, who I rarely saw, telling me my parents were gone, and that I was coming to stay with her."

I rub her skin, trying to think of the right words to say. How do I express that I think she's wonderful, smart, and so fucking strong without coming across as a simpering fan boy?

"You don't have to say anything. I know it's not the easiest thing to respond to. I don't need condolences or pity, I just wanted to tell you the truth."

"The last thing I feel for you is pity, Kate," I reply, leaning forward. I kiss her scar again, letting my actions speak for me, because clearly I suck at words. These scars are a part of her that deserve tenderness. Maybe that's Kate in a nutshell, someone who needs to be shown that she can be both soft and strong. Either way, I have no issue telling her with my body how I feel about her. Words? If I even tried to string together the words I was feeling, it would probably haunt me with embarrassment forever.

"You're too sweet for your own good, you know?" she says.

I'm smiling, but who knows if she can see it? "How bad is your vision, anyway?" I ask.

"You're very blurry."

"Mmm. Then just lie back and close your eyes," I say, as I shift further down the bed, lifting the hem of my shirt that covers her body and I kiss up her soft thighs toward her core. If she has any issues with me going down on her first thing in the morning or after she confided in me, she doesn't let it be known as she tangles her fingers in my hair and holds my head right where she wants me.

It's different from the other times we've been together, yet it's still the same. We both know Kate is in control of what happens here, that I want to please her...no, that I need to please her.

She has no qualms about taking her pleasure either; it's so fucking sexy the way she grinds her pussy on my face and moves me where she wants me.

"A little harder," she says on a pant, and I do just that, sucking slightly harder on her clit. "Fingers too."

I eagerly comply, and I'm a happier man for it as she whispers out, "Good boy." The phrase has my cock weeping. I'm achingly hard.

"Touch yourself. It's just a shame I can't fucking see it," she groans.

I smile against her cunt, wrapping my fist around my length as I stroke myself while devouring her.

It's not going to take me long to come, not as she holds my hair, or her flavor drips into my mouth. I'm a goner as her thighs press against the side of my face, my tongue working overtime to please her.

"Stop touching yourself," she pants out and I groan against her pussy, not slowing my tongue or fingers for a single moment. "Make me come on your face and I-I'll make it good for you," she stutters her words as her back arches off the bed.

Her thighs are shaking and her grip in my hair is tight as she lets out the softest moan, her eyes squeezed shut as she shifts her hips up and down against my face, taking what she wants.

I swipe my tongue over her pussy again, and she shivers, lightly tugging on my hair.

"Straddle my stomach," she whispers, and I do as she asks, holding my weight on my knees, her hand slides between us though, sliding over her pussy.

When she pulls back, she's cupping my balls, coating them with her warm release.

"Do you want to explore a little?" she asks, her fingers sliding from my sac, and gliding over my taint. Her other hand is slowly stroking my dick and I think I might just combust then and there.

I was nearly ready to come when I was eating her out.

Now that she's underneath me, eyes heavy-lidded with desire and she wants to please me? I'm going to be a fucking goner.

"Whatever you want to do to me, sweet Kate," I say and she smiles.

Her hair is still a mess from the way she slept as she slides her fingers a little further, sliding easily with her wetness.

"Is this okay?" she asks, rimming her finger around my asshole as she slowly jerks me off.

"Fuck, yeah. That's more than okay," I say, just staring down at her, knowing I'd let her do whatever she wants to me.

"Are you going to come if I push a little further?" she asks. "Are you going to come all over my tits the second I slide into you?"

"Probably," I say, admitting defeat. Even as I tower over her at this moment, I'm the one wrapped around her finger.

"Good," she says, her finger only slightly penetrating me as her other hand picks up speed, jerking my cock.

"Fuck...Uhh...I...That's so fucking good." I'm not even able to string my words together as her finger tilts forward hitting the right spot that has my balls tightening and my will crumbling to pieces. "I'm gonna..."

"That's it. Let me see what I do to you."

Her finger inside of me moves in tandem with her hand, and I have to hold on to the headboard, my forearm straining so that I don't collapse on top of her as I watch in complete fascination as my cum shoots out, splattering against her perfect breasts.

She doesn't stop fingering me or stroking me until I'm whimpering with over sensitivity. I'm not sure I've ever had a harder orgasm in my life.

I'm still straddling her, as she slips out of me, her hands gripping my thighs as I enjoy a few moments of seeing her happily covered in me.

"You okay?" she questions.

"I'm broken, but in the best way. That was...that was so good."

"You still owe me since I wasn't able to watch with perfect vision." She smirks, knowing that she's completely shattered me.

"Kate. You can have whatever the fuck you want," I agree, pushing a strand of hair away from her face.

"I think I'd like to stay in this bed all day with you, but I think it's probably best that I head home," she says, and I almost consider convincing her to stay.

"Shower, a quick breakfast, and then I'll take you home?"

"Deal," she repeats my earlier words as I take her into the shower with me.

It's probably for the best that she doesn't stay the entire day. I mean, we don't have family dinner until six, but spending the whole day together seems to go beyond the scope of friends with benefits. She's set her boundaries, and I have to do my best in following them, even if all I want to do is break the rules, just this once.

When we leave my bedroom, Gavin's nowhere to be found and I wonder if that's him solidifying his boundaries, too. Maybe I really am alone in feeling a deeper connection. Instead of saying anything stupid, like 'hey do you want to date me and my brother,' I shrink those nagging feelings into a small ball and swallow them whole.

IT'S Sunday dinner and the elephant in the room is Kate, and she's not even in the room.

"I'm so happy the grand opening went well. It's everything

you boys have dreamed about for the longest time," my mom says, and I smile back at her.

I don't think she had big aspirations for me and Gavin; we were truly the spares of her children. Aiden became a pro baller, and Lincoln took over the family business. In a lot of ways, it took pressure off mine and Gavin's shoulders. We could fail more and do whatever we wanted. I also think that it made us unmotivated in some regards.

If no one expects much of you, you can never really disappoint someone. Maybe it's aging, maybe it's the business going well, or maybe it's meeting Kate, but I want people to expect more out of me.

"They really did an incredible job," Penny says.

"Yes, it was a very enlightening night. It was great getting to meet some friends we didn't even know our brothers had. I always assumed they were each other's only companions," Lincoln says.

I think I want to stick my butter knife into his eye.

My mother is like a dog with a bone with this information.

"Which friends? Would I know them?" she asks.

"There were a lot of people there," Gavin says, trying to shift the conversation.

"There were, but some were more memorable than others," Lincoln says.

This is our penance, I realize. For all the shit we gave him for being with Penny, my older brother is serving us our payback.

"Oh, well, now I'm extra curious. Was it a female friend?" my mom asks. She's nearly exploding with joy over the thought of me and Gavin dating someone seriously.

"You know, I recall a woman being there," Lincoln says, snapping his fingers. "What was her name?"

"Her name is Kate. She's just a friend," Gavin says sharply, glaring at Lincoln.

"Well, why just a friend? Is she pretty? Semi-normal?"

"Are those literally the only criteria you look for in finding me or Ben a girlfriend?" Gavin asks.

"Semi-normal?" I repeat.

"You're both thirty-five. It's time to start looking for something serious. Look how happy both of your brothers are."

"If I recall, Aiden was thirty-nine when he met Jessa and Lincoln was thirty-six when he ruined Penny's life," Gavin says.

Lincoln gives him the middle finger, while Aiden rolls his eyes.

"I'm sorry. Is it such a crime to want to see my sons happy and settled? Who knows how long I have left on this planet." She sighs and I grimace.

"Really, Mom. The death card?"

"If common sense doesn't work, maybe guilt will."

"You want us to find girlfriends out of feeling guilty?" Gavin says and mom takes a deep breath, taking a swig of her wine.

"I'm just saying that you both have a lot to offer someone and that life is hard and walking through it with someone else is a beautiful thing. I just want my kids to be happy," she says, holding my father's hand on top of the table.

"Mom, we are happy. You don't have to worry about us. Plus, you already gave me the best wombmate," I say, grinning at Gavin, who rolls his eyes, but there's no heat to it.

"Sometimes I really think I should've been an only child," Aiden says, and Jessa lightly smacks his chest.

"Alright then. I'll let it go for now. I just want you two to think about it. You have all this success and, of course, you have each other to share it with, but I can promise you, it's a magical thing being able to share your success with a romantic partner."

"We'll take it under advisement," Gavin says and the chatter around the table finally goes in a different direction that no longer involves our dating life—thank fuck.

My phone buzzes in my pocket, and I pull it out discreetly under the table.

KATE

I think I need some material to get myself off tonight.

Is the memory of my head between your thighs not good enough? I clearly need to up my game.

KATE

I need visuals. With sound.

I'm at family dinner.

KATE

Is that supposed to make me want it less? Because it's kind of the opposite now. Don't you have a childhood bedroom you could sneak off to?

I'm going to need some motivation so I can get this done quickly.

KATE

Not too quickly ;)

Image of her biting her lip and showing me her tits

"Fuck," I grumble under my breath.

"Everything okay, Benjamin?" my mom asks and I give her a quick nod.

"Yeah, something's just not sitting right in my stomach. I'll be right back," I say.

Gavin arches a brow at me, but lets me leave as I scurry away, trying to hide my hard-on. As soon as I've escaped to my childhood bedroom I plan out how I'm going to film this cinematic masterpiece.

As much as I trust Kate, putting your face in a masturbation video is just a bad idea. No one wants a taint-ball combination angle either. So I place the phone on my nightstand, my old high school baseball trophies and a family photo sitting on top. I turn the family photo face down as I adjust my phone and hit record.

I shift my T-shirt under my chin, and pull my cock out from my shorts and underwear, avoiding the ball situation all together.

My body takes most of the screen up, but you can still see some of mine and Gavin's trophies and memorabilia in the background, and I wonder if it will make it even hotter for her. The fact that she told me to do this, and I didn't even question it, I got up in the middle of family dinner and obediently did what she asked. I imagine her watching the video, touching herself as she listens and watches me jerk off, knowing I'm thinking about her.

It reminds me that she specifically wanted sound and I aim to please.

"God, Kate. I wish you were sitting on my face right now," I say as panted breaths slip out of my lips.

My strokes are fast and hard. I'm not trying to make the video longer than it needs to be, or risk one of my nosey ass brothers interrupting my cinematic glory.

"I'm not gonna last thinking about how good you tasted, how lucky I was to wake up between your thighs. Fuck, I want to do it again."

My thighs flex and I have to work to keep them straight as I think about Kate. Picture her ass in my face as I eat her pussy and she watches me jerk off and she lets me come on those perfect, perky tits when I'm done.

"Kate," I whimper out her name, fucking my fist faster and faster.

A strangled but muffled moan slips out of me as I finish, spurting cum over my stomach, clinging to my happy trail as I end the video and hit send before I can second guess myself.

Video attachment

KATE

Good boy.

The door to my bedroom flings open as Gavin shakes his head at me while I'm cleaning myself up.

"You fucking degenerate," he jokes.

"Completely worth it," I reply back.

Kate

This is Florida

I WATCH Ben's video too many times, and come twice while touching myself, just listening to him say my name along with his heavy breathing and gentle whimpers.

No one has ever made me feel as in control as Ben does. He got up in the middle of his family dinner and jerked off for me. If that isn't power, I don't know what is.

Part of me wants to text him again and ask him to come over, but it feels out of bounds to what we agreed to—what I was insistent on. The more time we spend together, the more I wonder if this can actually work.

I find Ben endearing, sweet, and easy to talk to. When I told him about my scars I didn't see pity in his gaze, just sadness that I had to go through something like that. Maybe it's my imagination, but I thought he wanted me to stay at their place for the rest of the day. It's that desire to be around him constantly that scares me. Even if it isn't sex, I just enjoy spending time with him, no matter what we're doing.

I wanted a video of him, so I asked for it. As much as I'd like for him to come over, this seemed like a good compromise.

Things with Gavin are more clear, his line is drawn deep in the sand. We're just fucking, and yet, even with him, there's a part of me that wants to crack his hardened shell and figure out why he won't let anyone in.

It's all fucked and I can't stop.

I can't stop hooking up with them and I also can't stop the way these feelings are growing. I kind of hate myself for it. I promised myself that I would take this time to grow, to be single, and just enjoy men as a delicacy. But it's becoming impossible to see Ben and Gavin as just men who fulfill my sexual needs. They're so much more, and I have no clue on where to go from here.

The sun has long set and as I sit in my empty house, for the first time in a long while, I wish it wasn't so quiet.

There's the slightest movement out of the bay window and I pull back the curtain to take a look. Sure enough, the SUV Pat warned me about is idling down the street, just far enough to not be on my property, but close enough to monitor my house. I swallow a bit of dread and keep an eye on the vehicle. Five minutes, ten minutes, twenty minutes pass and they don't leave.

Genuine fear is licking up my spine as I wonder if this is a threat, or is it worse? Would it be pathetic to leave my own home and hide at Savannah's or Chelsea's? Would it be even more desperate to depend on one of the brothers I'm fucking to come stay over? Is that even on the table?

Before I second guess myself, concern wins out.

Either of you still up?

GAVIN

Ben had to go to the bar to handle a situation, what's up?

I bite my lip and consider lying and getting over myself. It could just be someone who lives in the neighborhood. I'm just being paranoid, right? No, deep in my gut I know that I'm not being paranoid.

> I think my ex is canvassing my house. I'm not sure what I should do.

GAVIN

> I'll be right over. Do not leave the house. Wait till I get there.

> Okay, thank you.

He doesn't respond after that, and I just sit at the window, watching this unmoving vehicle, hoping that I made the right call. Each moment that ticks by I feel even more anxious. The second Gavin's white car pulls into my driveway, a soothing sense of calm fills me.

That's until I see the baseball bat in his hand and he begins striding toward the vehicle parked on the street. I'm up off the couch in a heartbeat, swinging my front door open.

"What the fuck are you doing? You don't know who's in there. They could have a fucking gun," I yell at him.

He doesn't turn to face me as he speaks. "Get back in the goddamn house, Katherine."

"No way. Please come inside. Please," I beg him.

He takes two more steps forward with the bat and grabs his phone out of his pocket. The SUV speeds off as Gavin holds his phone up, recording the vehicle and hopefully getting their license plate.

"I told you to wait inside," he says when he turns around. He's now lazily holding the bat as he approaches my house.

"This is Florida, Gavin, land of the crazy. You can't just stroll up to anyone holding a baseball bat, you don't know what level of unhinged you're possibly dealing with. If you think I'd let you get hurt because you came over here to help me, you're delusional."

"I'm delusional?" he asks, pointing to himself like there's another man in my yard holding a baseball bat.

"What were you going to do? Smash the fucking windshield? I'm not even sure if it's Will or not," I blurt it all out.

Gavin takes an exacerbated sigh, his head tilting to the night sky as his nostrils flare and he seems to ask the universe for patience, like I'm the problem here.

"Can we go inside?"

"Do you want something to drink or eat?" I ask as he follows me into the house, and I lock the door behind us.

"Just water," he says, and I fill us both glasses of water as we sit at my dining room table.

Mikey comes up to him and sniffs him, clearly sensing it's not his favorite twin, before walking away.

"You've got to be shitting me. Even the cat likes Ben more."

My brows furrow and I tilt my head. "Do you really feel that people like Ben more?"

"No. I know people like Ben more. I'm not insecure about it, it's just a fact. Ben is gentler, kinder, easier to be around."

"I don't think you're giving yourself enough credit."

He waves me off, taking a sip of water, his fingers turning the glass as he looks back up at me.

"So, the SUV. Is this the first time? What makes you think it's Will?"

"You remember my nosey neighbor, Pat? She told me she's seen a black SUV outside of my house a few times now. I think at first she was just trying to get information to see how many male night time callers I have, but her mentioning that she never sees anyone get out or in of the vehicle had her realizing it could be something more serious. Along with the chance encounters with Will on multiple occasions it had me panicking. Maybe I'm paranoid, but I don't think I'm being delusional here. No matter if it's him or not. Someone's been watching my comings and goings. I asked Pat to record anything she finds. She was working on getting a license plate."

"I think I captured it in the video. I wasn't asking because I think you're paranoid or don't believe you. I just wanted facts, so we can talk to the police."

"The police?" I question.

His face softens, all the hardness and frustration from earlier slipping away as he grabs my forearm, his thumb delicately rubbing my skin as he speaks.

"You shouldn't be scared to be in your own house. Especially being a woman who lives alone. You need to get a restraining order. It's difficult in Florida, but if we can prove that he's stalking you, we have a case."

I bite the nails of my free hand and Gavin reaches across the table and grabs it away, cradling it in his own hand.

"My sister-in-law, Jessa, she had a psycho ex who broke into her home when she was alone. It took a long time for her to feel safe again. Fucker even drew a gun on my brother. I'm not taking this lightly because I've seen first hand how bad things can go. He's intimidating you about the part of the company you own, and I think we have a good case for stalking. If he's under their radar, the more protected you are. We can go to the station right now."

"Jessa's ex really did that?" I say, avoiding everything else in his statement.

"He was obsessed. While I think this thing with your ex is more money motivated, they're both dangerous."

"I should just sell him the fucking company."

"You don't have to make that decision now, let alone let

him threaten you into doing it. Let's just talk to the police and see what they can do."

"Can we go tomorrow? It's late," I say, not wanting to spend endless hours at the police station, and if it is Will, he knows Gavin is here. He won't show up again.

"Fine, tomorrow," he says, grabbing his water and walking toward the sunroom.

Shit.

I go to stop him and he opens the door and the first thing that draws the eye is my work in progress painting of him and his brother. I started it before I even knew they were twins, back when I thought it was one man making all my fantasies come true.

His footsteps falter and he stares for a long moment, and I wonder if he's going to freak out and think I'm an absolute creep. Instead, he steps closer, tilting his head and observing the painting with a critic's eye.

"That's Ben, and that's me," he says, easily picking out who is who.

"I actually started this painting before I knew you were two people."

"After you were with Ben?"

"No, actually. It was the night we were together. It felt cathartic. You're right about that night. I was desperate to hand over control and let go of everything that was going on. I tend to live in my head a lot. Sometimes I let things fester and rot to the point I've poisoned my mind. But you, you shut it off."

"It's incredible," he whispers in awe.

"I hadn't painted anything in nearly two years, but that night I came home and had the urge to create. I stayed up until the sun came up painting this beautiful man with two person-alities that didn't seem possible in one human body."

"That's why we look conjoined?" he says.

I laugh and stand next to him. "Yes. This side, your side, embodies confidence, strength, and dominance. This one is eager to please, softer, looking for permission."

"Do you have more of your own art around here?"

"Oh, you don't want to see that," I say, waving him off.

"If I didn't want to see it, I wouldn't have asked."

Okay, then. "Follow me," I say, leading him to my studio. It's a bit messy in the space, but what artist's area isn't?

"Everything in here is mine," I say, wrapping my arms around myself. I'm used to critique, taking high-level art classes will make your skin thick. I get shivers thinking about presenting my piece to a class full of pretentious art students and the way they would shred the most beautiful, soul-crushing piece to shreds.

It's not that I'm worried about Gavin judging my technique, maybe I'm just worried about what he'll see in the paintings themselves.

"Is this supposed to be a self-portrait?" he asks and I clear my throat. I don't even have to look at the piece he's talking about.

"I painted that when I was in a really dark place with Will. About three years ago."

"Is this how you really viewed yourself?" he asks, and I shake my head.

"Not on the outside, no," I reply, staring at the painting. It's me sitting at a vanity, the back of my head in the foreground as I brush my hair. But the reflection is a stark contrast. It's a gaunt version of myself, tears welling in my eyes, dark circles framing my too tight, too pale skin. "I felt like I was withering away from the inside and no one but me saw it happening. This piece reflects that."

Gavin stares at it for a long time, almost to the point where

I'm uncomfortable. The need to know what he's thinking is near desperate, until he finally speaks.

"You know what's interesting? I called it the first day I met you."

"What's that?" I ask as he turns around.

"That he didn't know how to appreciate what he had right in front of him."

"And you do?" I question.

"Nope. I don't have a single fucking clue," he says, turning around and moving canvases around left and right, looking at everything.

I clear my throat and the suggestion that tumbles out of me surprises even myself. "Do you want to paint something?" I ask him.

He stops his pursuing, the crease between his brows deepening. "I'm not an artist."

"Anyone is an artist," I disagree.

"You promise not to judge my painting?"

"Cross my heart," I say, making a motion over my chest.

"Okay," he agrees and I grin, setting him up at my station with a smaller twelve by sixteen canvas, while I take the floor.

I put on music and Gavin and I work on our pieces in companionable silence. I have no idea what he's working on. He doesn't want me to see it until it's completely finished. I respect the creative process and sit on the floor painting a portrait of Mikey, except he's a pirate, eye patch and all.

"Why don't you sell your art?" he asks, nearly startling me.

I rest my hand on my chin and shrug. "Sometimes monetizing things takes away all the joy of something. I like teaching the history of art. I'm good at it. It's a job. This is a release. There are no expectations, deadlines, boundaries. I can just do whatever I feel like. Plus, it's not like I need the money. If I wanted to, I could decide not to work at all."

"Me either," he says and I tilt my head and he sighs, his hand still on the paintbrush. "My family is well off. Ben and I had large trust funds. If we wanted to we could fuck off and travel, never work a day in our lives.'"

"So, why don't you?"

"Don't get me wrong, we did in our early twenties, but it felt empty."

"Empty?"

He nods, but doesn't elaborate, and I don't make him. We go back to silence, but as I'm painting a sword in Mikey's paw, I keep glancing over at Gavin, trying to figure him out. There are moments that he's so serious. I wonder if he's wound up too tight. Then there are moments, mostly around Ben, where he seems lighter, more easy going.

It makes me wonder who Gavin really is, and why he might be hiding his true self from the world.

Gavin

Critique & Protection

FUCK. Now I know how she felt when I stared at her painting for way too long. It's the same way I feel as I ponder how I'm going to show her my piece. It's nowhere near as good as her paintings. I think the last time I picked up a paintbrush was junior year of high school for a mandatory credit and it shows.

But it was relaxing. More cathartic than I ever thought it would be. But as I look at my painting, I realize how brave Kate was to show me hers to begin with. Of course, hers looked realistic, mine is definitely more abstract, maybe she won't even see what I meant or what I was feeling when I created it.

I clear my throat. "I'm done."

"Can I see?" she asks.

"You first," I say and she smiles, standing up from where she was sitting on the floor and turns her canvas. I can't help but let out a laugh. It's her orange cat, only he looks like he belongs on the high seas with his pirate hat, eye patch, and sword with the ocean in the background. Beyond the humor, it's well done, it looks exactly like her cat in a non-cartoony way.

I swallow as I turn the easel around, and she takes a few steps closer. Her analytic gaze searches over my painting, and she just stares for a long moment.

"I'm not an artist, but I had fun making it," I say, trying to make sure I don't sound insecure. The last fucking thing I want is her changing her mind about what she said about me earlier when I saw her painting of Ben and I.

She thinks I'm confident and strong; I don't want her perception of me to change.

"It looks like shit," I say, going to grab the painting and turn it around but she grabs my hand.

"It doesn't. This is you?" she asks as she points to the man sitting at the edge of the bed, his head in his hands. A looming shadow hovering over him.

I shrug and Kate hums.

"I would analyze it as anxiety following you, fears, stress?"

"Something like that."

"Always so mysterious," she hums, tapping her chin.

"The composition is great, and so are your proportions. The message is clear. It makes you feel something, it makes you contemplate what it's about. What was the artist feeling? Are they taking in their surroundings or showing something within themselves?"

"So what was Mikey as a pirate supposed to represent?" I ask, trying to bring some levity into the situation.

"That he's handsome and a little naughty when he wants to be, of course. Not all art has to have a powerful message. Sometimes inciting happiness in the viewer is all you need. I'd say I accomplished that, just like you accomplished making me feel something."

"I made you feel something?" I ask.

Her big blue eyes are locked in on mine and I feel like she

sees me. All the shitty pieces I try to hide behind one-night stands and pretending I don't give a fuck.

"Something like that," she says.

It all feels like too much and all I want to do is cut and run, go the fuck back home, and not worry about her seeing too much. Not stress about her being home alone at this house while that prick is out there doing god knows what. But I can't, I won't. I'm trapped here and I'm not sure how to handle it.

Like she sees right into my insecurities, she grabs my wrist.

"Would you be open to a different kind of art?"

"I'm not sure I have it in me," I admit, hating the idea of being even more vulnerable tonight.

"I promise it'll be a lot more fun. I bought this stuff a while ago but haven't trusted anyone to try it with," she says, dragging me by my hand to her bedroom and then into her closet where she begins rifling through some boxes.

"Have you ever played with wax?" she asks, shocking me.

"Twice. I forgot that was on your list"

"So did I. I had more pressing matters at hand."

"What kind did you get?" I ask, leaning down as she finally finds the box she was looking for.

"Oh, look, your favorite," she says, handing me handcuffs and a blindfold. The handcuffs are more restrictive than the ones we played with at Avalon. She has a pair of nipple clamps and she cringes as she shoves those to the side. I suppose those are out.

"Here we go. I got three kinds. All of them are low melting points. Oh, this one is coconut and turns into a massage oil. These two are more for painting and peeling, and then this one...seems more advanced," she says, tucking the last one away.

It's late, far too late after spending so much time in her

studio, but she's giving me control. She knows I need it. Is it because she has similar urges of needing control?

I slide my hand into her hair, holding the nape of her neck and she sighs.

"How about I drip that coconut wax on your hot little body and give you a massage to help you relax, before I fuck your ass," I suggest, accepting the fact she might say no, and I'd be fine with it.

Instead, she licks her lips with an enthusiastic yes.

"Towels, lube, a small vibrator, and a hair tie," I tell her.

She blinks at me a few times. "A hair tie?"

"Do you want wax in your hair?" I ask and she smiles, shaking her head.

"Good, then go get everything," I tell her, and she's quickly on her feet, going to collect everything we need. "Oh, where's your lighter?" I shout as she's in the hallway.

"Nightstand."

I open the nightstand and find not only the lighter, but two other crucial items I requested. I press the button on the side of the small bullet and appreciate that she had the foresight to charge her toys. I place the lighter, toy, and lube on the nightstand as Kate walks into the bedroom, face flushed and a stack of towels in her arms.

We strip her bed down to the sheets and one pillow before protecting everything with a layer of towels.

I read the back of the candle quickly, and light the wick, knowing it's going to need about ten minutes to melt enough wax.

"Hair tie?" I question Kate.

"Oh," she says, holding out her wrist.

I slide the elastic off her slender wrist, sliding it on to mine, before fisting a handful of her shirt and dragging her toward me to kiss her. I told Ben that it wasn't that deep, that I only kiss Kate because I like it.

I'm a fucking liar. Especially after tonight. When I kiss Kate, I feel light. I feel like someone's favorite, and I can't even stop myself. She makes me feel needed; I love the idea of protecting her. She likes the same things I like, while also showing me new things. What we did tonight, the moment of peace we shared while creating art, had me feeling more unguarded than I've been in a long time.

I don't hate it as much as I thought I would.

Am I scared shitless? Fuck yeah. This small, smart, complicated woman has the power to destroy me and my brother, but I also think she's capable of doing much more, and I think I'm going to let it play out.

Maybe I can fuck her into liking me. Maybe she's feeling the same way I am. That this could be more, and fuck if I know what that looks like, but I'm not going to think about it too much right now.

At this moment, I'm going to put that all to the side and give her what she wants and what I need.

Her tongue tangles with mine as her wrists rest against my neck, her fingers playing with the soft ends of my hair. I part the kiss briefly to lift her shirt over her head. A simple white sports bra covers her chest, her hard nipples straining against the fabric. I drag my thumb against the bud, before gripping the elastic and she helps me pull it over her head.

My thumbs trail down her abdomen until I press her shorts down.

"No panties? This whole time?" I joke.

She shrugs and I take a moment to admire her body, every single inch that I want to kiss, own, and please.

I lean down, the scruff of my jaw brushing lightly against the softness of her cheek. "Turn around," I tell her.

She immediately complies, and I glance down at her ass, not able to control myself as I grab a handful of the soft flesh, kneading her ass. Knowing I'll be leaving my marks all over her tonight.

I brush my fingers through her hair, not really knowing what the fuck I'm doing. In theory, I thought it would be attractive to put her hair up, but now that I have her thick strands in my hand, I have no fucking clue what I'm doing.

I bundle her hair to the best of my ability and stretch the band around it a few times. It looks like shit, and when I turn her back around, I have to bite my lip to not burst out into laughter.

"What?"

"I've never put a woman's hair up in my life. I have all brothers, your hair looks insane."

She pats her head, feeling all the lumps and loose hairs, giving me a smile before pulling out the tie and redoing it, making it look completely effortless.

"Better?"

"Better, now face down ass up on the bed," I say, swatting at her ass making her laugh.

It feels lighter than all the other times we've been together, comfortable, more intimate as she seductively climbs onto the bed, making sure to not shift the towels too much as she lies down flat, her pert ass and delicate back on display as I glance over at the candle.

Since it turns into an oil, I'm not worried about my body hair, and I undress completely. If we use the other wax that hardens, I'll have to be careful, but it's all up to what Kate wants. Those have a higher heat point, and there's a possibility she won't even like this.

I run a hand down her spine, kissing her ass cheek, before

grabbing the wax and testing a drop on my forearm. It's warm, bordering on hot, almost like when you first get into a hot tub, but it's soothing and smells strongly of coconut.

"You tell me if it's too much?"

"Yes, sir," she says.

As if my cock wasn't already hard from the moment she showed me everything in the box she hides in her closet, it's now aching. Pre-cum is leaking out of the tip as I hold the candle firmly and drip the small amount that's melted between her shoulder blades.

Her muscles stiffen for a moment, before she goes completely pliant and I'm rubbing the warm rich coconut over her soft skin.

My thumbs drag around her tight back muscles, and she moans into the mattress with each press and roll of my fingers. I'm the reason all the tension is slipping away from her and why she feels safe. The feeling is heady and has me ready to come before I'm even inside of her.

"More?" I ask.

The oil is a little messy, and I'm glad we covered her bed as she nods into the towels and presses herself against my crotch.

I smack her ass, which only makes her do it again.

"Oh Katherine, the more you try to top from the bottom, the more I'll make you wait for it," I tell her, before dripping the melted wax on her skin. "God, this fucking ass."

I knead her cheeks, rubbing in the oil and spreading her wide, looking at the hole she's going to let me fuck. I want to make it as good for her as it will be for me.

Despite wanting to take what I want and fuck her until she's begging to come, I take my time, repeating the same motions.

Her skin is shiny and slick with the oil and I can tell she's desperate for more. While she's enjoying my relaxing touch, a true release is what she really needs.

I want her more than I've ever wanted anyone else, I'll just have to figure out how to make her want me and my brother in the same way.

Kate

Anal and Unrelated TBRs

MY MUSCLES ARE LOOSE, and I feel relaxed, while also feeling completely on edge. I crave more. The anticipation has me needy and rubbing my thighs together.

It's not that I don't like anal, it's just never been something that the other men I've been with have taken the time to ensure it was also good for me.

I know Gavin is going to make it good; I know that I'm going to enjoy myself and it's going to be an experience I won't forget. I'm not even nervous about the what if's or what could go wrong. No, far from it. I'm excited.

Excited to give him something that he wants from me, eager to actually enjoy the act.

His hands are strong and firm against my back, his fingers working out every point of tension. There's no doubt that he knows how wet I am, just like I know how hard he is when his cock just so happens to slide against my ass. We're both aching for it, and the buildup is half the experience.

The heat of the melted wax barely registers anymore, just a warm, comfortable liquid covering my body. The scent of coconut is thick in the air, and I think I'll correlate this moment with the scent for the rest of my life.

Next time we'll use the hotter ones that harden and need to be peeled off my skin, but I can't imagine doing it now. I need him so fucking bad, and I realize that I'm not above begging.

"Please, Gavin," I say, as he rubs my lower back.

"What, is there a spot I missed?" he says, and I know the smug bastard is smiling as he says it.

"Please fuck me," I say. Maybe if I'm direct enough with my pleading, he'll give me what I want.

"Are you aching for it, Katherine? You want me to fuck you in the ass that bad? Then ask for it," he says, his thumb teasing my back entrance.

I swallow thickly, and he applies hardly any pressure, doesn't even try to push into me.

"Fuck me in the ass...please," I say, giving him what he wants.

I'm rewarded immediately as his thumb presses harder against my hole.

"I love it when you're needy for me. Don't worry, I'll always take care of my girl."

My. Girl.

Fuck, I like it more than I should. I like this all too much. It's no longer feeling casual. This is cresting over sexual exploration to a level of intimacy I've never experienced. I like needing Gavin too, and Ben. I keep getting these small nuggets of who they are as individual men and I like what I see...too much.

It would never work out, it would never be socially acceptable. What we have is behind closed doors. We've all agreed to it, and I have to take what I can get.

He grabs one of the extra towels on the bed, wiping down his hands and my ass and hips, cleaning up some of the oil, and doing it far too slowly in my opinion. I want him so bad, and I feel like he's making me wait, building the anticipation for how good he's going to make this for me.

Gavin grabs the bottle of lube from the nightstand, drizzling the cool liquid, a stark contrast against the oil, against my crack, using his thumb to rub and tease. I don't feel as tense as I have in the past. I'm not clenching or stressing about every single thing.

Gavin's a good man, he's in charge, and he'll take care of me.

He pushes his thumb in, and I automatically push my ass against his hand. He laughs lowly, and firmly grabs my ass cheek, holding me still.

"You should see how fucking good your ass looks covered in oil and me pressing inside of you," he says, giving me a rough smack against my cheek before squeezing the flesh.

I live for the combination of pain and sweet words. His thumb is pressing in and out of me, the build of pressure is nice, and equally torturous as I wait for more. He's taking his time as he stretches me slowly before moving on to using more fingers, preparing me for the size of his length.

"This ass is mine, you got that?"

I nod, which apparently isn't good enough, making him spank me again.

"I'm gonna have you addicted to taking my cock here. You'll be begging to take me and Ben at the same time," he says.

I swallow, and instead of fear, I feel completely turned on. That wasn't in the realm of possibility for me before, but could I really? Could I train my body to take them both at the same time like that? Sure, I've seen it in porn, it's possible, but could that be me?

The visuals are too clear; me straddling Ben, petting his

hair and kissing his face as I warm his cock, and then Gavin slipping in my ass, making me feel so wholly full.

"You like the idea, don't you?" he asks.

"I want that," I whisper.

He grabs my small bullet vibrator off the nightstand and hands it to me.

"Lowest setting only," he says, and I press the button, following his directions, which is a foreign concept, because usually I have this sucker on level 3 to come in a matter of seconds.

The low hum of the vibrator fills the room as I slip my hand between my legs and place it on my clit. It feels good, but doesn't give me what I need to finish.

Gavin is using more lube, and I'm pretty sure I've never been more oiled up in my entire life as I feel the head of his cock pressing against me.

"Relax for me. That's it. Fuck," he says, as he so slowly presses the tip inside.

The stretch doesn't hurt, and he takes it so slowly, pressing just a little more in with each thrust. I can hear the way I'm sucking him in, and with the way he's gripping my ass, I know he's trying to control himself.

"You're taking me in so good, baby. God, this ass looks so pretty with my cock in it."

I know that if I turn the vibrator up even one setting, I'll come on the spot. It has me panting as I ride that edge of euphoria.

It feels better than any of the other times I've tried the act, and when Gavin pushes deeper, I can't help but to moan. My thighs are shaking and all I want to do is collapse on the bed.

Gavin notices, of course he notices.

"Lie down," he says, keeping his dick inside of me as he

helps adjust me so that I'm lying flat on the bed. "Fuck, this makes you even tighter," he hisses.

His hands are pressed on my lower back as he continues his slow thrusts. The vibrator rests against my clit, the pressure of lying like this making the vibrations stronger.

He's slow with the way he fucks me, and I imagine the way he watches where were connected, his eyes never leaving the spot he's claiming for his own. It's ridiculously hot and has me on edge.

"More," I beg against the towel I'm holding on for dear life. "Please," I say, feeling like I'm nearing tears. Not from pain, this feels far from it, but from being on the precipice of orgasm for so long.

Gavin's fingers dig into my skin roughly as his strong thighs straddle my body and he pushes harder into me, his pelvis crashing against my ass as he fucks me. I moan into the bed, gripping the towel.

"Fuck," Gavin whimpers out, his hand sliding to the nape of my neck where he holds me down. "You're going to come for me while I fuck you in the ass, Katherine? You want it so bad don't you, sweetheart? Tell me how bad you need to come like this."

"So bad, Gavin. Please," I say, slipping up and saying his name. I expect a swat to the ass, but all I'm given are sharper thrusts and a tighter grip against the back of my neck.

My body is pressed so tightly against the bed I can't escape and I relish in the feeling of being completely dominated while filled. The bouncing of his hips has my pussy hitting the vibrator in just the right way.

I finally...fucking finally, fall over the edge. A near cry of bliss slipping out of my lips as I come, my pussy clenching around nothing as I suck in Gavin deeper.

I can't even hear what Gavin is saying. It's like black spots are fielding my vision and my hearing is going out. Maybe I was holding my breath.

But before I know it, he's pulling out of my ass, making me moan from sensation and the sudden emptiness as more warm liquid splatters against my back.

"Goddamn," he says, collapsing on the bed next to me, one of his large hands placed on my lower back as I turn and face him. "A work of art if I ever saw one," he says, admiring his painting and I can't help but to smile at him, one he gives me right back. It's charming and sweet.

He looks thoroughly exhausted and satisfied.

Maybe the moment after having the best anal of your life isn't the time to realize it. But as I look at him, his lips parted, eyes closed, and his dark hair messy with sweat, it's clear as day. I think I'm falling for him, while also having feelings for his brother.

I turn the vibrator off, leaving it somewhere in my bed.

Gavin is taking a few deep breaths before his blue-green gaze meets mine. He doesn't say anything, he just leans down and presses the softest kiss against my forehead.

"You okay?" he checks in.

"Yeah, more than okay."

"I hate to sound like my brother, but I have to know what you would grade your experience?" he jokes.

I bite my lip and shake my head. "I guess we'll never know," I say, sliding off the edge, my body covered in oil as Gavin hops up and chases me into the shower, making me squeal as he picks me up around the waist and smacks my ass lightly.

We're under the spray of the water as he cups my cheeks and kisses me.

"Do you need anything before we finish up here and go to sleep?" he asks and I just shake my head, kissing him back.

Being taken care of by him, being in his arms, is all I want right now.

❀ ❀ ❀

I THOUGHT I hated sleeping next to men. I realize now I just hated sleeping next to Will. Maybe it was because my body knew he was wrong for me before my mind did, or maybe it's just that we were incompatible.

Gavin and Ben hardly move or wake in their sleep, and thankfully neither snores, so I wake up feeling refreshed, if not confused.

I wake slightly before Gavin, but when he does wake up, he does it with a smile.

"You can not be a temptress this morning. We have shit to do."

"Me? A temptress?" I joke and he pushes me down on the bed, the back of my head cushioned by a pillow as his chest covers mine.

He pushes a rogue piece of hair out of my face.

"A temptress indeed," he says, his eyes searching mine. He looks at me for a long time, it feels so domestic, like I just woke up with a partner, not my friend with benefits. I wonder if he feels it too? "I have to meet Ben in a few hours for an employee meeting. We have just enough time to go to the police station."

"You were serious about that?"

"Kate, you called me over in the middle of the night and I had a baseball bat at the ready. You don't feel safe in your own home. So, yes, I'm dead fucking serious."

I swallow thickly, and just let my hands slide up the expanse of his chest, enjoying the softness of his chest hair. "Maybe I'm overreacting."

"Maybe you're underreacting. I'd feel better if you did this. It would make me feel more comfortable," he says.

"You play dirty, Mr. Carlson."

"I'm sure you say that to all the Mr. Carlsons," he says with a smirk.

I shove at his chest. "Only the two best looking ones," I say, and he leans forward and places a soft kiss against my lips.

"Go get dressed before we get distracted," he says, not moving right away, before he lets out a heavy sigh and falls on to his back, his arm resting above his head showing off his strong biceps.

I think I could paint him like this: debauched, hair messy, muscles and chest hair on full display, giving me that panty dripping smile that has me thinking insane thoughts. Could I enter a real relationship with these brothers? I know I wouldn't be able to decide between the two of them; I want them both. Does that make me a sex crazed, selfish cunt?

It doesn't matter, because until they give me any indication they want more, I'll just harbor my twisted little crushes.

I get dressed, tossing on a simple sundress, and tying my hair up before applying sunscreen and just enough makeup that I don't look like I didn't sleep at all the night before.

When I step out of the bathroom, Gavin is wearing his clothes from last night with his keys in his hand.

"We'll grab something to eat on the way," he says, and with my stomach in my ass, we drive to the police station.

The idea of speaking to police brings back memories of the accident with my parents, and having cops in my hospital room asking questions. It makes me feel uneasy, and if Gavin wasn't here, I know I wouldn't be here. I'd continue being freaked out in my home and suffering over it.

Gavin's hand reaches across the dash and kneads my thigh.

"I'm here with you. I'll be with you every step of the way," he says.

I place my hand on his and squeeze, because that's exactly what I needed to hear. Promises that things are going to be okay are bullshit, and it's the last thing I want. He's giving me facts, that he's here and that he cares. It might just be as a friend who he fucks, or maybe it's more.

We do as he says, eating along the way, though I can't stomach much and stick to my iced coffee.

When we get to the police headquarters, Gavin takes my hand, interlacing our fingers. I feel a sense of safety when we touch, and he explains to reception why we're there.

We sit in the waiting area for far too long. Gavin is texting about work things and I have a text thread with Savannah and Chelsea, keeping them updated on everything going on. They both seem to be fully on board with the plan, and are praising Gavin on pushing me to come and get a restraining order.

We're finally called back by an officer and I have to explain everything that's happened over the last few months. I feel like an idiot, but Gavin reassures me with gentle touches, and chiming in when my details don't seem sufficient.

"I've had my phone checked, they didn't find any tracking software," I tell the officer.

"Have you checked your car?"

"My car?" I reply, and he nods with a sigh.

"Very common tactic of stalkers to use airtags or other devices on a vehicle to know where their victim is. Based on everything you've said, we'll be granting you a TRO, temporary restraining order. It will be valid for three months. He can not come to your place of employment, five-hundred feet in front of your home—"

"Five-hundred feet, are you shitting me?" Gavin interrupts and the officer gives him an irritated look.

"This is a standard TRO. If you both so happen to be in the same place, he will need to stay three-hundred feet away. If any of these agreements are broken then there will be more discussions of expanding or making the restraining order more permanent. I'll send an officer out to look at your vehicle."

"My vehicle isn't here."

"You can swing by the precinct at any time and have an officer look at it."

"We have video of him driving past her house," Gavin says, holding out his phone to the officer, who looks like it's the weakest piece of evidence there could possibly be.

"What if there was an instance of physical abuse in our marriage?" I say softly.

Gavin looks pissed, and the officer looks like he pities me.

"Did you file a complaint when it happened, and do you have any evidence?"

I shake my head, feeling like an idiot for bringing it up. It was one time things got out of hand, but that one time is what has this sense of fear creeping up my spine. He slapped me one time when we were married and the way he gripped my arm at the restaurant.

"He hit you?" Gavin says in shock.

The officer taps the table once and gives us a tight-lipped smile. "I just need you to sign a few things."

I nod, and give him a weak smile, but when I look over at Gavin, he looks lost. He doesn't question the man as I sign a few things. Before long I have a temporary restraining order in my hand, and Gavin's fingers interlaced with mine in the other as we leave the station.

He opens my car door for me. He doesn't slam it, but when he rounds the vehicle and takes his seat in the driver's seat, he glances over at me.

"You should come and stay with me and Ben."

"What?" I blink at him no less than eight times.

"He's put his hands on you before, and clearly, they aren't taking this seriously. What the fuck is that? They have no plan to enforce this TRO or whatever the fuck. This man has been stalking you. Fucking harassing you and making you feel unsafe. You should move in with us."

"I...Gavin. I can't move in with you guys."

"Why not?" he demands.

"First and foremost, I have four cats who would be a nightmare to move to a new home. Second, I really love my house. Third, that's a big fucking step, don't you think?"

He clears his throat, his sunglasses hiding his face as he shrugs.

"Let's just check my car, let them serve him papers, and see where it goes."

"Can you honestly tell me you think he isn't capable of hurting you?" he asks.

He is capable. He's already done it.

"I'll be fine, Gavin, I promise."

"I don't like it," he grumbles, and for the first time in a very long time, I feel like someone is truly looking out for me and not afraid to put me in my place. I'm not sure if I've felt this way since my Aunt Helene was alive.

"I'll get a security system and I promise to tell you about anything suspicious."

He glances over at me, my reflection in his sunglasses.

"For now," he says, as he turns into my driveway.

"For now. What does that mean?"

"It means for now. I'll send over the guys who did security for the bar and marina. Maybe they can come out today," he says, as he types away on his phone, before starting the engine and driving back to my house.

I stare out the window the whole ride and think about

Gavin's reaction. Have I not been taking this seriously enough? How dangerous is Will? Would he escalate things further? Should I take Gavin up on his offer and go live with them until everything is sorted out.

Before I know it, we're parked in my driveway and he's turning on the flashlight of his phone and getting down on his knees.

"I'm going to take a look around your car before I have to leave," he says.

"Yeah...I'll be right back."

I go inside of my home, grabbing us two bottles of water and give the cats a few headscratchers before going outside. I'm about to hand Gavin some water as he's crouched under my car when he makes a guttural noise in his throat.

"You've got to be fucking kidding me," he curses as he rips something from the bumper of my car. "This is how he's been following you around. Do you see how serious this is now?"

I'm not sure why my first reaction is for tears to well in my eyes. Gavin's face softens as he stands off the ground and wraps his arms around mine.

"Stay at our place until they get your security up, at least? Please," he whispers against my hair, his tone soft with me.

"I can have Pat feed the cats," I mumble against his chest.

"Thank fuck. Go pack a bag and I'll drop you off at our place before I head into work."

"Okay," I whisper.

Gavin kisses the top of my head, and it makes me want to cry all over again. My feelings for him only get deeper and I'm not sure what's going to break me more, the moment our arrangement is over or when I won't have him to protect me anymore.

Benjamin

Domestic Bliss

GAVIN IS in the world's shittiest mood as we go through our employee meeting. We've nearly tripled how many employees we have over the last month with staffing for the club and the need for more reliant boat captains.

It's been a lot to manage, but it's more fulfilling than I thought it would be. I feel a sense of pride knowing that we employ so many people and are a part of them providing for our families.

Plus, I get to work with my brother, who's my best friend and we're doing what we love. Working on the water and offering a safe, comfortable place where people can come together and socialize and celebrate life.

I feel happier than I ever thought I would. I'm not delusional enough to think Kate isn't a big part of why I'm feeling so hopeful about everything lately. God, I feel like some kid who got his first hard-on for a girl, jerking off twenty-four seven thinking about what it would finally be like to fuck her.

I've had crushes before. No, I've had infatuations before, but this is different. I could see Kate in my life, and beyond that, I could see her in *our* life. There's always been this lingering fear that one day Gavin and I would be all grown up and I wouldn't have my twin anymore—at least not in the same way we've always lived our lives. Maybe that's codependent and unhealthy as fuck, but I love our life. We're thirty-fucking-five. We're not going to change when it comes to how much we need each other any time soon.

But Kate...Kate likes both of us, and she doesn't treat either one of us like we're better than the other. Something I know that eats away at Gavin. He's so convinced that people prefer me over to him and he's so fucking wrong.

Gavin is the most loving and understanding person out there and anyone who doesn't see that isn't worth his time. Kate sees it. I know she does. Just as she sees me. She sees the soft side I keep hidden along with the fun loving man I am.

I'm so absolutely fucked over the woman, and I don't care.

Rick hands out the schedules for the week and goes over boat safety with our captains and once he's done, everyone leaves the bar, except my brother, who pours—over pours—himself a glass of whiskey.

"Uh, you good?"

"Kate's at our house," he says and I can't decipher his tone. Is he pissed about it? Happy about it?

"Why?"

"All they did was give her some bullshit temporary restraining order. You know what happens if he breaks it? It just gets extended or made permanent. He was outside of her fucking house. He's been threatening her," he says, downing the glass and swallowing heavily.

I know my brother almost as well as I know myself and I can see it in the way he speaks now. He's not upset that Kate's at our house. He's upset because of the circumstances. He cares more deeply about her than I realized.

"Is she okay?"

"I'm not sure. I think the reality of it all is hitting her. She agreed to stay at our place until I had Mitch and his guys set up security at her house."

He pours himself another glass, but this time he sips it.

"This all happened last night?" I ask.

"This morning technically."

"You stayed at her house, in her bed?" I clarify.

It was one thing when we both spent the night. It was clearer then. We were giving into our desires and it was agreed upon, friendly, casual sex. Well, for them, for me, I think this stopped being casual comically early.

"Yeah," he says with no explanation, taking another sip from his tumbler.

It's then I realize just how emotionally inept me and my brother are. I've already asked him this before, but I decide to go a different route.

"I think I have feelings for her beyond our arrangement."

I search his eyes as he places the tumbler on the counter with a soft clink.

"Fuck. I think I do too," he says, running a hand through his hair. "It doesn't matter, though. She's made it pretty clear what she wants. Not to mention her ex is clearly a fucking psycho. I don't think she's going to go from divorcing that freak to dealing with the public scrutiny that comes along with what it would look like being with us."

"We could, I don't know, ask her?"

Gavin furrows his brow at me. "That's the dumbest shit I've ever heard."

"Yeah? Well, what's your plan? Making her addicted to your dick and hope that maybe she might grow in affection towards you?"

"That sounds like a pretty good fucking plan."

"What's the worst that she could say? No?"

"Yes, that is the worst that she could say. She could say no and then we wouldn't have her at all. She's a professor. You saw how freaked out she was with her nosey ass neighbor and those girls at the bar. Imagine that on a grander scale," Gavin says, waving his arms while he talks.

"She came to us at the club opening. She seemed to work through that fine," I say with a shrug.

"Really? She seemed fine? She seemed like she wanted to run out of the club and never look back until Penny plied her with drinks. She's not ready. She might never be. Go figure, the one woman I finally want I can't have."

"That's really dramatic, even for you," I say with an eye roll.

"It's not a joke."

"I didn't say it was. I just think maybe you need a feelings board or something so you can communicate better. She's at our house. She feels safe there with us. She came to our club opening. When she was scared last night, who did she text? Us. I'm just saying, maybe she's scared, maybe she's not ready, but there's no way she doesn't feel something."

"Does it really matter if she feels something if she isn't willing to act on it?"

"I think you're doing a lot of speculating on how she feels," I respond.

"Maybe, but I think we need to play this smart. She's going through a lot and the last thing we need is to spook her. We're exclusive with this fuck agreement, at least there's that."

"So you really are trying to manipulate her with your dick?"

He tosses a rag at my face, and I laugh.

"Alright, fine, we'll just be two yearning fucking assholes, walking on eggshells in our own house wondering if the girl likes us back. Maybe we should write her a little note and leave it on the fridge. Do you have feelings for us? Mark yes, no, or maybe."

He tilts his head like he's open to the idea and I toss the rag right back at him.

"You're an idiot."

"That means you're also an idiot."

"Probably," he agrees. "Either way, I know you worked late last night. Why don't you go home and make sure she's okay? I'll cover the bar tonight."

"You sure?"

"Yeah, I think I need to stay busy," he says, and I know what he really means. If he doesn't keep his hands or mind at work, he might do something stupid, like tell the full grown woman staying in our house that he has feelings, or worse, going and beating the shit out of her ex-husband.

"You're sure this is what you want to do?"

"Yes. Keep things how they are and we'll just go from there," he says like it's simple and I realize then that Gavin truly doesn't know what the next step in this process is and neither do I.

"Maybe we should ask Lincoln or Aiden what to do," I suggest.

Gavin grimaces at me like I've said the most inconceivable shit on the planet.

"Aiden I'd consider. But there's no way in fuck I'm taking relationship advice from Lincoln."

"Fine. Just text me and let me know when you'll be home, and sort this mood out before then, yeah?"

He brushes me off, and I sigh. I know my brother well enough that he needs time to come to his own conclusions and I'll honor his wishes. I won't say how I'm feeling or how he's feeling to Kate, however it won't stop me from doing everything in my power to make sure that these feelings aren't unrequited.

That would honestly be the biggest fuck you the universe could throw us right now. It would be our punishment for being so slutty for so long.

Maybe my confidence is over inflated, but I don't think that's the case. Kate might have mixed feelings and could still not like the idea of entering another relationship, let alone a complicated one with me and Gavin, but there's no way she doesn't also feel this connection. I just need to prove it.

🐚 🐚 🐚

I MAKE sure that I'm louder than I would normally be as I unlock the door and walk into the family room.

Kate's on the couch reading a book, her big round glasses perched on her nose as she places the paperback on her chest and gives me a smile.

"Hey, Ben. I didn't think I'd be seeing either of you till later tonight."

"Not much going on. I worked late last night, so Gavin has it covered. How did you know it was me?" I ask, sitting down on the couch, and propping her legs on my lap before kneading her calves.

"Well, Gavin's hair is slightly longer than yours right now and also the way you walked in here with a big smile on your face."

"Fair enough. You doing okay? Gavin told me about last night and this morning."

"I'm still processing. It's hard to imagine that this person I spent so much of my life with could be this vicious. It's almost like the person I was married to doesn't even exist anymore.

The tracker really..." She stops speaking and shrugs like she can't find the words.

"Do you want to go out and get your mind off everything? We could go out to eat, take the boat out? Or we could order a ridiculous amount of food and stay in."

"Would it be tremendously boring to just stay in?"

"Do you want to get high and order takeout?" I offer and she bites her lip, a wide grin taking over her face.

"I haven't smoked pot since college."

"Oh, innocent Kate. No one says that anymore and I have edibles. No smoking necessary."

"I probably shouldn't."

"We could just get food, watch some mindless show and enjoy each other's company."

She swallows thickly before shaking her head. "No. Let's do it."

"What are you feeling? Pizza, Chinese, Indian?"

"How do you feel about chicken tikka masala on pizza?" she asks playfully.

"I think you're onto something," I say, placing the order on the app for both restaurants, before going to my room and grabbing the small plastic cylinder of edibles I picked up for my clearly medicinal use.

When I come back to the living room, Kate's sitting there with a blanket on her lap, and I plop down next to her. She holds out her hand and I put it in her palm.

"You could cut it in half—" I say too late as she drops the small candy into her mouth and chews.

"So, how long does it take?"

"Like forty-ish minutes?"

"Hmm. What should we watch until the food gets here?" she asks, clicking through the different streaming services we have.

It's odd how comfortable it is having her on our couch, how much I like her being in our space. I don't even like having our brothers over, but Kate feels like she truly belongs here.

I just stare at her side profile, thinking how beautiful she is, and how much I want more. How much I want this on a daily basis. I don't know how much longer I can wait to let this guise of friends with benefits go on for.

Because the fact of the matter is I have feelings. Big ones that I've never had before and it feels like the longer I keep them bottled up the more likely I am to explode.

"What?" she asks, turning to face me.

"Nothing. We can watch whatever you want."

"Hmm. Oh, have you watched this?" she asks and I shake my head.

The first episode plays and suddenly I'm watching a rom com about a podcaster and a rabbi who fall in love. It's a funny show, but it has me thinking about my dating situation and what I want.

Beyond liking Kate, and having these big feelings, where could I see this relationship going?

For the first time in probably ever, I think about the future. I could see us in Kate's house. I could see myself waking up to that orange cat sitting on my chest every morning. The imagery is clear as day as I picture me and Kate and her and Gavin. There wouldn't be a compromise for me and Gavin to separate. We could still live our lives together, but it would be even better with Kate in the middle.

"Are you okay? Is it hitting you?" Kate says, running her fingers through my hair as I look into her pretty blue eyes.

I want to blurt all these emotions out as a knock on the door sounds.

"There's dinner," I say, kissing her cheek before getting up and grabbing the ridiculous amount of food I bought.

It takes about twenty more minutes, and then suddenly all the food tastes better, and I feel all my riddled anxieties slowly slip away.

Kate must be feeling it too, the way she's moaning around her pizza dipped in chicken tikka masala sauce.

"Oh fuck this is good," she says.

My smile is so wide that I can feel the stretch of skin around my eyes.

"God, I love your smile," she says dreamily, taking another bite of food.

"What else?" I say, greedy for compliments.

"Hmm. What else do I like about Benjamin Carlson?" She taps her chin like she's deep in thought. "This dimple for one," she says, pointing to my chin. "I like how you listen, your kindness, your sweetness. You're a good man, Ben."

"Even though I did what I did?" I ask, knowing I've apologized, but not knowing if it will ever be enough.

We put the food down, lying face to face on the couch, my arm underneath her neck, her head resting on my biceps as she nods.

"Yeah, even though you did what you did. Is it weird that I think it was meant to happen?"

"You really think so?"

Her eyes are heavy-lidded as she smiles up at me.

"Yeah, I think we're just what each other needed."

"What is it you need?" I ask her, wanting to be everything she expects of me.

She shifts on the couch and blinks at me. "Just this."

I lean forward and press a tender kiss against her lips, her tongue lashing out and licking my kiss off her mouth.

"What about you? What is it you need?"

"Just this," I reply, because it's easier than saying those three little words I've never said to a person that want to come flying out of my mouth. "And maybe you fucking my brains out," I say, trying to cut the tension and Kate belts out a laugh, throwing her head back.

"Hmm, can you picture me with a strap-on?" she says with a big smile and my cock is already rock hard.

"I picture it often."

She shifts so that she's on top of me, stroking my face, her pupils are huge as she leans down and presses a soft kiss against my lips.

"I'd do just about anything for you, Ben," she whispers against my lips, making me shudder.

Her hips shift to where she's grinding on me and she closes her eyes hefting out a soft breath. "Fuck, I think I could come like this," she says, moving back and forth on my cock, even with our clothes on.

I hold her tight against my body, thrusting my own body against hers. She stares down at me, and as she does I feel lost in my body but completely sure that I'm falling for her.

The pressure builds higher and higher as we rub against each other, our fingers tangled in each other's hair as we share our breaths and kisses.

Her grip in my hair tightens, her hips grinding against my length faster as a moan rips out of her. She looks so beautiful and it has me going over the edge with her, as I come in my pants like a teenager.

She moves her hips twice more, her body shuttering, as she blinks at me with heavy-lidded eyes.

"Yeah, I think I could get used to just this," she says.

I'm a fucking goner and I don't think I ever want to come back to reality.

Kate

Back to Reality

I SLEEP FOR SO LONG, I'm not even sure the last time I got that much uninterrupted sleep. I wake up feeling refreshed, and it isn't even strange that I'm not in my own home.

Don't get me wrong, I prefer my space with my books, furniture, and cats. But their place feels effortlessly comfortable in a way I didn't expect.

There's a note on the pillow next to mine and I grab it.

Had to go to work early. Make yourself at home, see you later tonight.

-B

We didn't even have sex last night, we just cuddled, ate, watched TV, and shared each other's company. It felt so nice, better than nice, actually.

My feelings for Ben are slowly uncomplicating themselves, while also making the situation ten times more complicated in itself.

I like him. No, I really like him. I want more cuddles, movie nights, and tender moments. I think he wants the same too, but there's another factor. Gavin.

I have no idea how he feels, and that makes everything so complicated. There's no way I'm willing to let this arrangement go, but I'm also not sure how much longer I can keep holding back.

After I wash my face and brush my teeth, I'm wearing nothing but Gavin's shirt as I head into the kitchen.

An embarrassing yelp squeaks out of me as I clutch my chest and stare at a disheveled Gavin, sitting at their small dining room table, drinking a cup of coffee. He's only wearing his underwear and Jesus Christ. These men have turned me into a horny nutcase and I do my best not to ogle him for too long.

"Didn't mean to scare you." He smirks, taking a sip. "Want a cup?"

"Please," I say, taking the seat next to him.

He makes me a cup of coffee and places it in front of me before sitting back down in his seat.

"The security guys will be done this afternoon," he says, and he doesn't sound pleased.

Does Gavin Carlson want me to stay here? I mean, sure, he's the one who extended the offer in the first place. But he's been absent this whole time.

"You don't sound happy about it," I remark, taking a sip of my coffee.

Needs more sugar.

Gavin stands, grabbing a small white jar, and placing it in front of me. How the fuck did he know I needed more sugar? I swear I didn't think I made a face when I took a sip.

"I like you where I know you're safe," he says, which just has all different parts of me squealing.

"Well, I'm right here," I say, standing up and walking between his legs.

He adjusts his body to accommodate mine, his strong legs spreading wide as I grip his firm shoulders.

"You are. Right here, safe at my house." His hands grip my hips and I search his eyes, trying to find some puzzle pieces to slot it all together.

We don't feel like just friends, not after the other night. None of this feels casual, but there's no way in hell I'm going to be the one to change the pace of things and potentially ruin everything.

"Safe in your house, ready to do anything you want me to do," I whisper.

He fists the way too large shirt covering my body and drags me closer, causing me to stumble against his body. I expect him to tell me to get on my knees and fuck my face, but instead he tugs my face down against his.

The legs of his chair scrape against the tile and I find myself straddling his lap.

Gavin and I have never had sex this way. He prefers fucking me from behind, or at least I thought.

He kisses me roughly, it feels like a claim in a way, that I'm his, and isn't that a dream?

There's no toys, no bondage, no club. It's just us and it has my arousal climbing by tenfold.

I nearly dig my nails into his shoulders, like I'm holding on for dear life, praying that this moment doesn't end. To my surprise, it doesn't. He just keeps kissing me, his large hands grabbing my hips like a lifeline.

There are no dirty words, only our mouths on one another as he lifts the shirt up slightly, before freeing his cock from his briefs. He drags the head through my wetness and I stretch on my tiptoes, slinking down on every inch he gives me.

He doesn't stop kissing me and it isn't rough or rushed sex, either. I'm nearly warming his cock as I sit on his lap and we make out like we just discovered the act of french kissing.

Gavin grabs my ass, making me shift against his length. I'm moaning into his mouth, just as he's panting into mine.

This feels different. This feels like everything I knew but was trying to shove down. The sex without feelings was good, phenomenal even. But this? This feeling curling around my heart and squeezing while our bodies are connected feels revolutionary.

I'm falling in love with both brothers and have no idea if they feel the same. They have the power to break me, and that scares me even more than this feeling I couldn't stop if I tried.

But when we part from our kiss, Gavin nearly lifts me up and down on his hard length and I look into his eyes.

I'm not sure it's unrequited at all.

That look in his eye, and his hand sliding between us to rub against my clit, has me falling over the edge in every way possible.

Gavin follows suit, bucking his hips and fucking into me, a masculine whimper slipping through his lips as he rests his head against my collarbone. I keep my arms wrapped around him.

Neither of us moves until his cock is soft and I shift my body so that I'm sitting on his thighs.

"You should come to The Bahamas for Labor Day with us. It's something we do every year with our family," he says, and I'm surprised.

He said nothing during sex and the first thing he said postcoital bliss is that he wants me to fly out of the country with his family.

I swallow thickly and search his eyes. "The semester starts before labor day."

"My parents have a private plane. You wouldn't miss any of your classes and it's over the weekend."

"You want me to come?"

"I asked, didn't I?"

I pinch his shoulder and he grins. "Your parents will be there?"

That has him making a scrunched face. "I'll get me, you, and Ben a rental. We won't even stay at the house."

"What exactly would you tell your parents about my reasoning being there?" I ask, mostly prying for my own knowledge.

"That you're our friend?" he says it more as a question and I wonder why.

The magical moment feels gone as lead sinks in my stomach. "Right. Can I think about it?"

"Of course you can think about it," he says, and he almost looks remorseful.

"Let's shower and maybe you can take me home before you have to go to work?" I ask.

I need breathing room, time to think. Can I keep doing this knowing that my feelings are only going to grow stronger when Gavin still just sees me as a friend? There's no Ben without Gavin, and I wouldn't want there to be. I can't simply make myself stop feeling this connection between both of them, but I'm also greedy and want every moment I can get.

"Yeah. I'll take you home," he says like he's unhappy about it, lifting me off his lap and leading me to his bathroom.

I try to ignore the fact his cum is dripping down my thigh, almost like I'm ignoring the fact that I've fallen hard and I don't know if I'll be able to get back up.

❧ ❧ ❧

BEING BACK in my home feels odd. It feels quiet. But it was necessary. I need to figure my shit out, plus the semester starts back up soon.

Luckily, my plans are ready to go with years of teaching under my belt, but somehow this feels different. Usually there's a mix of mourning that the summer is over along with the excitement of having new students, but this year I find myself pouting more than usual.

This was the best summer of my life, and it was because of Ben and Gavin. I'm not sure why, but it feels like when the summer ends, so does everything we had together. I know how I feel, but have no idea where they stand. Beyond that, what does it even matter when I'm not sure how this translates into the real world?

What would people say? Think?

As much as I wish I didn't give a shit about the optics, I do. Yet, part of me feels like if they told me this was beyond a friendship, it would be worth getting past.

Ugh, it's all too much.

So instead of doing anything about it, I head to my art studio and let all these pent-up feelings out on a canvas. Maybe the scent of acrylic paint will help give me some clarity.

At least I felt safe in my home again. The security system Gavin had installed is top-notch, and there haven't been signs of the SUV in the neighborhood according to Pat. Even though I feel secure, there's still this lingering notion of how much safer I felt with Ben and Gavin.

I didn't want a man; I didn't want a boyfriend, and here I am pining after two.

What the actual fuck?

I start the painting; the thought came to me the other night. It's a reflection of the one I made of Ben and Gavin, except it's me. The two sides that make the woman, the two sides they made me see.

Surprisingly, as my brush strokes get smaller, I see the composition coming together before my eyes, hoping that some clarity will flow through me. Yet, the longer I paint the more confused I get wondering what the hell I'm doing and if I'm strong enough to withstand our friends with benefits situation.

Gavin

The Fine Art of Falling for Your Friend

I FEEL a yearning I've never had before when it comes to Kate. I'm not sure exactly when it happened, or why it's so deep, but this need to be around her is unlike anything I've ever experienced before.

The night I spent at her house was a game changer for me. I'd never let a woman dig that deep, and she seemed to like the fact that I was letting her in.

She says she's our friend, that she isn't sleeping with anyone else, well neither are we.

"Should we just tell her we canceled our Avalon membership?" Ben asks.

"No, she doesn't need to know that," I say and he rolls his eyes as we wait at the museum entrance.

It's almost like I can feel her presence before I see her. She's wearing a sundress, sunglasses covering her eyes as she strolls up to us.

"You guys didn't have to come," she says, and Ben bites her lip, leaning down and giving her a kiss.

"We wanted to," he says, pulling away from their embrace.

I swallow thickly, wanting to do the same, but I hold back. What if she doesn't want more? What if I finally have feelings for someone and they aren't reciprocated.

I'm not sure if she senses my uncertainty, but she takes a step toward me, wrapping her arms around my waist, squeezing me and giving me a hug.

"Chelsea and Savannah were busy and this exhibition is only here for the week. Maybe we can grab dinner after?" she asks.

I find myself nodding, agreeable to whatever she wants. Fuck? Is this how Ben feels all the time? It's a foreign concept.

"I'd like that," I agree as I let the woman scan my phone with our tickets. The event itself was cheap, but Kate seems grateful anyway, it has nothing to do with the monetary value.

"Sculpture isn't my main field, but I can still appreciate it," she says as we stare at a life size egg that's cracked around the exterior, human fingers attempting to get out. The egg is painted gold, and I tilt my head as I try to gather the meaning out of it.

Ben goes to touch and Kate swats his hand away, and his cheeks heat. Instead of scolding him further, she squeezes his hand, him no longer having access to it. They hold hands through the rest of the museum and a sense of jealousy riddles through me.

I've never been jealous of Ben in this way, and it's not that he's affectionate with Kate, it's that they're openly in public being affectionate and I want that too.

We're looking at the next piece, a present with a bleeding heart inside of it, the blood spilling over the sides. Now this piece I get. It was probably a man who had feelings for a woman and she sent his heart back in a box.

A soft hand glides down my back and I look down at Kate.

"Are you okay?" she asks softly.

Am I okay? Not particularly. I'm lost and I'm never lost. I'm supposed to be the steadfast one between me and Ben, the one who keeps their shit together.

Meanwhile, I haven't been holding it together at all. No, instead I've been thinking about how sweet she was on my lap before breakfast, and how much I toss and turn at night, wondering if she's okay in that giant house of hers all by herself.

I didn't know how bad I needed to be needed until Kate. Maybe that's the moment she sucked me in when she came to Avalon with near tears in her eyes, asking me to make everything better.

I crave it. It's an addiction now, and I don't see a way to quit her. The most horrifying part is I don't want to either.

"I'm fine," I say flatly and she continues rubbing my back, soothing me, and she doesn't push it.

We finish the exhibit and as we leave, she holds Ben's hand and grips my forearm with the other.

I wonder if this is something friends do or if I never stood a chance in hell.

⚜ ⚜ ⚜

MY COCK IS in Kate's mouth while she rides my brother. She looks up at me with her bright blue eyes and I can't imagine not having this.

It's not that I haven't shared with Ben on multiple occasions, or even been with some incredible women, but none of them looked at me the way Kate does.

"You're going to swallow every drop. You've been craving it, haven't you?" I ask her.

She moans around my cock as my brother sucks on her breasts and she rides him at the pace she sets. Her nails are digging into my ass as I slip deeper into her throat and I can't hold it any longer. Finishing in her mouth and she eagerly swallows every drop.

I don't loiter in the bedroom, instead I go to Ben's bathroom and start showering, letting them have their moment together.

My eyes are closed as the warm water trickles down my face and small arms wrap around me. I like it too much. I like having her at our house, the way she shows me affection.

I don't know if it's easy because we're friends with no strings attached or if it's because we're meant to be more.

She kisses the middle of my back and I turn around in her arms, shifting my body so that she's getting some of the spray too.

"You staying the night?" I ask her.

She bites her bottom lip. "Do you want me to?"

I could lie, tell her that it's up to her and it doesn't matter, or I could let myself have what I want.

"Yeah, I like you here."

She leans in, pressing the side of her face against my chest, running her hands down the expanse of my back.

"Have you thought any more about The Bahamas?" I ask her.

I'm not sure why I can't let it go, but the idea of going out of the country without her seems wrong. It used to just be my brothers and Penny who went, and it was simple, but then Aiden met Jessa and Lincoln and Penny realized they were meant for each other. I always had Ben, but the idea of her not going with us seems like a lie.

Honestly, this is all starting to seem like we're lying to ourselves.

"Not yet," she says, not lifting her head off my chest, and I worry that she doesn't feel the same way.

Maybe this is unrequited, and I'd be an idiot telling her how I feel.

🐚 🐚 🐚

IT'S Sunday and we've already had dinner. My brothers, Penny, and Jessa are sitting out by the firepit and it sinks in my chest how Kate should be here too.

"So, did you convince her to come?" Penny asks me and Ben.

Lincoln and Aiden are talking about boring business shit, and Jessa seems like maybe she had one too many of my mom's margarita's and is falling asleep on Aiden's shoulder.

"Working on it," Ben says.

"Well, why is she hesitant? You guys are dating."

"We aren't dating," I say and Penny squints at me.

She holds up one finger. "You all are exclusive with one another." Another finger. "You two are obsessed with her." A third finger. "You guys go on dates." A fourth. "She's clearly falling for you guys, too." Once all five of her fingers are up, she stares at her hand. "I can't think of a fifth thing, but this whole not telling her your feelings shit is ridiculous."

"You're one to talk," Ben says, taking a sip of his beer.

"We're not talking about me right now. We're talking about you two and how kismet this all is. You both never wanted to date someone because you didn't want her coming in between your relationship with one another," Penny rambles and I won't admit that she's right, that was a big part of the hesitancy, plus a lot of women wanted marriage and kids and those things aren't on the table for me. "Then you find Kate, who likes you both equally, doesn't pick favorites, and it somehow works. You can't be boneheaded enough to let this go. Just tell her how you feel."

"She's been through a lot," I say, and Penny rolls her eyes.

"So has everyone."

"What if she doesn't feel the same way?" Ben asks, and Penny rubs her temples.

"She feels the same way."

"And how would you know?" I ask, and Ben leans in, both of us acting like Penny is some sort of fortune teller, leading us in the right direction.

"A woman can tell these sorts of things."

"Maybe having her meet mom is too much," Ben suggests, shrugging.

"Or maybe you all just need to jump right into the deep end and stop pretending she's just a friend," Penny says as the baby monitor app on her phone goes off and she excuses herself.

I look at Ben, and he stares back at me.

"I want to show her off. I want our family to see that we're happy," he says, and I nod my head.

I groan and rub my face, not knowing how to handle the situation. "If she's not ready to go with us, she's not ready."

Ben arches an eyebrow at me, but he nods, even though I have a feeling he's going to take matters into his own hands.

This trip with our family has been a major milestone for both of our brothers in the past and I'm not sure why, but something tells me it could be the same for me and Ben too.

Benjamin

Professor

KATE'S BEEN busy with the semester starting and I've been incredibly greedy of her time. Gavin told me I should give her space, but I've decided I'm tired of Gavin acting like a dictator. I think he's wrong.

I think the last thing Kate needs is space. Or maybe I'm just the needy fuck going through withdrawals about not being around the woman I think about constantly.

I'm a love sick puppy and it's rather pathetic, but I have a plan in place. I simply just have to make an offer that Kate can't refuse.

Did I look at her course schedule online? Yes, very stalkery of me. Am I also meandering around the campus searching for her lecture hall? Also yes.

I'm fully committed at this point, I know it's something she wants and it's something I've been thinking about nonstop. I look back at our texts with one another and decide that this is in fact a good surprise and a risk worth taking.

I think we should check pegging off your wishlist.

KATE

Is that so? Tell me more.

I think you'd love being in control, and it felt so good what we did the other night, I can't imagine how good it would feel with a toy.

KATE

You know I would love to do that with you Mr. Carlson. Maybe we can talk about it later tonight, when I'm not in the middle of teaching a class.

I smile reading the texts over and over. She wanted to talk about it tonight, but I'm thinking actions are stronger than words. Plus, the fact she called me Mr. Carlson and going all professor mode on me is giving me too many ideas. I pocket my phone and ask two college students for directions, finally finding her building.

I slip into the hall, sitting toward the back. Her class is nearly over, full of mostly women, minus a few men. Not a surprise, since this is her Women in Art History class. She owns the classroom, while still giving off warm, down-to-earth vibes.

Most of the class is engaged, no one is watching a show on their laptop, they're actively taking in and absorbing her lecture.

God, she looks so pretty, so in control of the classroom. I've missed her more than I'd admit to anyone out loud. Not even just the sex, just her. Even if my plan is to lure her in with sex right now, it seems to be the thing that keeps us on the same page.

She clicks through the presentation, turning off the projector.

"Any questions?" she asks.

I raise my hand and she squints at me. She's trying to keep a smile off her face.

"Yes," she says pointing at me, all her students turn to face me. Half of them are probably wondering why a thirty-five year old man is at their lecture.

"Will this be on the midterm?"

"I guess you'll just have to wait and see. Make sure you all submit your artist of choice for your assignment. Remember, everyone has to choose a different artist, so you don't want to wait and have last dibs," she says as her class packs up their bags and begins to funnel out of the hall.

I sit in place as Kate sits at her desk and starts tapping away at her computer. Is she playing along or is she ignoring me?

I wait till most of the students are out of the hall before I make my way down the steps to her desk.

She keeps typing for a few moments before she looks up at me from her glasses. Fuck, I'm hard already.

"Mr. Carlson, if this is about your failing grade, I'm sorry, there's nothing I can do for you," she says.

Oh, I'm hot for the fucking teacher.

I lean down on the desk, my palms pressed against the wood. "You're sure there's nothing I can do?"

"You'll have to take the class again next semester, I'm afraid."

I glance around behind me. All the students have left. It's the last class in this hall for the day, I checked. I turn back to Kate.

"I'm willing to do whatever it takes."

"You should have considered that before now. Your performance in my class was inadequate."

I'm fighting back a smile as I walk around the desk, invading her space, nearly towering over her.

"Please, Professor Morley, I promise this isn't a reflection of my adequacy," I say, pulling at the white bow around her neck.

She looks so fucking hot. The sheer white top she's wearing with a bow around the collar and the prim, tight black skirt that cinches at her waist.

"Like I said, there's nothing you can do, Mr. Carlson."

I use the desk for leverage as I get down on my knees. Kate looks at me with a shocked expression, her gaze shifting over the doors of her classroom.

"This is inappropriate," she says.

My hands go to her pantyhose-covered legs, shifting over her tight black skirt.

"I told you I was willing to do anything. I can prove to you that my performance is far from inadequate," I say, rubbing my face against her skirt-covered lap.

"I'm not sure how falling onto your knees is going to get you a better grade," she says, as I shift her skirt up her thighs.

"Then let me show you. I'll do anything, professor. Let my mouth make up for my grades. Let me show you how good I can be."

"Fuck," she hisses, her eyes closing softly, before she blinks a few times, staring at the entrance of her lecture hall. "Ben. We can't do this here," she says, fisting my hair, breaking character.

I expected as much. As sexual as Kate is, she's still a professional. Anyone could walk into this hall and catch us. Not that I'd care if I got caught with my mouth devouring her, but she would, and I'd never want to jeopardize her career.

"Then come with me somewhere instead?" I say, my hands still rubbing along her thighs.

She runs her hand through my hair, looking at me like she misses me and feels conflicted about it.

"Where?"

I knead her thighs, wishing she was sliding those tights down her legs and holding my head between her thighs. She seems withdrawn and I hate it.

Why can't I figure out how to navigate this?

"I think we should tick that item off your list tonight," I say, instead of saying, *"hey, so I think I'm in love with you, and trust you, so let's try this new thing."*

Her nails drag along my scalp. It's soothing, and I missed it.

"I thought we were going to talk about it tonight?" she says, smirking.

"I haven't stopped thinking about it and neither have you, have you? I want it bad, don't you?"

She takes a deep breath before nodding. "Yeah, I do."

"Then let's go," I say, standing to my full height and holding out my hand.

She seems so reluctant, but packs up her things. I carry her bag for her as we leave her lecture hall and walk across campus to the parking lot.

"I'll text you the address. You can meet me there," I tell her.

Kate arches a dark eyebrow at me, but doesn't fight it as she gets into her vehicle and I walk to mine, dropping her the pin.

KATE

What are you up to, Mr. Carlson?

Whatever it takes to pass, Professor M.

I put my phone down, grinning to myself as I drive over to the store I have in mind. I'm nervous, but I've planned my entire day around what I want to do with Kate tonight. There's been an endless amount of research and prep. But I want this—with Kate—and only Kate.

I park in the designated parking lot and when she pulls up, I'm waiting for her.

She takes in the big sign and gives me a questioning look.

"Let's go, professor," I say, grabbing her hand and walking inside.

We're visually assaulted by a wall of dildos as soon as we're inside, but the store is clean and organized. A woman in her mid-fifties greets us with a wide smile.

"Welcome. My name is Cortina. Is there anything you need help with today?"

"Yes, we're looking for a strap-on for beginners," I say.

Kate's mouth parts next to me, and I pet down her dark hair as she gives the employee a kind smile.

"Of course, follow me," the sex toy shop worker says, leading us down an aisle with different types of harnesses. "Are you looking for something detachable?"

"Yes," I say. "Easier to clean," I whisper down to Kate.

"Well, there are a few options. Is there a price point, or anything you're specifically looking for?"

"No price point, willing to buy a few things to see what works best," I say, and Kate is gazing at the shelves, the initial shock of where we are overtaken by excitement.

"Does this work well?" she says, holding up a dual pleasure strap-on, one that would penetrate her at the same time. The dildo itself doesn't look large, but slightly intimidating.

"Yes, the only complaint I've seen for that one is the harness itself. If you're looking for dual pleasure, I would suggest this one." The attendant holds up a new package, and I'm relieved that the toy is slightly smaller. "This one has more straps than the thong harness, so more support," she says happily.

It's honestly impressive the way she doesn't judge the fact that I'm about to get fucked by this beautiful, petite woman. I decide right then and there that I'll leave a review and mention how helpful sweet Miss Cortina has been this evening.

"This is so helpful, thank you. I think we have it from here," Kate says.

Cortina gives her a nod. "Of course, just note that you only want to use a water-based lube with these toys and I have a toy cleaner upfront that I recommend. If you need anything else, please just give me a shout," she says, before walking back to the front of the store.

"You're sure?" Kate questions, glancing up at me. "This is something you want, right? It isn't something you want to do to make me happy?"

This is how I know I'm in love with her.

"There's never been anyone I trusted enough to do this with. But with you, it feels right," I tell her, instead of confessing my undying love in the strap-on aisle.

"Okay," she says, clearing her throat. "I like the idea of this one, but I don't like that it's a thong harness. That seems uncomfortable."

"And big," I say.

"How about this one, then," she says, picking up the harness and toy combo that Cortina suggested.

"Let's do it," I say happily as we go to the front.

Cortina already has the suggested toy cleaner and a few lube options for us. We go with something straightforward and simple. Cortina upsells us on a lubrication launcher. Damn this lady is good.

I take my credit card out to pay, and Kate refuses, paying for the items.

We leave the shop and are standing in the parking lot.

"My house?" she asks.

"If that works for you?"

She places a hand on my chest. "You're really sure this is what you want?"

"Kate, I didn't give myself an enema and eat straight up fiber for the last twenty-four hours for nothing."

"What if I wasn't free?" she says, her eyes wide with my preparation.

"I didn't really think of that as a possibility," I say with a shrug, and she bites her lip, grabbing my shirt and bringing me down for a kiss.

Someone honks a horn and we break away.

"Alright, I'll meet you at my house," she says, and I can't tell which one of us is more nervous, but we part ways.

When I get into my car, I put on the playlist that always gets my heart pumping as I make my way to Kate's house.

We're really doing this.

❧ ❧ ❧

I'M NOT sure what I expected? Maybe Kate opening the door with nothing on but the strap-on and telling me to bend over the couch. But instead she's thoroughly sanitized the toy and has a video on about anal prep.

"I've watched plenty of porn. But watching porn and doing it are two different things. I want to make sure it's good for you," she says from the bathroom, where I can hear the lecturer talking about lube and technique.

Meanwhile, I'm completely naked on her bed, hard and eager.

Waiting just makes it that much better, though. I don't touch myself, just stare down at my hard cock, trying to let it know that good things come to those who wait.

When Kate walks out of the bathroom, my breath hitches.

She's wearing the harness. It's a stark contrast to her smooth pale skin, the small black toy curving slightly upward. She's wearing a bra that's slightly see-through, giving me a glimpse at her hard, perky nipples. She has her dark hair up in a messy ponytail, her glasses still on, and I'm not sure she's ever looked hotter.

I swallow thickly and she smiles. "I think...I think maybe I like the idea of you being on your back," she says, and I nod eagerly.

Not only are we going to do this, but I'm going to get to watch every second of it.

She crawls up the bed, the hard press of the silicone hitting my thigh as she cups my cheek and kisses me.

My heart feels like it's going to beat out of my fucking chest and my cock is pouring pre-cum in anticipation.

She doesn't stop kissing me as her hand grips my shaft, her thumb sliding around the mess on the tip and I pant into her mouth.

"You might just get that A after all, Mr. Carlson."

I smile into the kiss, loving that we're picking up right where we left off.

"I told you I'd do anything."

"Your dedication doesn't go unnoticed. Look how hard you are for me. You want to be mine in every way, don't you?" she whispers in my ear, making my flesh pebble and my ass tighten.

"Yeah, I want that," I reply, knowing that I mean it in every sense, not just what she's going to do with me.

She leans over me to pump the lube into her hand from the nightstand. I can't help myself when I suck on her breast through the material of her bra. Her breath hitches, but she pulls away, holding my gaze as she shifts her hands under my balls and begins circling my hole with her fingers.

"Fuck," I hiss.

The sensation is new as she touches me and watches every single expression on my face.

"Okay?" she checks in and I nod, spreading my legs wider.

She keeps just toying with me, my cock weeping and my ass begging for her to do more, and she enjoys it. Her nipples are hard and I notice the way she's tilting her hips, shifting the toy that's inside of her against her g-spot.

I just know when she's fucking me the pressure is going to be more. It's going to feel good for both of us.

"You want more, don't you?" she asks.

"Please," I'm nearly begging as I hold on to her thigh with one hand and fisting the sheets with another.

Her finger slides into me and I lick my lips as she keeps eye contact with me, making sure that everything she does is good for me. I'd been thinking about this since the first night she touched me like this, how much I wanted more, and knowing that she's going to give it to me is nearly about to send me over the edge.

"You can take more can't you, baby?"

"Yeah, anything for you," I tell her and I mean it.

"Another finger?" she asks, and I nod eagerly, before the pressure increases and she has two fingers scissoring inside of me.

"Touch yourself. Slow."

I do as she says, stroking my cock while she fingers my asshole.

"You're always so good for me Ben. You like pleasing me? You like having me fuck you?"

"So much. Wh-whatever you want it's yours," I promise her as she continues fingering me and I hold the base of my cock, knowing that edging myself is going to be worth the wait.

She grabs my hand that was barely stroking myself, and moves it to grip my balls as she grabs the lube again. Dripping some along the top of the dildo as well as my ass, sliding her fingers in and out.

"I know you need more, you want me to fuck you so bad," she says, slipping her fingers out of me and teasing my hole with the end of the toy. "You're gonna take it so good for me and let me know if anything doesn't feel right."

"Yes, Kate," I swear.

Her hand strokes the dildo, covering it with a sticky sheen, before adjusting her body.

Fuck, she's so much smaller than me as she kneels between my legs. My thigh is nearly the size of her waist, as she fists the toy at the base, her brows furrow and she glances to the side of me.

She wipes her hand on her stomach, the tackiness of the lube shining against her skin as she grabs a large pillow.

"Lift up," she tells me and I do immediately as she slides the pillow under my hips, giving her a better angle. "Much better," she says, pressing the toy against my hole.

Her olive green nails slightly dig into the skin of my thigh.

"Relax, baby, I got you," she says. "You're going to take me so well and you're going to love it."

I take a deep breath, my hand tightening on my balls as she presses in. I groan loudly as she thrusts slowly.

The toy isn't big, maybe comparable to three fingers, but holy fuck, does it feel good.

She makes a soft little moan as she presses further into me.

"Look at you, Ben. Fuck, that's such a good boy."

I squeeze my balls tighter so I don't come and I watch this small woman I'm obsessed with fuck me.

Kate

Shell Shocked

I DIDN'T KNOW that I would like it this much. There was no way to know it would feel this good. Not just the toy rubbing against my g-spot, but truly dominating this strong, amazing man beneath me.

I didn't know what to expect when it came to wearing a strap-on but I like the way it feels. The cool leather is tight against my skin, nearly digging in but in a pleasant way. With each thrust the toy on my end rubs the inside of my walls, but the harness itself doesn't move much to provide friction on my clit.

"Please don't stop," he begs.

His one hand is cradling his balls while the other is holding my rib cage.

It's hard gauging each thrusts of my hips and I accidentally slip out of him, which has him groaning and me gripping the base of the toy, lining it back up against him and pressing in.

"Okay?"

"Yeah," he replies in a pant.

I move slowly, watching where I'm entering him, knowing now how far not to go so that I don't fall out.

"What feels better? Slower or faster?"

"You can go faster," he tells me and I shift my hips, my ass flexing with each thrust, and the small toy inside of me is hitting a delicious spot. It has me moaning, and that has Ben's eyes rolling in the back of his head.

"That's okay?" I check in, knowing that I need this to be good for him, and that he's been wanting this just as much as I have. I wouldn't want to hurt him, or for him to not speak up if something didn't feel right.

"Yeah, it feels so fucking good. You give me just what I need, you're perfect," he says, giving me the praise I needed to go faster, the toy moving in and out of him while he holds the base of his cock.

"You're taking me so well. You needed this, didn't you?"

"So fucking bad. I don't think I'm going to last," he says, his hard cock weeps at the tip as he whimpers with every thrust.

He's so ridiculously sexy like this I can barely handle it.

"Don't come, not yet," I tell him, wanting this to last, wanting to remember this moment forever. "I want to watch you longer."

He nods his head, his abdomen rigid as he holds his breath in and out and I slow down my thrusts, no longer giving him the faster thrusts that had him on the edge of coming.

"Does it feel good, Mr. Carlson? Does it feel like you deserve an A?"

"Fuck," he hisses, his fingers digging into my skin. "Yes. So good. You're so good to me."

"That's right. Are you going to take it deeper for me? If you take it deep, I'll let you finish."

"Please, please. Fuck. Please let me come," he begs and it breaks my resolve.

There's no way I can edge him any longer.

"Are you going to make a mess for me? You love being my good boy, don't you?" I ask.

The hardest part is keeping the right rhythm as I thrust in and out of him. Each time I push all the way inside of him, he's moaning with pleasure. It's fascinating watching the toy slip in and out of him, knowing it's hitting just the right spot.

I slide my hand from his quaking thigh and slowly stroke his cock.

It has his hand slipping away from his sac, tangling in the sheets as his abdomen flexes and softer, sexy whimpers slip out of his mouth.

"You're taking it so good, baby." I thrust a little harder, letting the toy go deeper and drag against his prostate with each thrust. "Come for me."

His grip on my ribcage is tight, but welcome, as he tosses his head back, his Adam's apple bobbing with pleasure.

Harsh breaths slip in and out of his nose as his lips part. His thighs are shaking and his stomach is taut.

My fist is stroking him and my thrusts are uncoordinated, but it's hard to focus when all I want to do is watch him fall apart, knowing that I'm the one making those soft slips of euphoria fall out of his mouth.

Me. Only me.

The toy inside of me feels good, but it's not enough to make me come. It doesn't matter though, because watching him tipping over the peak of his orgasm is all I need.

"Kate," he says my name like a prayer as warm cum shoots out of the tip of his cock, falling over my knuckles and spurting onto his happy trail.

I don't stop fucking him with my fist or the strap-on. Not until his hand reaches out, grabbing my wrist and his spine is lurching off the bed because it's too much.

He looks at me with those pretty blue-green eyes like I'm a goddess.

"Good?" I ask, slowly sliding out of him.

He gasps when the toy leaves his body.

"Good?" he questions, laughing and shaking his head. "Kate, I think I saw God. Now please take that thing off and ride my face," he says.

It's the most demanding I think he's ever been, and it has me wanting to laugh as well.

He straightens his legs, and I climb onto his stomach.

"Take it off for me."

Ben's hands are a little shaky as he grabs the leather straps, unlatching them from the loops. I rise on my knees as he gently pulls off the harness and toy from inside of me.

His hands go to my hips as I shimmy up the bed, pressing my pussy against his face. It's reminiscent of our first night together. I close my eyes and replay everything I just did to him, and how edged I felt the whole time.

Ben licks me fervently, his gaze locked on mine, and his fingers digging into my thighs.

"Right there," I tell him, shifting my pelvis, so his mouth is just in the right spot. I'm so close, so soon, and I'm not sure if I want to ride the wave or pull back so I can make this last longer.

But when he moans against my pussy, there's no pulling back as I ride his face.

"Fuck, you make me feel so good," I tell him, his eyes shutter and his hands glide to my ass, as his fingers roam the indents of where the harness was pressed against my flesh.

His tongue is too much, and I'm too worked up, I didn't stand a chance in making this last. When his lips wrap around my clit, I fall apart, coming faster than I have in my whole life.

I don't move for a few moments, my chest heaving as I

catch my breath and pet Ben's hair before I slide down his body and he cradles me against his chest. I stroke his chest, arms, and throat as we lie there.

"How are you feeling?" I ask him.

He squeezes me a little closer. "Exhausted in the best kind of way."

"Was there anything that was uncomfortable for you? Anything you really liked or didn't like?"

He turns to his side, so that we're staring at each other. My hand is flat on his chest as he rubs down my arm.

"I think I like just about anything as long as it's with you," he says, and it has me licking my lips and swallowing down all these feelings.

Instead of responding, I pull his head to my chest, petting his hair as we lie there in tender silence.

🌰 🌰 🌰

A SHOWER, two water bottles, a bag of Doritos later, and Ben and I are lying on my bed naked, a random show on in the background.

I don't ask him to leave, and he doesn't make some excuse to skedaddle the fuck out of here either, so we just lie there. His head is on my lap as I flip through my emails, approving the artists my students send in for their papers.

I can feel Ben staring at me as I glance down.

"Yes?"

"One, you look really hot in professor mode. Two, have you thought about The Bahamas? We both really want you to come."

Had I thought about Gavin's offer? Only a thousand times. I thought about why it was a poor decision, how I'm already in too deep and if I met their mother, it would only make it ten times worse. Then I thought about how much I missed them and how nice it would be to get away, how it would feel like the summer never has to end.

"I don't know."

"Can I ask what's holding you back?" he asks.

Oh, only that I'm in love with you and your brother and I'm not sure if you feel the same?

"It's just a lot with it being the start of the semester and taking a trip."

He doesn't seem to believe that answer, and I guess I don't either.

"Please? Gavin already got us a condo, so we won't have to stay the whole time with my family. It's our favorite place. We want to share it with you."

I pet his hair, putting my tablet down.

They've shared so much with me, been vulnerable and there for me when I need them, if this is really what they want...

"Fine, I'll go."

Ben grins, nearly leaping out of the bed.

"Where are you going?" I ask.

"I gotta tell Gavin. Pack up your bags. We leave tomorrow at 5," he says.

This is definitely not a good idea, but I can't deny that I loved putting a smile on his face. So, instead of answering more emails, I'm tossing on a T-shirt and packing a bag for a long weekend with my friends who are also brothers who I happen to fuck, and their family.

What could go wrong?

❧ ❧ ❧

"ARE YOU SURE? I mean I could get a ride share home. It's not a big deal," I say as we're walking to the private section of the airport.

Gavin has a death grip on my luggage as he shakes his head.

"Nope, you're at the airport. There's no going back now," Gavin says in his bossy tone.

"Everyone already likes you. It'll be fine, Kate," Ben says, trying to be reassuring, but all I feel is complete dread.

I'm nervous about the questions their parents are going to ask. Are they going to wonder which brother I have a crush on? Are they going to buy the whole "Kate is just our close friend" bullshit?

Granted, their brothers and sisters-in-law probably have an idea, and I liked them all a lot, but this seems like a big step when this can't go any further than it already has.

Suddenly Gavin stops mid step and grabs my chin, his gaze locked in on mine.

"What are you worried about?" he asks.

"Are they really going to buy that I'm just your friend?" I say, and maybe, just maybe, I say the word friend like a slur.

"No. Because you're not just our friend. Now we need to move our asses so they don't take off without us."

I blink at him, and he grabs my wrist, nearly dragging me through people as we finally get to the private gate.

Ben speaks with the attendant and we're taken down to a golf cart that will bring us to the plane.

"Gavin, what does that mean?" I finally speak up, some of my brain cells coming back online. As wind whips through my hair, I see the smaller plane that we're driving towards. My nerves were already fried, and now I feel like I might throw up.

Could he really? Could they both feel what I feel?

"We'll talk about it later," he says, which has me wanting to have an absolute meltdown.

But there's not a single moment for that as we enter the plane and I come face to face with the entire Carlson clan.

"Kate, you've met the delinquents. These are my parents, Maggie and Jeff, and my aunt and uncle, Holly and Tim," Gavin says, like he didn't just drop a massive fucking bombshell on me a few moments ago.

Instead, I put my hand up in the stupidest wave. Everyone probably thinks I'm an idiot.

"It's so lovely to meet you," an older woman with dark hair says, and I know instantly it's their mother. "I can't wait to get to know you better on this trip, but right now I'm going to need everyone who was late for the gate time to park their asses in their seats so we can make our takeoff time," she says, clearly scolding her sons who are probably late more often than they are on time.

Gavin grabs my hand and plants me in the seat next to him, Ben across from me, and an older gentleman sitting next to him.

Ben looks just as shocked as me, giving Gavin glances of confusion, but Gavin doesn't give us anything. Per usual, he's unreadable as fuck and I'd give just about anything to crack his head open and figure out just what's going on in there.

"Glad to see you made it, somewhat on time," the older man says with a crinkle of his eye.

Definitely their father.

"Kate, it's lovely to meet you. Neither of my youngest boys have brought a friend on vacation before. They were kind of built in best friends, same with Lincoln and Aiden, I suppose. So what is it you do?"

"I already told you, she's a professor, dad," Ben says.

"Oh well, spoil all the small talk, why don't you?" his dad

jokes and then the two of them start talking about the marina and bar, meanwhile I'm sitting here absolutely fucking shell shocked.

I look over at Gavin and he shakes his head.

"You can't be that surprised can you?" he asks and I just blink at him as he reaches across my waist and buckles my seat belt.

The captain lets us know that we're headed to the runway and all I can do is stare at Gavin and wonder if this trip is going to be an even bigger clusterfuck than I realized.

Gavin

Bahama Disaster

ON OUR WAY to the plane probably wasn't the best time to drop that bomb, but I just couldn't hold it back anymore.

After that morning in the kitchen, I just knew I couldn't hold back anymore, and I took a risk. She was either going to pull away and tell me that we were just friends, or she was going to get on this plane ride with my family and suffer because we're so much more than friends.

She got on the plane and I'm feeling smug about it.

We're in the air, and I can tell she wants to ask me a million questions, but with my dad sitting across from us, she bounces her leg instead. Ben is making the same exact motion across from us and I hold back a smirk.

I unbuckle my seat.

"Where are you going?" Kate asks.

"Bathroom, be right back," I tell her.

Except when I get to the lav door, Ben's pushing me inside and locking us in there together.

"What the fuck was that? We didn't discuss this," Ben says,

running a hand through his hair that's just slightly longer than mine at the moment.

"She got on the plane, Ben."

"Okay, and?"

"I told her we weren't just friends, and she got on the plane. She feels the same way," I say, and my brother blinks at me.

He rubs the back of his neck, looking at the door and back to me.

"She got on the plane," he says in awe.

"She got on the fucking plane. She's probably talking to dad about the parallels of fine art and architecture right now. The fact she agreed to come in the first place. She feels the same about us."

"Well, you," Ben says.

I roll my eyes. "Shut up. You're the one who got her to agree to come. Don't be obtuse. We're a package deal. She knows that."

He takes a deep breath. "She's probably freaking out."

"Oh, she's definitely freaking the fuck out. Tonight, after dinner, we can get away from the family. We'll lay all our cards out for her."

"So your plan is to trap her on an island to tell her you have feelings for her and she has nowhere to run," Ben says.

"Exactly."

He rubs between his eyebrows. "What if...what if she has feelings but doesn't want to publicly be in a relationship with us?" I ask.

It's no doubt something I've considered. Kate has a job that's important to her. She presents herself in a way that she cares what other people think.

"We could pretend to be one person again," I say and my brother punches my arm. "Ow, fucker. Fine. But that's just something we'll have to talk to her about. I can't keep doing this."

"Me either. But what if we lose her?" Ben asks, his face softening and I shake my head.

"Then we'll have to convince her. We're Carlsons. When we know someone is the one, we don't stop till they're ours. And Kate? She's ours."

Ben takes a deep breath, nodding his agreement. "Then let's get through this weekend. It's either going to be the best or most awkward family vacation ever."

"I do actually have to piss, if you don't mind," I say, and he rolls his eyes before leaving the bathroom.

While he's gone, I mentally prepare myself for what Kate has to say about my declaration. She got on the plane, I remind myself. No matter what she says, she got on the fucking plane.

❦ ❦ ❦

KATE IS jittery the entire party van ride to the house, and part of me feels guilty. Then there's a sick part of me that enjoys seeing her squirm.

Because she's made me crawl out of my skin more than once over the last six months. She left an impression on me that night at the bar and it's never gone away. She's only dug deeper, imprinting herself under my skin and not leaving. I tried to fight it, maybe not hard enough, but I just couldn't take it anymore.

I couldn't pretend that I wasn't obsessed with her, that I didn't want to take care of her, that I didn't want her around me all the time. It's a completely new feeling, and it scared the absolute shit out of me. But watching her slowly disassociate herself from our lives was an even worse thought.

So, for the first time in my life, I've been vulnerable with a woman and I'm terrified about how it's going to turn out.

Granted, I didn't tell her the exact extent of my feelings, but I'm going to the moment we're alone.

So, in true me fashion, I make sure we're not alone to the very last second, starting with a family dinner prepared by the chef we always use on the island.

We're walking up to the house, and Kate looks in awe as she takes in the home, though she's still nervous. Not that I did anything to help on that front.

"Kate, I'm so sorry we didn't get a chance to speak on the plane. We're so excited to have you. I hope you don't have any allergies or foods to avoid?" my mother asks her.

"No, not at all. I'm sure everything will be delicious. Thank you again for inviting me."

"Of course, it's just silly that my sons felt the need to stay elsewhere," she says, giving me a pointed look. I in return just blink at my mother, who rolls her eyes. "You'll have to tell me how you met my boys. You're the first girl they've ever brought on vacation," she redirects to Kate.

Kate coughs into her fist.

"Right. Um, I met them at the marina one night when I was out with my friends," she half lies.

"Oh, we're just so proud of them. All our sons, really. Do you have family back in Tampa?"

"Mom," I complain. "Why don't we sit down for dinner before you grill her with eight hundred questions," I say, placing a hand on Kate's back and leading her inside the house toward the dinner table.

She sits between me and Ben at the table and I really should've prepared her for how off the rails family dinners can get, but Lincoln beats me to it.

"It's great to see you again, Kate. So, which one of my

brothers captured your full attention to have you join us on family vacation?"

Kate had her glass of water pressed against her lips, but stops, staring at my older dickhead brother, before glancing at Ben and then me.

"So, what's for dinner?" I interject, wishing I could kick the shit out of Lincoln's shin under the table.

"Lobster risotto, for a starter," Chef says, giving Kate a slight reprieve.

This family hasn't had anyone new to harass since Jessa joined the family, and it shows. They all seem like eager sharks, ready to pounce at the first sight of blood. Maybe this was an absolutely horrible fucking idea. Yet...having someone I care about at the family dinner table for a change feels right.

No matter how invasive and ridiculous my family can be, I love them more than anything and it feels right having Kate here.

We're all presented with our food, which is fantastic as always.

"This is amazing, thank you," Kate directs to the chef and our mother.

"Chef always does an amazing job. I'm just happy to have one of the empty seats at the table filled. Going back to Lincoln's question, so you're all just friends?" my mom asks.

Kate's cheeks are bright fucking pink as she clears her throat.

"If you'll excuse me. Where's the restroom?" she directs the question at my mother, who points down the hall.

Kate places her napkin politely on the table, looking down at the floor as she scurries away to the bathroom.

"What the fuck is wrong with you all?" I ask collectively to the table.

Lincoln rolls his eyes. "Oh, please. This is on you. Why did you invite her if—"

"Please, just stop being a dick," I say, pointing at him.

"Dick," Brynn repeats in her seat next to her mother, happily eating her risotto.

"We really have to work on the bad language," my aunt Holly says from the side of the table.

"Well, if everyone would f-u-c-k-ing stop cursing," Penny hisses under her breath.

My mother clears her throat. "Are...are things more complicated with Kate?" she asks, glancing between me and Ben.

"Mom," Ben whines and she throws her hands up.

"Listen. We love you no matter what."

"Yeah, I mean look at Lincoln," Aiden says, speaking for the first time since sitting down.

I rub my temples and sigh. "If everyone in this family could just be friendly to Kate, not scare her off and just be polite, I would appreciate it."

"But..." my mom says. I know she doesn't like my non answer.

"As soon as I know where we stand with Kate, I'll let you know," I reply, leaving it at that.

It's not a shock to my brothers or their wives, and also not surprising to my parents or aunt and uncle?

"You boys always did do everything together," my dad says unhelpfully.

Everyone at the table is snickering and laughing under their breath as I run a hand through my hair.

"Can you go make sure she's okay?" I ask Ben.

He swallows thickly but nods. He's better with comfort, with smoothing things over, and I know he'll be able to calm her nerves better than I will.

"Now, when she get's back, everyone is to be on their best fucking behavior, got it?"

"Fuck," Brynn whispers under her little toddler breath, and I get a sick little sense of satisfaction when Lincoln seems slightly irritated.

Serves him right.

I take another bite of my food and wonder if I could have fucked up any worse than I already have.

This is a disaster of a family vacation.

Kate

Double Your Standards

AM I having a breakdown in this bathroom that looked like the beach threw up in it? Yes?

How the hell am I supposed to go out there and show my face when their mother just politely asked me if I'm fucking both of her sons. The answer? Yes, clearly I'm fucking them both, but are we more?

I'll just die in this bathroom. At least there's pretty baskets full of shells for me to admire in my last moments.

Here lies Doctor Katherine Janette Morley, cause of death? Embarrassment mixed with confusion.

Why...why the fuck did I agree to come on this trip? Part of it was post-pegging bliss with Ben and how sweetly he asked, in combination with the tender sex I had with Gavin when he initially asked me to go.

When I pulled away from the situation, my plan was to take a step back and just accept that this could never be anything more than it ever was. And then...then I gave in, because I didn't want this to end. Then Gavin shocks me on the way here, saying we're not just friends and then his mother asks me which one of her sons I'm fucking.

What a complete nightmare.

I'm scrolling on my phone, seeing when the earliest flight out of paradise is when there's a little tapping of knuckles against the door.

"Kate, can I come in?" he asks.

I know it's Ben, because Gavin wouldn't have asked.

I take a deep breath, cracking the door open, and go back to sitting on top of the closed toilet seat.

"You okay?" he asks, getting down on his haunches and rubbing my thighs.

"I shouldn't have come, Ben. This is...it's too much."

"My family or what Gavin said?" he asks, and I search his face before looking away.

"I don't know, both."

"If it's about my family, that's just how we express our love by giving each other shit. My parents aren't blind and they aren't judgmental. Even if I want to slap Lincoln right now, I really owe him a thank you for breaking them in when it comes to out of the box relationship dynamics."

I clear my throat and look at him. "And what Gavin said?"

"I don't know if talking about how I feel about you in the powder room is the best place, but I feel the same, Kate. You haven't been just my friend for a long time. Is...do you not feel the same?" he asks, so softly if I wasn't so intently watching him speak, I'm not sure I would have heard it.

I immediately run my hand through his hair before cupping his jaw.

"No, you're right, we haven't been just friends for a long time."

He takes a deep breath of relief, nuzzling against my hand and squeezing my thighs tighter.

"Are you worried about what my family thinks, about what other people will think?"

I know my face is flushed; I hate admitting that I care what people think and instead of saying anything out loud, I just nod.

"Alright, well, I think that's something we can work through, if you're willing."

Am I willing? The answer is a resounding yes. No one has ever made me feel the way these two do. I know Savannah and Chelsea won't be going anywhere, so I shouldn't give a shit about people who don't affect my daily life.

"Now, what do you say we get out of this bathroom and get back to dinner? Gavin and I will protect you from our family," he says, and I squint at him. I'm not sure there's a human shield large enough to protect me from the Carlson family.

I put my hand in his, and it feels like I'm taking the biggest leap in this relationship. There's still so much more to be said between the three of us, but if I want this to work, I'm going to have to put this fear to the side.

There's not only the fear of what people will think, but also the fear that by giving my heart to both of them, if they break it, I don't think I'll ever be able to piece myself back together. Deep down I know the fracture they would cause would be twenty times worse than the scars Will left behind. If I fully commit myself to them, they truly have the power to destroy me.

It's a horrifying notion, but the way Ben's warm hand holds mine, and the soft press of his lips at the crown of my head soothes me, I know they're worth the risk.

I said I wanted to live my life and I thought that exploring my sexuality was the way to do that. In a way it was, it led me to Ben and Gavin. But truly living feels like taking the risks, loving myself and opening myself up to loving others. I owe it to myself to try.

So even though I'm dreading the conversation at the dinner table, I take each step against the dark hardwood floors until I'm back in my seat. Polite smiles are directed at me, and Gavin's hand lands on my lap, giving my thigh a reassuring squeeze.

"So what's the plan for tomorrow?" Gavin says, acting like I didn't have a complete melt down during dinner.

"Steve's going to take us out for a catamaran and snorkel," his dad says excitedly. "I was thinking about taking the spear fishing equipment. What do you think?"

"I think you're sixty-eight years old and taking a weapon on a rocky vessel is a dumb fucking idea," his wife snaps back and I smile.

"Damn, Maggie, can't a retired man enjoy his life?" he says back.

"Yeah, only if he's still alive to live it. No spearfishing."

The older man grumbles as Aiden and Jessa talk about the snorkeling equipment and Lincoln worries about the safety of his children on the catamaran. The chatter is loud and animated and even though I ran away from this earlier, it fills a hole in my chest. I instinctively knew this part of me was missing, but seeing it laid out at a table makes it so clear.

I've missed the banter of a family. Sure, growing up when it was me and my parents, it was quiet, but we still had our moments where we were the ideal family unit. Then there was aunt Helene, and we were a family of two, but the sense of community and comradery that came along with being her niece was visceral. When I married Will and his family became mine. That one was the most contentious out of the three, but it was still a family. There were inside jokes, memories, and laughter that connected us all.

It's been years, Chelsea and Savannah have been my family, which I couldn't be more grateful for, but this feels like a different sense of the word.

"You know, I was thinking about spearfishing tomorrow. Maybe dad can just so happen to watch while I'm doing it," Ben says, his arm resting on the back of my chair.

"Benjamin, don't you start with me," his mother Maggie says.

"What?" Ben says innocently.

"Don't *what* me. Don't encourage him."

"Just what we need, my children watching their grandpa get stabbed in the chest with a fish spear on our dangerous family excursion," Lincoln deadpans across the table.

"That's enough talk of fish spears. They're banned from the catamaran. The picnic and drinks will be packed in the morning. Kate, do you have any drinking preferences?"

I shake my head, realizing I'm now part of the conversation.

"Nope, I like everything."

"She sure does," Lincoln whispers, and his wife clearly steps on his toe as he nearly jumps out of his seat.

I smirk to myself. Maybe I made the right decision to stay after all.

🐚 🐚 🐚

I DON'T GET a moment with Gavin alone, and that brief conversation with Ben in the bathroom was hardly enough to put me at complete ease.

Luckily, though, it's just seven of us out on the beach now. Gavin and Aiden are getting the fire going as I sit with Jessa in beach chairs, my feet buried in the sand, waiting for Ben, Penny, and Lincoln to come back with drinks and snacks.

"You hanging in all right?" Jessa sweetly asks.

"Yeah, I think so?" I reply, it's more of a question because truly I'm not sure.

I mean logistically, I'm alive and not running away. But mentally my head is still a mess trying to figure out how the rest of this weekend is going to go, let alone what life looks like when we're back in Tampa.

"You know, I met the family on a trip to the vacation house, too. I like to think of it like a Band-Aid. You get it over with and then they become your family right away," she says, her dark brown hair flying around her face from the sharp breeze flying over the waves.

I take a deep breath and appreciate her words. The idea of also inheriting a family along with letting myself really fall for Gavin and Ben is an enticing thought.

I may ogle Gavin as he stands next to his brother, joking and laughing while discussing the best way to start a beach fire.

Jessa clears her throat. "If you don't want to talk about it, it's fine. Aiden told me you've been having problems with your ex and, well, I've been there if there's someone you want to talk to, someone who can understand the betrayal."

I blink and turn and look at her. It feels wrong to unload on a somewhat stranger. But when I'm around Jessa and Penny, I feel like I do around Savannah and Chelsea. It's a sense of ease and trust. That I can be myself without judgment.

"How did you stop worrying about getting your heart broken again?" I ask, low enough that I know Gavin wouldn't hear.

Jessa nods a few times, like she's curating the perfect answer.

"It's difficult giving yourself to someone when you've been hurt before. When I met Aiden, I had this crush and, of course, I was attracted to him. Then the more I got to know him, the more I realized how gentle and kind he was. I knew that even if I gave him my heart, even if we didn't end up together forever, he would always treat me with kindness. But lucky for me it worked out and I never have to think about that again. Aiden is my person."

"I thought Will was a good person. I'm still not sure how we wound up here. I'm afraid that if I let them in, the same will happen. That it will be good at first and then at some point, the same thing happens. We stop caring and fall into these routines we can't get out of. That the person who was once my world becomes the person who hurts me the most," I say, not knowing why I'm getting so deep with her, but I need someone to talk to or I'm going to lose my mind.

Jessa taps my hand. "Maybe it's time to double your standards, literally." She laughs. "Gavin and Ben aren't Will. Do they do any of the things that your ex would do?"

"No," I shake my head. "I couldn't see them going and getting another woman pregnant or staying with me out of duty. I also definitely don't see them harassing me over company shares, so there's that."

Jessa blinks at me. "Oh, Kate, we have way more in common than you can imagine."

She tells me about her father, and how he was never in her life but gave her shares of his company when he passed. Her half-brother couldn't stand it thinking the shares all belonged to him. The relationship between her half-brother got so bad that she sold her shares to Aiden, making him the biggest share owner and him taking over the business and buying her brother out completely. She doesn't talk to her half-brother anymore, but it seems like he took that money and found something he enjoyed versus the obligation of continuing his father's legacy. It's wild seeing how different and similar we are.

We make sure to exchange phone numbers, and I do the

same when Penny comes back to the beach holding a basket full of supplies to make s'mores, while Lincoln and Ben are carrying the cooler.

Ben brings me a seltzer of some sort and leans over the back of the chair, wrapping his arms around my collarbone.

"You doing okay?" he asks with a kiss to my cheek.

"Yeah, I think I'm going to be fine," I say, and I actually mean it.

Gavin

Confessions of an Emotionally Stunted Twin

I'M MAYBE STALLING the inevitable in talking through everything with Kate and Ben, but sue me.

It's not like I'm scared to talk about my feelings, it's just... well, yeah I'm fucking scared.

She's still here, joking with my family, smiling and drinking a fruity canned drink. She didn't run away. She could be back in Tampa by now, but she's still here, and that's all I need.

I think I've been hiding this sense of anxiety that fills me on a nearly daily basis. But when I'm with Kate, it quiets. I'm not sure how to tell her that without sounding insane. Or asking her to be with me and my brother—openly in front of the world. She's been through so fucking much and I'm not sure if what I want to ask is even feasible.

She's sitting across from me at the bonfire and she tilts her head, staring at me, before standing up and dusting off her legs.

"Gavin, can we take a walk?" she says.

"Ooo, someones in trouble," Lincoln sing-songs and Ben smacks him in the chest.

She glances over at my brother, and even though I can't see her face, I just know she's reassuring him as she grabs my hand, interlacing our fingers and we begin walking down the shoreline. Warm gentle waves caress my feet as my toes dig into the sand with each step, and we don't speak until the laughter of my family is far behind us.

"So," she says.

"So."

She squeezes my hand and turns to face me. The moonlight kisses her feminine features as she stares at me. Her thumb rubs over my knuckles.

"We're not just friends?" she asks, a small smile appearing on her face.

"No. We're not just friends."

"What does that make us then? What does this mean to you?"

I run my free hand through my hair and try to take a moment to collect my thoughts, unfortunately none of the eloquent words I want to say slip out of my mouth.

"It means I fucking love you, okay?"

She blinks at me a few times, shock taking over her features, before she tilts her head back up to look at me. Her eyes are crystalline as the Caribbean sea as she stares at me.

"You love me?"

"Yeah. I...God, I've never done this before, okay?"

She grabs my other forearm so that both of my hands are in hers and I can't fidget.

"What does love mean to you?" she asks.

I wonder when she became a shrink, and I think about saying that, but that would be the part of me that self-sabotages things speaking.

"It means I hate when you're not around. It means that

when you're with me I feel calm. The only other person who ever makes me feel that way is Ben, but it's different with you. I want to tell you my secrets, I want to share my day with you, and I want to learn more about art from you. You're beautiful and smart, and fucking complicated, but I like that. I was happy being single, beyond content with it, but the thought of being single and not having you in my life makes me feel like shit. The idea of you just thinking you're our friend, of just thinking of me as a friend makes me want to scream. You're not my fucking friend, you're so much more and I wanted to wait and make sure that it was something you wanted before I said anything. But I knew that if I came here without you the whole time, I would be wondering what you were doing back home and if you were missing me too."

I take a deep breath, realizing I absolutely spilled my guts to her, and look down. A small tear falls down her cheek, and I use the back of my knuckles to wipe it away.

"I love you too and it also scares the shit out of me," she says and it feels like I can exhale, like this fear I've been holding on to is washed away and I don't have to worry anymore.

Instead, I grab both sides of Kate's face and lean down so I can kiss her frantically.

She returns my kiss tenfold and I know without a doubt I've never felt a kiss like this. I didn't know a kiss could feel like this, all the emotion of us spilling our feelings is wrapped up in this one press of our lips.

Her arms wrap around my neck and I slide mine down to her waist, lifting her off the ground and kissing her passionately.

We part from the kiss, our chests rising and falling as she hugs me and I hug her back.

"I'm scared that you two could break me worse than Will ever could. Please don't break me, Gavin."

"I won't," I tell her honestly.

Now that I have her in my arms, now that I know she feels the same, I'm never letting her go. Nothing will ever be this good, ever.

"I'm scared of what people will think."

"My family will accept us. Your friends will. Fuck what anyone else thinks," I say.

She nods against my neck. "I'll try. For you and Ben, I'll try."

I place her down on the ground, leaning forward and kissing her again, before we part and stare at each other.

"What does this mean when we go back home?" she asks, biting her lip.

In the bedroom, I have no issue with taking control, setting the stage. Usually in life I don't either, but navigating this relationship feels different.

"We make our own rules. We do what feels right. Our agreement was exclusive. Things stay that way. We take you on more dates for sure. We have more sleepovers, and no more of this *just friends* bullshit."

She smiles, grabbing my hand and squeezing.

"I can do that. Yeah, I can definitely do that," she says, her head leaning on my shoulder as the beacon of the fire leads us back to my brothers.

My chest feels lighter. This lie no longer looming over me as I wrap an arm around my girlfriend's shoulder and we drink way too much and I can't control the grin on my face as we stumble back to the house as the night comes to a close.

Kate's hands are gripping both mine and Ben's shirts as she pulls me down for a kiss and then does the same with Ben.

"I'm a lucky lady," she says, pure happiness radiating off of her. I feel guilty she hasn't had a chance to really sit down and talk with Ben, but it seems like she's ready to talk with her body. "I need you both so bad."

"What do you want?" I ask her as Ben starts kissing his way down her collarbone.

"Both of you," she whispers out and I shake my head, grabbing her jaw and kissing her.

"Gonna need more time for that," I tell her, plus I'll need her not to be drinking and love drunk when we both take her at the same time. "You want to be fucked so good you don't even know what the word friends even means?" I ask, tugging on her hair and exposing her throat more for Ben.

"Fuck yes."

"Then get on your back, Katherine. We're gonna fuck that word out of you," I tell her and she complies as we do just that.

The term friends with benefits gets completely fucked out of all of our systems.

🦢 🦢 🦢

"KATE," I whisper, attempting to wake her up.

We stayed up too late fucking, even my thighs are sore. So much for renting a condo, hopefully no one in the family heard the noises coming out of our room last night.

Ben is pouting in the corner. Mostly because everything is settled with me and Kate and he hasn't gotten to say his peace just yet.

"I'm sorry. You have all today," I tell him.

"Kate, baby, you gotta wake up or we're going to miss the boat," I say, ignoring my brother's petulance.

"Ugh. The boat," she moans into the pillow.

I slap her ass, which just makes her groan even more. "I've

got ginger ale and motion sickness patches for you, just in case."

She lifts up from the pillow, her eyes slightly puffy as she looks around.

"Where are we?"

"My parents' place. We didn't make it over to the condo."

"Oh god," she groans. "Five minutes," she whispers as she gets ready for the boat ride.

She puts on a bathing suit, puts on an insane amount of sunscreen and wears a long sleeve flowy cover up and pants, along with a massive sun hat and sunglasses.

When she comes out of the bedroom, she places a hand on her hip.

"What?"

"Nothing. You're just fully protected from the sun."

"Yes, as you two will be. Prepare to be sick of me when it comes to SPF. Ben, come here," she says.

My brother hops out of his chair like his ass is on fire as she has him sit on the edge of the bed. She smooths sunscreen on his face like he's a child and I can't help but grin as I watch.

"Oh, don't think you're not going to get the same treatment in a few minutes," she says, as she makes sure my brother's ears are coated as well as the back of his neck.

"It's nice," Ben says, shutting his eyes, letting Kate do whatever she wants to him.

"See, Ben is such a good boy," she jokes.

"Do we really need to go on the boat? We could just stay in all day," Ben says, his hands lightly gripping the back of Kate's thighs.

"You know, that's a good idea."

"Nope. We're going on the boat. Sunscreen me up and let's go. I don't want to spend the next four months hearing every Sunday how we hid Kate away from the family and didn't participate," I say, knowing my family way too damn well.

Skipping out on a family activity is a sure fire way to have my mom up my ass, and she's already going to be with her interest in Kate.

"I hate to admit it, but he's right," Ben grumbles as we switch places and she lathers me up. I won't admit it, but it does feel kind of nice.

"Alright, now where do we need to go to catch this boat?" Kate questions as we climb down the deck and I point out to the ocean, where a catamaran is anchored in the distance.

"Uh?"

Ben laughs, grabbing her hand. "There's a tender to take us there," he says, as we walk in the previously made footprints in the sand and climb into the dingy.

Kate holds on to her sun hat as the small boat whips across the water to the back of the catamaran.

I get out first, helping Kate up the ladder, and my brother follows suit.

The second we're on deck, my mother is ushering us over to the table and plying us with fruit enhanced water and nearly forcing us to eat a solid breakfast.

"I don't need anyone passing out on the boat. Don't think I didn't hear you and your brothers stumbling into the house well past midnight," she scolds with no heat.

There's a lot I could say for my family, that they're loud and invasive as fuck. But truthfully, I couldn't be anymore grateful for the parents and siblings I have. I love them and I love Kate. Part of me can't believe I still said it to her, that I said it to anyone.

There must be a stupid, not usually present smile on my face, because my mother stares at me, her eyes hidden behind sunglasses, but I can feel her happiness radiating through her.

She's happy because she can feel my joy and that joy is in the form of the woman who's covered every inch of her skin away from the sun, and my twin brother who helped me build the life I have today.

Maybe it's a vacation bubble, or possibly I'm still living off the high of finally saying those three words, but the smile stays on my face for the rest of the evening as I spend the day with the people who mean the most to me in the entire world.

Kate

Bliss & Blackmail

GAVIN AND BEN'S DAD, in fact, brought a spearfishing kit.

The guys are all in the water playing with their very dangerous toy. Maggie is yelling over the edge to make sure no one dies, along with her sister Holly. Penny and Jessa are getting the kids situated in life jackets as our captain sets up this insane inflatable dock that has a net for the kids to swim in.

I take a moment of reprieve, grabbing a pillow, my book, and towel, and go to the front of the catamaran, lying down on the net. The Caribbean breeze hits from the bottom, as I just take a few moments away from the madness.

The Carlson family is filled with life and excitement, but it's been forever since I've been around a big family like this, plus, I may be slightly hungover from the night before.

I have a thin beach towel over my face, lying on my back, considering taking a nap or reading my book, as a throat clears and the net jiggles with someone's weight.

"Any room under the towel for me?" Ben says.

His body is glistening with salt water, and it drips in rivulets down his chest and abdomen.

"There's always room for you, Ben," I say.

He grins, lying his wet body next to mine, placing his wet hair on my chest, making me laugh.

"No casualties with the spearfishing?"

"Just everyone's ego, because we can't catch shit," he says, adjusting his body so that his head is next to mine.

The towel makes us feel like we're in our own little world as he looks at me. I cup his face, rubbing my thumb against the warmth of his sun-kissed skin.

"I love you, Ben," I tell him plainly, knowing he needs me to say it.

Him and Gavin are different and have such different needs, while also giving so much that I need in return.

Ben takes a deep breath, kissing my wrist and soaking it in for a moment.

"I love you so much, Kate. I know you're scared. Fuck, I'm scared too. But I think we could make this work."

"I want to. More than anything," I assure him.

"Whatever speed works for you, whatever you need," he says, his hand placed over mine.

"Right now, all I need is you and Gavin, everything outside of that we can figure out together," I say honestly.

I lean forward, kissing his lips tenderly. It's always soft and delicate with Ben and I treasure it. I treasure him.

He's everything I didn't know what I needed and wanted in a man. Ben's opened my eyes to so many things, not even just what we've done behind closed doors. I never knew I needed a kind, soft man in my life, that I would yearn for gentleness and effortless companionship.

I'm the luckiest woman in the world to have found the best of both worlds. I didn't walk into Avalon with anything besides a list and motivation to explore my sexual boundaries, but I came out with so much more.

The kiss with Ben gets heated, and both of my hands are on his face, hoping that my kiss says everything I'm thinking. That he's worth it, that this is real, and I'm not letting him go.

He's holding me tightly too, as the towel covering us flies away with a gust of wind. Exposing our moment to his entire family.

There's a loud whistle as we part, and I use my book to cover my face.

Ben grabs the book, his honest gaze meeting mine.

"No more hiding, right?"

I take a deep breath and run my hand through his salty, wet hair.

"Yeah, no more hiding."

He leans down, kissing me one last time, and I'm fully aware that his family is watching. I let myself live in the moment, hoping that they accept this relationship, but deep down, knowing that it doesn't matter.

As long as Ben, Gavin, and I accept what we have, that's all that matters.

We part from the kiss, and the grin on Ben's face is contagious. It's reassuring that I'm doing the right thing. A large shadow creeps over us, and it's a dripping wet, very happy Gavin in all his glory.

He shakes his wet hair at us and I can't deny that the water feels good on my hot skin.

"So, everyone saw you making out. What do you have to say for yourselves?" Gavin jests.

"Hmm...that this is turning out to be a very good vacation?" I say, scrunching my nose.

"Well, it isn't a vacation unless you get into the water," Gavin says and Ben agrees, nodding his head frantically.

I arch an eyebrow at each of them.

"Pretty please get in the water with me, Kate?" he asks, looking too fucking cute for his own good.

"Fine," I agree, as he helps me off the netting, where I take off all my sun clothes and place them in my beach bag.

We go to the port side, Gavin on one side of me and Ben on the other.

"Okay, ready?" Gavin asks, squeezing my hand and I squeeze his back.

"Ready," I agree, as Ben takes my other hand and we jump into the water, a very girly squeal may or may not have escaped me on the way down.

The warm salty water hits my skin in a rush as we swim to the surface and I laugh, my face tilting up as I let the sun glisten against my face. It feels like my life, finally taking that leap of faith and knowing the end result, is going to bring me more happiness.

Gavin resurfaces last, and he looks lighter too. He's smiling more, I realize. The man who used to be mainly smirks and so hard to read looks happy.

It's a visceral feeling of pressure and joy knowing that I'm the reason he feels that way.

"So, we should probably sneak off back to the beach and fuck all day," Gavin suggests.

I splash him, and he avoids my assault, scoop me into his arms. Ben floats right next to us.

"So, we're all in?" he asks.

"We're all in," I repeat, and kiss him too, not caring who's watching. "Now, how do we get back to the condo to show you just how all in I want to be?" I ask, feeling like a sex-crazed delinquent with how bad I need both of them constantly.

🐚 🐚 🐚

IT WAS a long day on the water, a joyous one, but a tiring one nonetheless. We didn't even bother using the condo Gavin rented; we stayed at their family's place and I just pray we've been quiet enough with our extracurricular activities no one noticed how often we snuck away.

I showered and got dressed for dinner. We have plans to go to their favorite island bar tonight, so the lightweight floral dress works for both occasions. I know when we fly home tomorrow night I'm going to be exhausted to teach on Tuesday, but it feels worth it, so fucking worth it.

Ben's in the shower and Gavin's helping his dad with something around the house, so I wander into the living room. Maggie is there, brushing Brynn's hair and I almost back out of the room and hope she doesn't see me as Brynn holds up her hand.

"Hi, Kate!"

She's lucky she's cute, because she totally just blew my cover.

"Come take a seat, dinner should be ready soon," Maggie says, and I do, taking a seat on the opposite couch, shoving my hands between my thighs and doing my best to not bounce my legs or play with my hair. "You don't have to be nervous."

I fail at not letting my nerves get the best of me, my leg bouncing frantically and I'm a little lost for words.

Maggie continues to do Brynn's hair as she speaks, putting it in two little braids. Brynn is watching a kid's show on her tablet, zoned out as Maggie's soft eyes meet mine.

"We raised our boys to not let anything ever hold them back. We taught them they could be anything they wanted to be. I pride myself on raising them right in knowing that the world isn't black and white and to not always adhere to what society tells you is right or wrong."

"You've raised great sons," I say, wondering where the

conversation is going. Ben told me they would be accepting, but I thought it would be like Will's family where people gossip behind your back, but in the end, deal with whatever fractures there are in the family.

"Gavin and Benjamin were the easiest and toughest in a way. They were always together, literally inseparable. They tried to put them in different classrooms and they would act out until one of them got switched. I didn't have to worry about them as much, because they, no matter what, always had each other to fall back on. Similar and different in so many ways."

"I can definitely see that," I say with a nod and a smile.

"The one thing any mother wants for her children is for them to be happy. While I always knew they had each other, I worried that they wouldn't have more. That their codependency would stop them from ever seeking something beyond their tight sibling companionship. I may not fully understand your relationship, but you make them happy and that's all I care about. You're not being judged here. Who am I to judge the woman who has my sons so happy? You're welcome here, and you're family if you want to be," she says.

I realize then I'm holding back tears. She's finished with Brynn's hair, the little girl scurrying away as Maggie and I stand. She surprises me by taking a few steps and opening her arms to me. I accept her hug and take a deep breath.

I try to remember the last time I've been hugged like this and I think of Aunt Helene. I know she's smiling at me wherever she is, as I hug this woman back.

Acceptance, happiness, and family were all I ever wanted and in a blink of an eye I have it all.

THE BEACH BAR is a bit of a hole in the wall, but it's cozy and the margaritas are fantastic. There's a man in the corner playing acoustic guitar and singing while people dance and drink.

I feel so fucking light.

I'm sipping on the straw, letting the tequila hit my bloodstream. Gavin's hand is on the back of my chair and Ben's side is glued to mine as the siblings tell all the stories of what exactly has gone down in this bar.

"I don't think I have to tell you what whores these two used to be," Penny jokes, pointing to the twins.

"Nope, you don't," Gavin says with a glare.

"Gosh, it feels so good being able to dish it back, doesn't it, honey?" Lincoln says, and Ben groans next to me.

"Can we maybe make a truce?" Ben suggests.

"Hell no," Lincoln says.

"It's really difficult to be the most normal person in this family," Aiden says with a smirk.

"Do you really want to go there?" Gavin questions as my phone frantically buzzes in my purse. I ignore it, but it just keeps sounding off to the point where I roll my eyes and pull it out. It's an unknown number and I worry it's something for work.

"I'm going to go take this really quick," I announce, holding up my phone and walking toward the beach. I'm still within sight of the table as I answer the phone.

"This is Dr. Morley," I say.

"Check your email. Deadline is one week from today," the deep voice says, before the line goes dead.

I swallow thickly as I glance down at my phone. My brows furrow and I scroll over to my email.

It's some ridiculous account with letters and numbers and with my stomach churning I open the email.

Kate,

Do the right thing, or everything gets leaked. I don't think the university would appreciate a deviant on staff.

Beneath the email is a link that I'm probably an idiot to click, but it's from a standard file transfer site. My mouth drops as I look at all the contents in the file. My payments to Avalon, Gavin and Ben coming to my house, me dancing with Gavin and Ben at their grand opening.

What's worse is all the other images of the other conquests I had prior to meeting Ben and Gavin are there as well. The images make me feel sick. But what's truly making me feel disgusted is the fact that Will has been watching me this long, that he's been invading my privacy for far longer than I imagined.

There's no signature on the email, but it's clear who it is. Part of me wants to act impulsively. But then that deep-rooted part of me that hates this motherfucker has me working through the best way to make my payback hurt.

My heart is racing as I flick through the images again, making my anger simmer even more.

He stole so much of my youth, stole so much of who I am, and he wants to take more? Will is so sure that he knows me, that I care too much about what people think, that I'd give into his demands. But little does he know that Gavin and Ben aren't just some fling and I'm not ashamed of who I love.

My heart is racing and the idea of this honeymoon bubble being popped so fast, having to deal with this fucking blackmail, has me sick to my stomach. But I won't let him bully me, I won't let him take anything else from me. Slowly, piece by piece, a plan forms in my mind, an eerie calm washes over me as I walk back to the table with a mission in mind.

"Everything okay?" Gavin asks as soon as I sit down.

I take a deep breath and face my gaze to Lincoln; he looks confused that my attention is set on him.

"How would you like to be the largest shareholder of Dennis Commercial?" I ask him.

He takes a deep breath, scrubbing his hand over his stubble as he takes in my words.

"Tell me everything," he says, and I place my phone on the table.

I'm ready to take the revenge I'm owed. Will Dennis doesn't know who he fucked with. That weak woman who was on auto-pilot is dead and he's about to face the new and improved Doctor Katherine Morley.

Benjamin

Lights, Camera, Action

LINCOLN AND KATE are listening intently to the lawyers as they discuss everything. Since Kate's the primary shareholder, she should get all financial documents without a problem.

We're just hoping that it doesn't tip Will off. Not knowing what he's capable of, she's living with us, all four cats and all. While Mikey has taken to the change easily, the other three mostly stay hidden around different spots. I don't hate it, and shockingly, neither does Gavin.

I'm not sure if the plan is to just keep her moved in? But I don't hate the idea. In fact, I'm hoping she agrees, whether we move into her place, her into ours, or we find something new that works for all of us. But maybe I'm way ahead of myself, we all just admitted our feelings, that's good enough...for now.

"I knew that prick was hiding something with these lowball bids. He's trying to liquidate the business and get all the proceeds, cutting out all his shareholders completely. He's been buying everyone off over the years." Lincoln questions.

"He used our shared money to buy off the other owners?" Kate asks, and I'm not sure I've seen her so pissed.

"It looks like he's been doing this for the last five years. Slowly taking sums and using it to pay off other shareholders," the lawyer says.

Kate's eyes look watery and she nods her head. "He was probably cheating for that long," she says and I rub her back.

"I still don't understand why he would want to buy my shares," Kate says.

"So that some poor sucker like me will pay him three times the amount to buy out the current contracts he has," Lincoln says, rubbing his chin. "If he's the only shareholder, he doesn't need a yes or no on selling, with you still in the mix he would need your consent to sell and you would get majority proceeds. Why wasn't she notified on the other sales?"

Kate's cheeks go pink. "Carl would send me updates, I just didn't usually read them," she winces.

"I think he was counting on that. I'm sure he thought you would've folded before now and that's why he's resorting to blackmail. He has the most to gain financially if he buys you out first and has a larger competitor buy him out," the lawyer says.

"I bet he thought we would buy for an astronomical price, or maybe another regional builder looking to expand," Lincoln says, looking pissed off.

Kate seems withdrawn, like she's taking all the new information in a haze.

"What about the stalking? What about her safety?" Gavin interrupts, grabbing her hand and squeezing above the table.

There's a second lawyer for this issue as she clears her throat.

"Unfortunately, all the images taken of Ms. Morley were in public spaces. However, we could go down the avenue of a civil lawsuit for extortion and blackmail. It would be a time consuming process and you would be at the helm of public opinion. However with the evidence we have and the current TRO in place I do think we have a case, not a home run of a case, but a case, nonetheless."

"So, he faces no consequences for the mental distress of stalking her."

"That would surely be a part of the lawsuit. We will also contact the police and get a permanent restraining order in place in the meantime," the lawyer says and Gavin huffs, and moves his hand from Kate's to place it on her thigh.

Kate taps her fingers on the table a few times, like she's contemplating her next move.

"What deal would hurt him most?" Kate says, and the lawyer gets a wicked grin on his face.

"A few options here. One is cut and dry, you sell to Mr. Carlson and then he goes to war buying out the rest of Dennis Commercial and will then own the majority share of commercial construction in the area or we could play safe—"

"I want to sell. I'm ready to sell," Kate interrupts.

"Then let's get the paperwork set up and prepare ourselves for the fallout. I think it should take about forty-eight hours to get this processed."

"That's enough time," Kate says with a nod, and I glance over at her in confusion. "Just send me everything I need to sign, and make sure you give him a good deal, he's family, after all," she says, winking at my Lincoln who looks happier than a pig in shit to take down his biggest competition.

"This definitely means we have a truce about talking shit," I say to Lincoln, who rolls his eyes, but waves me off nonetheless. "What do you need forty-eight hours for?" I direct toward Kate

"Are you guys ready to go public, like all the way in?" she asks and my brows furrow.

"Of course."

"All right, then let's head to campus."

⁂

I'M STANDING on the white pedestal in nothing but black boxer briefs as a series of photography students roll into the studio space.

"Oh, my god. Everyone is going to be talking about this photoshoot for years to come. You all look so hot," her friend Savannah gushes as she puts some powder on Kate's face.

"You sure this isn't a bit much?" Gavin asks, readjusting himself.

Kate's wearing a one piece that is slightly sheer around her middle. She looks fucking sexy and I'm a little irritated about everyone seeing how beautiful she is, while also being honored that she cares this much to make a statement.

"I want him to know. I want everyone to know that I don't care what they think. That we're together and it might be different, but it's still beautiful and us and no one can tell us otherwise."

"Stop or else I'm going to get hard," I say, and Kate and Savannah laugh.

"What will the pictures be used for?" Gavin asks.

My brother is asking too many damn questions at this point. Our girl loves us, she's all in and he's worried about semantics.

"Well, it's going to be a learning experience for my students in black and white portraits and I think Kate has something planned," Savannah says, keeping her lips tight.

"Trust me? I mean, I'm trusting you right now," she says with a smirk. Gavin takes a deep breath but gives her a sharp nod.

"Trusting with what?" I ask, and she curls her finger for me to lean down.

"I'm wearing a plug so that I can take you both tonight," she whispers.

So much for not getting hard during the photoshoot. I take a step back, turning away from our incoming audience as I think of horrible boner killer things. It works somewhat, and I'm grateful the boxers are black and tight enough to compress things and hide my potential embarrassment.

"That was mean," I tell her and she smiles.

"Don't worry, you'll be rewarded."

I whisper "evil" under my breath as Savannah claps her hands together.

"Okay. Ugh, you're all so gorgeous. Come here and pose yourselves in whatever feels comfortable while I get the class setup. Maybe you start by sitting, Kate?" she says, and Kate nods.

Kate sits on the small simple stool and I stare at her for a moment, just taking this all in. She wants to make a statement, and I feel overwhelmed with admiration and wonder.

So, I take a seat on the ground, placing her leg in my lap, kissing her calf.

"Hey! I didn't say to start," Savannah chastises, but Kate bites her lip as she looks down at me.

It's not even just the promise of the very dirty things we're going to do together tonight, it's everything. The way she makes me feel, how I've never been happier, how I'm still learning new things. I'd do whatever I need to in order to make her happy.

"Class, welcome. I'm so excited to have this special program for you. I'm sure many of you know Dr. Morley. Her and her boyfriends have graciously donated their time to help you work on your portraits this evening. I expect you to take as many images as possible. You will need to develop and turn in three of your best works within two weeks. I'm looking for four main factors. Quality, positioning, lighting, and emotion.

"The last one shouldn't be a problem with these three, so don't let me down."

There's some mumbling in the classroom, probably trying to dissect our relationship, but I don't give a single fuck.

Bright lights turn on around us, shining out the college students taking our picture as Gavin comes to stand beside Kate, his hand on her chin, forcing her to look up at him, while I kiss her leg.

Shuttering sounds are going off like crazy and somehow, despite the slight nerves of people taking our picture, I feel empowered. It's almost like encapsulating our love frame by frame.

I always admired Kate's passion for art, though I suppose I never understood it. But when I break down what's happening right now, the art that we're making, I finally understand.

What we found is art in itself.

We move positions a few times. One where Kate is standing between the two of us, ones where we're lying down. By the end of the shoot, I almost forget that cameras are flashing and that each moment has been documented.

The lights turn off suddenly, and I'm seeing spots, but then a round of applause rings out in the room and it makes me realize that I wasn't alone in understanding how powerful this moment was.

Savannah comes up to us with tears in her eyes, wrapping her friend in a hug before pulling back.

"Wow. Just wow. Thank you all so much for agreeing to do this. The photos are going to be amazing. I'll send you what I took with the digital camera tonight."

"Thanks, Savannah."

"It's good to see you happy," she says, and they hug again. "Take good care of her, okay?" Savannah says and we both nod at her.

The class is buzzing with excitement from the photoshoot as they funnel out of the room.

"Now please tell me we get to take you home and fuck you," Gavin says bluntly.

Kate bites her lip as I grab her robe, holding it out so she can slide her arms through. I help her put it on and place my hands on her shoulders, my need for her growing with every second.

It's only then I realize we haven't even had sex since vacation, not that it's been a long time. I just crave all the intimacy I can have with Kate.

Is this what being an adult in a relationship feels like?

"Please," she whispers it like a plea.

I'm tossing on my clothes as fast as I can, and so is Gavin.

It feels like we just stamped publicly that we belong to her, and now in the privacy of our home she's going to show us just how deep that devotion goes.

Kate

Sandwiches

WE BARELY EVEN PULL INTO their garage when the back door is swung open and I'm immediately tossed over Gavin's shoulder. His large palm lands on my ass with a thwack, making me moan as the plug shifts.

I thought about not wearing it at the photoshoot, but it felt like an incentive to get Gavin to agree to go in the first place. I haven't told them my big plan, but I'll have them approve it before it's fully public.

Ben's trailing behind us, his grin wide as he follows. Mikey greets him. He's basically his cat now, and I can't even blame the orange traitor.

Gavin carries me down the hall, my hands on his lower back to keep my head from dangling as he plops me down on his bed.

"Fuck. I'm all worked up," Gavin hisses, cupping his cock outside of his pants. He takes a deep breath, running a hand through his hair, while I shift my body so that I'm resting on my elbows.

"What can I do to make it better, sir?" I ask, tilting my head to the side, feeling mischievous.

"Don't push me, Katherine," he says and I bite my lip.

I pat the bed, my gaze meeting Ben's.

"Why don't you take your clothes off and wait till he tells me what to do so I can tell you what to do," I say.

Ben's trying to suppress a laugh as Gavin grabs my ankle and drags me down the bed, making me yelp.

"You're just looking for a red ass, aren't you? Where's my good girl at?" he asks, taunting me right back.

"I want whatever you want, sir," I say.

"Now you want to be sweet for me?" he asks, his thumb rubbing circles on my ankle.

"I always want to be sweet for you."

His rough hands slide up my thighs, making goosebumps pebble along my flesh as he grabs the silk belt of my robe.

"You are, aren't you? Show me how sweet. Take this off," he says, grabbing the lace of the lingerie and pinching it. "Show me where you want me."

"Can you help me get out of it?" I ask, turning on my stomach, his fingers diligently unlatching each hook of the bodysuit. He then tenderly slides each strap off my shoulders before slipping it off my body. I have to adjust my body weight as he slowly shifts it down.

Eventually I'm bare to him, my face pressed against the sheets, with my plugged ass high in the air.

His fingers toy with the flared base, never tugging or shifting the toy, just enough to drive me crazy.

"Did you spend the whole photoshoot picturing what we were going to do afterward? Is that why you looked so fucking hot?"

Instead of words, I just press my ass harder against his hand.

"I think you need to learn a lesson in patience," he says, and I groan.

"Ben, come here," I tell him, and he shifts on the bed.

"No coming. No penetration, not yet," Gavin says, but he doesn't say no to me playing with Ben. I can abide by those rules, while making my own.

"You want to make me feel good, don't you, baby?" I ask him, and he nods eagerly.

He's still in his boxer briefs, not completely naked as I grip his chin and place a delicate kiss against his lips.

"You want me so bad. Tell me how bad."

"So fucking bad. You're going to be so tight," Ben says against my lips.

"Do you think I'm wet enough to take the both of you?"

"Let me make you wetter, please. Let me taste you, let me make your pussy wet so you'll fuck me."

"You'd like that, wouldn't you?" I ask, running my nails through his hair.

"Yes. So much," he says, kissing down my collarbone, licking and caressing my scar.

I adjust the pillows on the bed, lying on my back as Ben kisses down my body. I make eye contact on and off with Gavin as Ben finally makes his way to my pussy. I grip his hair lightly.

"You can't leave my thighs out," I say, noticing he didn't pepper them with kisses.

"Of course not," he agrees with a smile, holding my thigh and kissing the soft flesh.

Gavin is hard to read as he sits on the chair across the room, but I can tell the build of anticipation is making him ravenous.

I truly regret agreeing to the no coming rule as soon as Ben's lips are kissing my mound and his tongue is spreading my lips to lick my clit.

My breathing hitches as Ben licks and sucks, moaning while he does so.

"Have you missed this?"

"So much," he mumbles against my core.

"Is she wet?" Gavin asks from the corner.

"So wet. So good," Ben says, his eyes meeting mine as his lips wrap around my clit and he sucks hard.

My chest rises and falls and I know if he would just slide his fingers inside of me, I'd be close. His tongue is the best torture, as I feel myself getting wetter with the combination of my arousal and his saliva.

"Right there, Ben," I tell him, cupping the back of his head, holding his mouth right where I want him. "Please," I beg, and I can tell Ben wants to give in, that he wants to slip his fingers inside me and curl them in that spot I like while he sucks and licks at my clit.

But I don't even get the chance to tell him what to do as Gavin's hand clamps on his shoulder. Ben pulls away. There's a glistening sheen around Ben's lips that he uses his forearm to wipe away.

"I think she's wet enough. She can come as many times as she wants while we both fill her up. Go lie down on the bed."

Ben follows his directions as Gavin curls a finger at me. Like a moth to flame, I'm crawling across the mattress and kneeling as he tenderly grasps my throat, bringing me in for a rough kiss.

"I want you to go sit on my brother's cock and get used to the stretch of having him and the toy inside of you and make sure it's not too much. Can you do that for me?"

I nod, and he smacks my ass hard. "Yes, sir," I say, correcting myself.

"You'll tell us if it's too much? Don't push your body too far."

"Yes, sir," I reply and he kisses me again as I move over Ben's body, straddling his hips and grinding my pussy along the length of his cock.

His breath hitches and his hands grip my waist.

"You did such a good job making me wet, didn't you? You deserve to be fucked."

"Please," he rasps out, and I can barely take any more waiting as I slide a hand between us, his length tacky with my arousal as I notch him at my entrance and slide down.

My breathing hitches as I slide down, the pressure of having the toy inside of me and his dick is new. Not unwanted, not too much, but I know that when I take Gavin, it will be twice as tight.

Ben's mouth parts with a whoosh of air slipping out of his lips and his hands tighten against my flesh.

"Oh, fuck. I don't know how long I'll last. You're already so tight."

I hold the side of his neck. It's too large for me to even wrap my palm around anyway, but just enough pressure so that he knows I'm in charge.

"You're gonna lie here and let me fuck you. You need me to come first don't you, Ben?"

"Yeah. Yeah, I can…I can do that for you," he says, like he's not sure.

"You're always such a good boy for me. I know you can," I say, placing a kiss on his cheek.

It's then that Gavin is behind me. His fingers toying with the flared base as lube drips along my crack, making the in and out of the plug smoother. He doesn't pull it all the way out, just enough for the largest part to push in and out of me.

I hold on to Ben, my fingers digging into his shoulders as his brother toys with me from behind.

"Ready for more?" Gavin asks.

I look down at Ben who seems skeptical, but he nods.

"Yes, sir," I say as he slowly pulls the toy out of me and I immediately miss the fullness that it provided.

But that feeling doesn't last long as his lubed up cock presses against my hole. The pressure is so tight with Ben already inside of me, but Gavin moves slowly.

"That's it. Fuck, look at you so full," he praises, even though he's barely inside of me. "You were made for this. I always knew it, didn't I? That you were made to be fucked?"

I shiver at the memory of our first night together as he presses further ever so slightly.

Ben's abdomen is tight under me, his fingers digging into my skin as he lets out a suffering moan.

"So tight," Ben rasps out.

"So fucking tight," Gavin parrots, his hand gliding up my spine where he holds the back of my neck so that I'm pressed firmly against Ben's chest.

Gavin decides how fast he moves, how much I can take as he slowly cants his hips. The head of his length teases me, almost slipping out, but he never does. The fullness is intense, bordering on too much, and I hold on to Ben to keep my grip on reality.

"I knew you could take both of us. You were made to be between us. So fucking full of cock, you should always be like this," Gavin says. "Are you ready to take me deeper? You can take it, can't you?"

The words have me relaxing more, and he's able to slide in further, a masculine groan rattling out of his chest.

"Holy fuck," Ben curses beneath of me, his hips slightly shifting upward.

"Not yet," I tell him and he takes a deep breath with a nod.

Before I know it, Gavin's thighs are pressed against my ass cheeks and I'm so deeply full of both of them. The moans that fall out of me are involuntary and loud, but there's no way I could control them.

"Okay. You...you can move," I tell Ben.

The moment I tell him that, both of them are thrusting in and out of me in tandem.

There are moments when I feel so fucking full I could scream and others where they're in sync and I'm filled in one hole and begging for fullness in another.

"Are you going to come from being stuffed with cock, Katherine?" Gavin asks between pants. "I need to feel you gripping both of us."

"Please, Kate. I'm so close," Ben pleads beneath me.

"Okay. Fu...fuck. It's so good," I say while adjusting my position only slightly, making my clit rub against the hair of Ben's pelvis.

As soon as they start thrusting again I know I'm going to fall apart.

There are hands everywhere, on my waist, on my neck, on my ass. I'm full to the hilt and the sensation feels almost other-worldly. For a moment, it's like my mind completely shuts off and all I feel is my body.

Euphoria floods me as I crest the wave of my orgasm that boards on pain as my pussy clenches around Ben.

His breath hitches and I'm probably holding on to him too tight, but I can't help myself, not as I let my body shatter at their hands, a gush of fluid making the friction between me and Ben wetter as Gavin fucks into me harder.

Ben is frantically fucking me from below as I shudder from my release, moaning loudly into his ear, whimpers falling out of him as he floods me with his cum.

"Fuck. That's it, beautiful. There's my good girl," Gavin says behind me, before he pulls out.

Suddenly the emptiness has me going boneless over Ben's

body. Gavin spreads me wide as he pants, shooting ropes of cum against my asshole.

Ben holds me against his chest as I take in everything that just happened.

Who would have thought my post-divorce sexual exploration would have led me to be sandwiched between two men I've fallen desperately in love with?

I can't help but laugh at the thought.

"Did we break her?" Ben says, and I laugh even harder, and he winces at the feeling of me clenching around him. I show him mercy by shifting my hips as he spills out of me.

"Not broken. Definitely not broken," I say, as Gavin grabs a warm towel, cleaning me up and we all collapse against the pillows together.

I repeat the words in my head. I'm not broken and I never was.

Gavin

The Sweetest Revenge

I ALWAYS THOUGHT I was less than. That I was the forgotten brother, not as big of a success as Aiden, not as driven as Lincoln, and not nearly as likable as Ben. Maybe it's the reason I pushed away the idea of having a partner for so long. This idea that if I didn't hold on tight to Ben, I'd simply be left in the dust.

Looking back, I realize that while some of those fears might have been true, maybe I was just waiting for Kate all along. Someone that showed me that I wasn't inferior, that I wasn't a consolation prize.

Do I think this relationship is going to always be flowers and daisies? No, but for now it is, and I'm going to soak up every single moment I can of this pure bliss.

Kate has her glasses on, her laptop on her lap, as she looks over at me on the couch. Ben comes strolling in straight from out of the shower, moving her laptop and placing his head on Kate's lap and instinctively she runs her fingers through his hair.

"So, are you going to tell us your plans from our photoshoot?" I ask, toying with a strand of her hair.

"Well, I'm waiting for a phone call and I do need both of you to approve this plan."

Both me and my brother give each other wary glances.

"What exactly do you have up your sleeve?"

"I don't know if you know this, but I'm a rather petty person," she says and I just give her an unamused look.

Her phone buzzes and I'm guessing that it's one of her friends, but she smiles. "Oh, I think it's the call I was waiting for." Kate answers it with a friendly "Hello?"

She listens intently on the phone, nodding her head and glancing between the two of us.

"He hasn't been made aware of the sale yet?" she says, nodding as the person on the other line speaks. "I understand that this isn't what you advise." She gives a few mmhmms and other sounds of agreement. "Yes I understand." A few more words are shared and she hangs up the phone.

Ben and I both look at her as a wicked grin that has me fearing this small woman for the first time takes over her face. "How would you guys like to take a little trip to Dennis Commercial?"

"Oh, are you going full on evil Kate?" Ben asks, his head not even out of her lap.

She shrugs her shoulders. "I'm making a statement. One that will hopefully avoid a lot of other legal bullshit down the line."

I clear my throat, not liking the idea of her going anywhere near that man. She reaches out and touches my forearm and squeezes.

"If you're not okay with it, I can call the lawyer back and have him notify Will and we can move forward."

"This is what you want?" I confirm. Not even truly knowing what kind of scene she wants to cause.

"He invaded my privacy, he broke me a little bit. I'm all put back together now, but it only seems fair that he gets it dished back to him. If anything gets out of hand we'll leave right away."

I scrub a hand over my face. "I really don't want to go to jail for strangling this dick," I tell her.

"That's why Ben will be on Gavin duty, and you'll be on me duty," she says smiling.

"Remind me never to get on your bad side."

"Then it's decided. Let's take a little field trip to see your brother's new company," she says, as she grabs an eight by ten framed picture of the three of us. It's actually a tamer image, where the three of us are laughing while standing next to each other.

The whole drive to Dennis Commercial I worry that we're doing the wrong thing, but Kate wants vengeance, and who am I to deny this woman anything?

❧ ❧ ❧

"MR. DENNIS IS IN A MEETING," the woman at the front desk says, and Kate doesn't even register her words, just storms past the desk and swings open the door to Will's office.

He in fact was not in a meeting. His darkened eyes look over me and Ben with disgust, before landing on Kate.

"Thought you weren't supposed to be within three-hundred feet of me. Do I need to call the police?" he asks sarcastically. "Or did you come here to beg me not to share your dirty little secret and give me back my shares."

Kate taps her chin three times. "None of those things actually," she says, placing the picture frame on his desk, and adjusting it a few times on the table. "What do you think? Too much for your brother's new office?" Kate asks me, scrunching her nose.

"You gave him a pretty good deal, the least he could do is admire our faces every day before work," I say.

"I still think we should've gone with the one with my face on your tits," Ben adds and Kate laughs.

"What the fuck are you talking about?" Will says, his hand already on his phone, ready to call security.

"Oh, that's right. It's irritating not knowing something, isn't it? Sucks to have someone you thought you knew go behind your back and do shady shit," Kate says as I watch her in all her glory; I'm pretty sure Ben is hard watching her tear this man to pieces.

"What did you do, Kate?"

She taps her chin a few times. "What did I do? Hmm. Well, I didn't stalk you, threaten you, or get someone else pregnant."

Will stands up abruptly and I take a step closer to Kate, and her hand grabs my forearm. Her ex-husband assesses us, adjusting his suit jacket.

"What. Did. You. Do?" he says, his voice raising.

"You better watch your motherfucking tone," I tell him pointing at him.

"Baby, what did I do?" she asks Ben.

Will looks over at my brother, seeming even more irritated over the fact that there are two of us in her corner versus one.

"Oh. You mean how you sold your shares to my brother, and Lincoln Carlson of Carlson Commercial is now the majority shareholder of Dennis Commercial. That thing?"

"Bingo, that's the one," Kate says, and Will grabs the framed picture of us, knocking it onto the ground, the glass shattering into pieces. "Don't worry, I really did the photoshoot more for myself and have prints I'm going to be putting up around the house."

"You fucking did what?" Will bellows.

Kate adjusts her stance. This man is taller and bigger than her, but she doesn't care as she takes a step toward his desk staring him down.

"Listen to me carefully because I'm not going to repeat myself. I know I was a wet blanket in our marriage, that I gave up at some point and we were no longer a good fit, but never once did I belittle you or ever treat you like I didn't care about you as a person. You hurt me, you threatened me and made me feel unsafe. I suggest you sell the remainder of your shares to Carlson Commercial and get the fuck out of Florida, because it doesn't end here."

"I'm not going to let you strong arm me, bitch."

That's it.

Kate can't even move before I'm rounding the desk and grabbing the asshole by the collar and shoving him up against the wall.

"Don't you ever speak to her like that," I nearly scream in his face.

His face is beet red and it seems like he wants to put his hands on me, but I'm bigger and I have back up.

"Sell to Lincoln, take your wife and kid and never contact me again. Stay here and I'm going to sue you for every cent you've invested in this company. I don't care if this civil lawsuit goes on for years. You stalked me, blackmailed, and threatened me."

"Isn't that exactly what you're doing right now, threatening me?"

Kate shrugs her shoulders, and I don't loosen my grip for a second.

"Yeah. I guess I am. You'll be hearing from my lawyer," she

says, tilting her head toward the door. "Let him go, he isn't worth it," she says.

I want to smash my forehead against his, but do as she says, forcibly shoving him against the wall as we walk out of his office as a united front.

"That was hot as fuck. I'm hard," Ben says and Kate laughs.

"Then let's go back home and take care of that," she says with a laugh.

🐿 🐿 🐿

WE'RE PILED on my bed, Kate's head on my chest as Ben spoons her from behind as her phone vibrates on the nightstand.

"Hello," she says in a breathy voice, a slow smile taking over her face. "He did?" I can feel her heart racing against her chest as she nods and listens to the voice over the phone. "But it worked, didn't it?"

Her weight is mostly on my chest as she agrees with the caller. "This is what I want. I just want to be done," she says, "thanks again for everything."

With a shake of her head, she plops down on the pillows, taking a deep breath.

"Who was that?" Ben says in a sleepy voice, and Kate lets out a small laugh.

"The lawyer. Will's selling Lincoln the company. He...he doesn't want a civil suit. He's willing to come to an agreement to avoid going to court," she says in a rush, her eyes nearly dazed.

I wasn't so sure about her plan of storming his office and making a scene, but it seemed like it got her message across loud and clear.

"I still think you should take every single cent he has," I say and she scoffs.

"Well, what do you want?" Ben asks, ever so pragmatic.

"I feel like I got the payback I wanted. Seeing the look on his face when he found out I sold the shares to Lincoln and that he couldn't manipulate me was priceless." She blows out a puff of air, playing with the sheet. "I think I just want to be free. I want to be comfortable in my home, in our relationship, and not worry about running into him again. I'm not tied to him anymore. He doesn't scare me. I'm free," she says, her eyes glistening with tears. "I'm free," she whispers again.

A nearly cathartic cry slips out of her and Ben and I look at each other in confusion before taking action. I cradle her in my arms, my brother rubbing her thighs as she lets it all out.

"I don't want to deal with a civil suit. I just want to live my life with the two of you, and our four cats," she jokes, wiping her face with the back of her wrists.

"I should have head butted him when I had the chance," I joke and she pulls back and looks at me.

"No. I mean, it was hot when you grabbed his shirt. But I needed that moment so bad, to show him I'm not the weak woman he thought I was. I'm done worrying what anyone thinks about how I live my life."

"And how do you want to live your life?" I ask her, thinking back on that painting I saw in her home when she was going through her marital troubles.

"Alive. Happy. Free," she says, with radiant bliss written on her face.

"So what now?" Ben asks.

"We celebrate?" Kate asks with a wild smile.

"I know just the place," I say.

"Tomorrow though, my calves ache and it's been a busy day," Ben says.

"Agreed," I say.

"Oh, so you don't want to do another round?" Kate jokes and I shake my head. She laughs snuggling back in between the two of us.

I kiss the top of her head, proud of her for standing up for herself and getting the justice she wanted. I feel so confident in the fact that it was just a matter of finding the right person at the right time with the way Kate fits perfectly between us.

Life is good and every day the weight on my chest lessens ever so slightly. This is what love is, and I treasure it more than I ever thought I would.

᷂ ᷂ ᷂

THE BAR'S filled with family and friends, and Kate looks more beautiful than ever. She has the slightest tan from our time in The Bahamas and her head is thrown back in laughter as Penny has all of the women laughing, retelling some story about a dryer mishap.

I'm hardly listening, just mesmerized by her, by this feeling.

"Guess you really grew up, huh?" Aiden says next to me and I turn to face my oldest brother.

"I guess I did."

"A good woman will do that to you. I'm happy for you, Gav. You deserve this," he says.

I have to hold back emotion and just nod my head. "Now I just gotta figure out a way to keep her."

Aiden laughs, shaking his head. "Stop thinking about the worst case scenario. You have her. Jessa showed me the article. She wouldn't do that if she wasn't all in."

"Thanks, Aiden."

"Okay. Don't cry about it, get me another beer, will ya?"

I roll my eyes, but walk around the bar and fill up a fresh pint glass for him. As the foamy substance pours down the glass, a woman holding a baby walks into the bar, looking around frantically.

"Oh fuck," Savannah says.

"You've got to be fucking kidding me," Chelsea adds in.

"What am I missing here?" Penny asks, as Kate just stares at this woman, confusion written all over her face.

"Satan's baby mama," Savannah says.

The woman is young, probably in her early twenties. Too young to have the heavy bags under her eyes.

"You can't bring a baby into a bar," Penny tells her, immediately hating the woman without any questions asked.

The woman scoots the baby on her hip. "Kate, can we talk please?"

Ben is standing beside Kate, taking her direction on how she wants it to go. I slide the beer to my brother and give the woman a once over.

"Do you want me to have her removed?" I ask.

"No, say what you need to say," Kate says, being far too fucking nice to this woman.

She licks her lips and glances around our small little crowd. "In private?"

"Everyone here is family. Whatever you want to say to me you can say in front of them."

The woman nods and the baby plays with her necklace. "I didn't know. I didn't know what he was doing. He said that he wanted to sell the company but that you wouldn't let him, and without your approval he was stuck with it. I swear I had no idea about him following you. I know you have no reason to be kind to me, I know what I did. I knew he was married," she says, her cheeks flaming red as she lets the truth fall past her lips.

"I came here to ask that you let us move, that you don't open a civil lawsuit. I promise that he won't bother you again."

"What makes you think you have any control over a man like Will?" Kate asks, being far too sympathetic.

"I don't know, but I don't have any other options, okay? I don't have a job, Danger needs a good life, both parents. He agreed to go to therapy, he agreed to move and start over. I know you probably hate me and you have every reason to want to make his life miserable. But I'm here to beg. Please, please just let us move and you'll never see us again."

Kate licks her lips, and glances over at me.

"Did you sign a prenup?" Kate asks.

The woman's brow furrows and she shakes her head. "I'll agree to not file a civil suit on the conditions that you do move out of the state and that you save my divorce lawyer's phone number in your phone if you ever find yourself in need of such a contact. How much did you buy Dennis Commercial for?" She tilts her head over to Lincoln.

"Enough for a hefty divorce settlement," Lincoln says with a shrug.

"Okay, I can do that," she agrees, and Kate inputs the number on her phone. She gives us all one last glance, shifting the weight of the child on her other hip, before leaving the establishment.

"Do you think she'll actually call the lawyer?" Penny asks.

Kate shrugs, taking a sip of her martini. "I wasn't going to file the lawsuit anyway, but if I get them the hell away from me, and put the idea of divorcing him in her ear, I'd call that a win."

"Diabolical," Savannah says.

The night continues on with the celebration of the sale of the company, the cut ties with her ex, and the promise of tomorrow.

I'm behind Kate, my arm wrapped around her collarbone as Ben sits next to her, their fingers tangled with one another's.

"You were too sweet to her earlier," I say, kissing the side of her face.

"Well, what is it they say? The sweetest revenge is living a better life? I think I've got that covered."

Ben lifts her hand, pressing a soft kiss on her knuckles. "So, what do you want to do now?"

"I just want to live," she says simply.

"Then we'll do just that," I agree.

It's exactly what we do—we live.

Kate

Epilogues are For Lovers

A Year Later...

I DIDN'T KNOW life could be this easy.

I dig my feet into the white sand at the family beach house and reflect on how this past year probably wouldn't have happened if I wasn't vulnerable and let go of all my fears.

Don't get me wrong, there have been some hard times. Most of my colleagues have been very supportive, especially after having met Gavin and Ben. I've also found some really amazing women online that are also in polyamorous relationships to confide in. It's been a part of how we've learned to make things work.

Truly it all boils down to communication between the three of us.

Will and his wife kept their word. He moved out of Florida and I haven't heard from him since he tried to blackmail me. Based on his wife's online profile, it looks like she's no longer wearing a wedding ring. All the images she posts are either of herself or of her son. I hope she got out of the marriage, and I hope Will is suffering.

I'm still working on some of my pettiness, but certain things take time.

What I do have now is a family, one that loves me unconditionally and I love them right back.

It's proven by the way I'm almost pinning down a nearly five year old to make sure she doesn't get sunburn.

"Auntie Kate, that's enough sunscreen," Brynn says, trying to push my hand away.

"It's never enough sunscreen. I plan on teaching you many things when you're older, but let this be your first lesson. Sunscreen is the most critical skin care product you'll ever use. Plus, if you don't wear it, your skin could shrivel up and you'll look like a dehydrated sponge."

"Like SpongeBob?"

"Exactly."

My niece blinks up at me, her blue eyes wide. Penny just snorts, going along with the lie, as I adjust the hat on the child's head before she runs over to the beach where her brother is currently building a sandcastle.

"That's a good one. Last week I forgot about the tooth fairy and told her she doesn't work on the weekend. The tooth fairies are obviously unionized. You do whatever works," Penny agrees.

"I can't believe you're giving me another niece," I say, and Penny smiles brightly.

Penny was meant to be a mom. She loves it more than anything and it shows. I can't deny that I've also fallen in love with Brynn and Hudson. I can't believe I get to be an aunt, a real aunt.

When I was married to Will, they always felt like *his* nieces and nephews not *ours*. I'll never remarry again, but they're absolutely my niece and nephew in every sense that it matters. I love them; I babysit on occasion and I plan on being the cool aunt that they come to when they're in their teen years and loathe their parents.

"Seriously, keep your paws off her for once," Gavin jokes, as the brothers and Jessa take their beach chairs.

"What can I say? We make cute kids," Lincoln says, resting his hand on Penny's stomach.

"I won't deny that," Ben says, as he hands me a cold drink and takes a sip of his own.

"Oh my god, Hudson, don't eat sand," Penny suddenly shouts. Both parents are up in a flash as Hudson cries, his fist and mouth full of sand.

Jessa is on Aiden's lap, laughing at something he said and I know without a doubt they'll be sneaking off somewhere in a matter of minutes.

"Do I need to get a spray bottle or something?" Ben jokes.

Aiden glares at his younger brother, giving him the finger. Some things will never change.

It's evident that the smitten gene is prominent in the Carlson family. Even their parents, for as much as Maggie and Jeff bicker, I've learned they're still madly in love. I hope that Gavin and Ben still feel that way decades from now.

If you would've asked me my first night at Avalon if I could ever picture decades with another man, let alone two, I would have told you that you were crazy. But with Ben and Gavin—I can see it.

I can see them arguing over what food we should order for the millionth time. I can see us on this same damn beach in our sixties reminiscing on all the trips we've had here.

We understand each other on such a visceral personal level, it's hard to explain to most people. Ben and Gavin have spent every day of their lives together. Their bond between one another is something I'll never truly grasp. But what I have with each of them is profound. There's no hiding. I never feel like I'm numb. I'm living life to the fullest and that's how it should be.

"Want to take a walk on the beach?" Gavin asks with a smirk.

"Only if I get to come this time," Ben says, and I grin at him.

I take one of their hands in each of mine, a position I've had to get used to as we trail footprints in the damp sand.

"I think next summer we should spend a whole month here, without all the riffraff," Gavin says.

"You mean your family?"

"Our family. Yes," he says, squeezing my hand.

"I think I'd like that."

"And the other thing?" Ben says, and I look between the two of them, wondering what they have up their sleeve.

"I think we should build a place that's ours together. I know you probably don't want to sell your Aunt Helene's place, but going back and forth between the two seems ridiculous when we all wind up usually sleeping at the same place anyway," Gavin says.

He's not wrong, and it wasn't something I brought up because things work the way they are now. But the idea of having a place where we can call home and not just a spare set of clothes and a toothbrush does sound pretty perfect.

"I think I'd like that," I say.

"Thank god," Ben muses, and I bump his hip with mine.

"So, where do we start?"

"I already have my realtor looking at lots," Gavin says, going on about what the ideal lot would have.

Maybe our relationship isn't the normal progression of things, maybe it's complicated. It's not how I ever pictured my life—it's even better.

ACKNOWLEDGMENTS

Well, that's it, the Carlson Brothers have come to a close. Thank you so much for sticking with this series. To date, this has probably been the biggest emotional rollercoaster of a series I've done.

Swallow Your Pride was a breeze. It was the daddy kink book I always wanted to read. I'm pretty sure I wrote it in under a month. It was just a book I had to get out. It didn't perform as well as my paranormal or omegaverse and I wondered if people wanted contemporary from me. All I knew is people wanted the adopted cousin fucking, and I had to oblige.

Forget Your Morals was the most stressful promotional period and release. I had a few reels that hit the wrong side of the internet. Truly, I didn't know if I was going to continue and give the twins a book. Then, as fate would have it, a Tik Tok by Bonnie (bonreviewsbooks) went viral and everything changed. This series just needed to find the right audience, and I'm so glad it found it or else there's a good chance we wouldn't have Double Your Standards.

I've loved writing the brothers and the women they're obsessed with, and dare I say I think the twins were the naughtiest yet. This series has been my summer release for the last three years, and while I'm sad to see it end I'm so proud to have made it to this point.

I want to give a huge shout out to Sandra (Maldo Designs)

for creating the covers for this series. I told her to make it dirtier with each book and she delivered.

Jade & Marielli for always reading while I write, I can't express how much you two mean to my process. You keep me motivated and headed in the right direction.

Tasha, your input hands down made this a better book. Thank you for your feedback and for pushing me to really bring the spice for Ben, Gavin, and Kate.

Jessica, Hailey, and Kaitlen, thank you for beta reading and always being the best cheerleaders. Fun fact: Kaitlen bid on an auction item for charity that included having your name in a book, thus Kate was born.

Stephanie, I shudder to think about you not reading before arcs *wink wink*.

Kay, thank you for putting up my chaotic schedule and your enthusiasm to work with me on every book.

Podium, thank you for taking a chance on my naughty little books to convert them into audio.

Other works by Sarah Blue

Omegaverse Romance

Heat Haven Heat Cutes

Mile High Heat

Heat Haven Omegaverse

Heat Haven

Omega's Obsession - (Jonah's Parents)

Protector's Promise - (Elliot's Parents)

Too Tempting

Heat Haven Holidays

Dead Palms MC

Nobody's Darlin' - (Axel's namesake)

High Roller Omegas

Queen of Hearts

Pucked Up Omegaverse

One Pucked Up Pack

Don't Puck With My Heart

Puck Around & Find Out

Lavender Moon

Lavender Moon

Lavender Moon Meets Las Vegas

The Carlson Brothers - Contemporary Romance

Swallow Your Pride

Forget Your Morals

Double Your Standards

Paranormal Romance

Celestial Witches

The Marriage Hex

The Fang Arrangement - coming soon

Charming Series

Charming Your Dad

Charming the Devil

<u>Charming as Hell</u>

Love in the Veil

Petty Cupid

Lucky Cupid

Daddy Cupid

Jolly Cupid

ABOUT THE AUTHOR

Sarah Blue is a USA Today bestselling author of paranormal, omegaverse, and contemporary romance. When she isn't writing you can find her nose buried in a book or picking up a new craft she probably won't finish. She lives in Maryland with her husband, children, and two cats.

www.authorsarahblue.com
@sarahblueauthor on Instagram and TikTok
Sarah Blue's Reader Group on Facebook

www.ingramcontent.com/pod-product-compliance
Lightning Source LLC
Chambersburg PA
CBHW030744310726
48969CB00005B/1312